Clan War

Highland Heroes Series: Book 1

Theo Mann

Invisible Publishing Company

Highland Heroes Series

Contents

Chapter 1

Lily Dindle shoved her revolver out of the way to retrieve her keys from her handbag. She took hold of the wrought-iron gate to unlock it. The brass plate on the wall read, *Ironforge*.

The key grating in the lock distracted her from noticing a filthy ragman shuffling up behind her. He laid his grimy hand on her shoulder and Lily spun around ready to fight. Her hand flew to her heart when she saw him. "You scared me, Lionel."

He mumbled between toothless gums and made incoherent burbling noises.

Lily relaxed and smiled. "Go around to the kitchen entrance at four o'clock, the same as every day. You can get something to eat then."

He interrupted her with more incomprehensible ramblings, but she cut him off. "You know I don't hand out cash, Lionel. If you want something to eat, you can go to the kitchen entrance at four o'clock. Otherwise, I'll see you at the Community Center tomorrow at nine as usual."

He started talking faster. He waved his hands in exaggerated circles and his bleary, bloodshot eyes rolled in their sockets. His matted, filthy hair waved across his head with every movement.

Lily nodded while she turned her key in the lock. The gate popped open. "I understand, Lionel," she said over her shoulder. "I already told you I don't hand out money on the streets. I'll see you tomorrow at the center."

He kept talking louder and making less sense. She continued nodding while she backed through the gate and inched it closed between them against his best efforts to slip inside. "Have a good afternoon, Lionel."

She slammed the gate shut and retreated far enough behind it that he couldn't reach her. She breathed a sigh of relief and hurried into the big brick house behind the wall.

She punched her code into the security system to unlock the front door and double-locked it behind her before she fully relaxed.

After more than seven years of serving the poor and homeless on the broken streets of Detroit, she still never fully let down her guard until she got behind several layers of defenses.

She dumped her handbag on the hall table along with her keys. Four other bags lined the same table with four keychains dangling on hooks on the wall.

The unmistakable thump of gunfire shook the house from under the floor. Lily smiled to herself. One o'clock and the Last Division was busy with their daily combat training.

Lily pulled her sidearm out of her handbag and ran her finger down the timetable posted on the wall. Echo Boxwood would be doing her rotation on the basement firing range.

Lily headed for the stairs to join her friend. A female voice called to her as she passed another room on her right. "In here, Lily."

Lily tracked the sound to Dead Betty in the dojo. When the Last Division leased this house, they converted a spare living room into a martial arts training room.

Betty brushed her long, curly blonde hair off her sweaty forehead. Five-foot-six and built of solid muscle, Betty posed a special challenge to anyone who dared to spar with her. Lily hesitated to enter the dojo and take up that challenge.

Betty grinned at the gun in Lily's hand. "You won't be needing that in here."

Lily chuckled. "I was on my way to see what Echo's up to."

"Did you check the roster? What's your station today?"

Lily lowered her gaze to the floor. "Recon."

Betty's face fell to match Lily's. "Oh."

Lily nodded and turned away. "I better get to it. See you later."

Betty went back to a padded post with several wooden appendages poking out of it. Betty started going through her sequences of strikes and blocks against her lifeless opponent.

Lily cast one last wistful glance into the dojo. She would much rather spar Betty than do the job she was rostered for.

She headed back down the hall. Metallic clicks and snaps made her stop at a bedroom near the kitchen.

A tall, athletic woman with chocolate brown hair worked at a table piled with weapons. She slotted open the magazine of an automatic rifle and let it spring back into place.

Lily sighed and headed for the tiny office near the back porch. She didn't want Snowflake, their commanding officer, to catch her shirking her duties.

The savory smell of chicken soup drifted to Lily's nose and Lily smirked when she heard the last member of their team cursing in the kitchen. Zero hated kitchen patrol more than any other detail. Most of the Last Division did, but the smell told Lily that at least Zero hadn't burned the soup today.

Lily passed the kitchen to the office behind it and flung herself into a squeaky swivel chair in front of a bank of computers.

The office window looked out over the compound's backyard to the electrified fence beyond. A dozen homeless people already milled around out there even though the team wouldn't hand out any food for another three hours.

Every day followed the same pattern around here. Only the team's rotation changed. KP. Shooting range. Weapons detail. Hand-to-hand combat training. Recon. Then the sequence started over again.

When they weren't giving out food and conducting job training and home visits to Detroit's most destitute and hopeless residents, the team kept up their military routine. They had to.

Drug addicts, armed gangs, and bored teenagers had broken into this compound twenty times during the first year after the Last Division took up residence here. Things only got worse with every passing year.

The team conducted this humanitarian mission like a military operation. They could help more people that way and do the job they committed to doing.

Lily and her friends had found their rhythm after so many years on the ground in this domestic war zone. They just hadn't found the peace they were looking for when they came back from the war in Afghanistan.

Lily punched a random button on the keyboard in front of her and seven screens flickered on. She typed in her password.

The computers responded by opening seven different search programs. One panel displayed ten identical black and white squares showing surveillance camera feeds from around the compound.

Another screen showed satellite heat signatures from the surrounding seven blocks. The computer monitored their proximity to the compound.

Seven wavy lines wobbled across the third monitor. Lily gave them only a passing glance and turned her attention to the fourth screen.

A continuous stream of code traced up the surface and disappeared into the void of cyberspace. Lily read it for a few minutes and scribbled some notes on a notepad.

She nearly jumped out of her skin when a hand clapped her on the shoulder. "Anything yet?"

Lily leaped out of her seat and whirled around to find Snowflake standing by her chair. "What do you think you're doing—trying to give me a heart attack? How many times do I have to tell you not to do that?"

Snowflake didn't take her eyes off the screen. "I'm keeping you on your toes. Did you turn anything up yet?"

"I already told you I didn't," Lily grumbled. "How long do you want to keep the crawler running?"

"As long as it takes—maybe forever." Snowflake pointed to a section of numbers and letters on the screen. "What's that?"

"A newspaper in Greenville, North Carolina, is running the story again. One of the refugees settled there and his daughter just got accepted to West Point. A local journalist found out, and when the guy interviewed her parents, her father told the story. The paper is repeating it so it's turning up here."

"Do they name any names?" Snowflake asked.

"They couldn't. The father didn't know any of our names, so he couldn't repeat them. He only knew about the Last Division. The journalist is doing every search in the book to find out who was on the team, but he hasn't turned up anything yet. I'm sure he never will. If he was going to find anything, he would have by now."

"Keep an eye on it. You can inform the others at the briefing tonight." Snowflake straightened up. "I gotta go."

Lily looked around at her friend. "What about the rest of the rotation?"

"I have to go meet a supplier of G36s in Forest Park."

Lily's jaw dropped. "Forest Park! Are you insane? You can't go there alone. You'd never make it back alive, especially not with a shipment of assault rifles. How do you think you're going to get them back in one piece?"

Snowflake aimed a menacing finger at the computer screen over Lily's shoulder. "Keep an eye on that news article. I'll be back around seven tonight. Echo can do the briefing."

Lily collapsed back in her chair. Just great. The team's illustrious leader was going off on a suicide mission to the worst parts of Detroit to pick up more weapons while her friends got stuck doing the drudge work of handing out soup to the local homeless. Lily never got to have any fun.

Lily flung her pen on the desk when, out of nowhere, the computer gave a deafening blast of alarm. Lily lunged forward with her heart in her mouth and wheeled her chair around. She stared in unblinking horror at the monitor in a desperate search for the source of the disturbance.

Snowflake rushed back into the room. "What's going on?"

Lily's fingers flew over the keyboard. "Someone tripped our proximity alarm. They're inside the fence, but they aren't showing up on the camera feed."

Lily swallowed hard and fought down rising tension. Ironforge hadn't had a break-in for years, so why was one happening now in the middle of the day?

The alarm kept blaring loud enough to wake the dead. Lily worked feverishly over the computer to locate the intruder, but she couldn't find the signal anywhere. The sound racked her nerves and distracted her from concentrating.

"The intruder must be out there somewhere," Snowflake barked. "Track him down."

"Of course he must be out there somewhere!" Lily yelled over the noise. "He's using some sort of electronic signal to mask his position."

"What the hell for?" Snowflake fired back. "Who is it?"

"It's one man." Lily pointed to the video camera feed. "He jumped over the wall here, by the southeast corner. He hit the ground and disappeared, but he's definitely still inside the fence."

"The laser monitors should have picked him up."

The alarm sent Lily into combat mode. "I'm telling you he's using a device to deflect the monitors. He's invisible as long as he stays inside the fence. We have to track him down the old-fashioned way."

Snowflake whirled away. She lunged for the bedroom with Lily on her tail. Snowflake snatched up the Remington Bushmaster she'd just been working on when Lily first walked into the house.

Snowflake shouldered the weapon just as Betty appeared in the door. "What's going on?"

"Intruder," Snowflake snapped. "Arm up and get into position. Lily, get word to Echo and you two take the back." She stuck her head into the kitchen. "Drop what you're doing, Zero. Intruder alert."

Betty ran to a cupboard on the wall and pulled out a headset. She slotted it over her head and positioned the earpiece in her ear. An adjustable arm held a microphone in front of her mouth. She handed another one to Lily.

Lily waited only long enough to get her hands on the device before she ran for the stairs. The team trained all the time for situations just like this, but that didn't settle her nerves when a real intruder attacked their compound.

How much damage could one man do against five trained soldiers? What man in his right mind would attack Ironforge alone?

Lily fitted the headset to her ear while she dashed down the hall. The sets' earplugs would protect the team's hearing from the noise of gunfire while still letting them communicate with each other across the house.

Lily's heart pounded. She raced down the basement stairs and didn't stop until she reached the shooting range.

A short, curvy woman with deep black hair lay flat on her stomach on the AstroTurf floor. She aimed a rifle on a tripod at a target thirty yards away. She didn't hear Lily through her earmuffs.

Lily ran up behind her. She waited until Echo squeezed off another shot before she tapped her friend on the shoulder.

Echo ripped off her ear protection and flipped over. Her eyes said it all. No one on the team would interrupt someone on the firing range unless it was a serious emergency.

Lily jerked her thumb over her shoulder. "Intruder. You're with me."

Echo hopped to her feet. She didn't bother to take off her safety glasses. She followed Lily back upstairs and the two women both grabbed weapons from the bedroom. Echo put on a headset and the two women returned to the office.

Snowflake's voice crackled in Lily's ear. "Any sign of him?"

Lily motioned Echo toward the back door. "Get out to the barricade while I take a look."

Echo exited the house onto the back porch. She rested her assault rifle on the railing and scanned the surroundings. She ran her gun barrel over the homeless people still clustered around the fence while Lily slaved over the computer.

She searched the system one more time but still came up with nothing. She depressed the call button to address the whole team. "He's still not showing up on the monitors. Any sign of him out front?"

"Nothing yet," Snowflake reported.

Lily cursed under her breath and hefted her weapon. How were they supposed to fight someone they couldn't see?

She put out her hand for the doorknob when an unholy eruption of gunfire exploded on the back porch. Lily plunged through the door, planted her feet next to Echo, and propped her rifle on the railing.

Echo's gun kept burping bullets into the air. Empty cartridges rained on the floorboards before Lily saw what Echo was shooting at.

A single man bolted across the yard in front of them. He burrowed through the shrubbery by the wall before he broke cover and made a mad dash for a tree in the middle of the compound. He dove behind it for protection against Echo's bullets ripping the bark to shreds.

Echo straightened up, ejected her clip, and plugged another into the magazine. "Bastard! He's damn good, that's for certain."

"Who is he?" Lily shouted back.

"He's got training. That's all I know." Echo dragged her forehead across her shoulder to wipe away sweat before she took a fresh bead on her enemy.

Lily trained her gun on the tree. She dropped her finger to the trigger and squeezed just enough to put tension on the firing mechanism. The guy would be a dead man the minute he showed his face.

He caught them off guard even with both Lily and Echo standing ready to fire at a moment's notice and even with all their training and preparation. He dove into view and completed three somersaults before either woman got a shot off.

Lily and Echo opened up at the same moment. Two trails of bullets ripped into the dirt. The man vaulted to his feet and made one reckless jump for a derelict car rotting ten feet from the porch.

Lily led him with her gun sight. She missed his ankles by a fraction of an inch and her bullets pocked the corroded metal before he cowered for safety behind the car.

Echo growled through gritted teeth. "That's it. I'm gonna kill that son of a...."

Snowflake, Betty, and Zero came barging through the back door. "Report!" Snowflake demanded. "Where is he?"

"He's behind the car." Lily checked her magazine. "I'd say he's done this before."

"He's damn fast," Echo snarled. "He could be Special Forces, but I'd say he's even higher than that. He's no tool from the neighborhood. He knew the whole layout of the compound. He must have trained for this. I'd bet any amount of money on that."

"That's impossible," Betty chimed in. "Who would train to break into a charitable organization?"

"Someone who knew we kept weapons and food and computers inside," Lily replied. "He obviously knew what he was getting into before he jumped that wall."

"I don't give a crap who he is. This is over right now." Snowflake propped her rifle on her shoulder and seized one of several grenades dangling from her belt. She clenched her fist around the lever and pulled the pin. "I'll deal with him, whoever he is."

She lobbed the grenade high. It soared in a perfect arc over the yard on a deadly path toward the car. Lily ducked behind the railing for protection from the blast when, without warning, the intruder rocketed into view.

The grenade hit the car and a plume of heat and thunderous noise boomed across the compound.

Lily jerked up her weapon and sighted down the barrel. The others did likewise, but they were too late. The guy already made it halfway across the yard. With one wild leap, he plummeted under the porch into the cellar beneath the house.

Snowflake whipped around. "Get down there now! Zero, you take the basement stairs. Betty, you go through the ventilation duct. It's the only way he might be able to get from the cellar into the house itself. Echo, you and Lily stay here and make sure he doesn't try to escape. If he shows his face in the open again, bury him."

"What are you going to do?" Echo asked.

"I'm going down the same hole he used." Snowflake barged to the steps leading from the porch down to the yard.

The others all turned away to their tasks. At that instant, while all their backs were turned, a scuffle reverberated through the porch floor.

Lily barely had time to turn back the other way when a tall man, taller even than Snowflake, vaulted over the railing and landed right in front of Lily.

Lily reacted on pure instinct. She tightened both fists on her weapon and slammed it upward into the man's face. He staggered back and hit the railing. He flailed both arms to catch his balance. His eyelids fluttered for a moment.

Lily didn't hesitate. She heaved her gun above her head and smashed the butt into the man's nose. He toppled like a ton of bricks and folded into a pile at her feet.

Lily crushed her weapon in a white-knuckle grip. She flipped it around and crammed the butt into her shoulder. She pounced on the man and stabbed the muzzle into his eye socket. She gasped for breath to steady her hands to fire.

Blood poured from the guy's nose. His eyes stared in a dead blank at the roof behind Lily's head. Her pulse hammered in her ears and she tightened her grip on the trigger to blow his brains out.

Her vision cleared and she saw him through the fog of blood and mayhem. Every instinct told her to shoot, to put this enemy in the ground.

Somewhere out of the distant reaches of time, another voice whispered in her ear. She blinked and the man's face came into focus. "Liam!" she gasped. "What are you doing here?"

Snowflake materialized at her side. "You know this guy?"

Lily panted in a painful struggle to get her mind to function. "I know him. He's my older brother."

Chapter 2

Snowflake jabbed a pistol in Liam's face. "I don't care what you say. You're a dead man."

"Finish him," Echo snapped. "Whoever he is, he came here to put us out of business."

"First tell us who you're working for," Snowflake demanded. "Start talking. The minute you stop making sense, I put a bullet in your brain."

Liam held up both hands. He tried to get off the kitchen stool to stand up, but Snowflake shoved him back down. "Don't move, punk."

"Will you calm down?" Liam snapped. "Just put the gun away and listen to me. I didn't come here to put you out of business."

"Then what are you doing here?" Betty asked. "You could have just knocked on the door like anyone else."

"I tried!" Liam yelled. "Don't you think I tried? Do you think I would go to all this trouble to see my own sister if I could find another way?"

"I don't buy it," Echo retorted. "You didn't need a laser deflecting shield to see your sister. You could have just stood out there with your hands up and waited for us to bring you in. You didn't need all that cloak-and-dagger stuff."

Liam swiveled around to confront Lily. "Will you say something? For Christ's sake, will you tell your friends to back off?"

Lily stayed where she was against the kitchen wall and kept her arms crossed over her chest. She watched the whole scene unfold with mixed emotions.

"They're right, Liam," she told him. "I was just outside an hour ago. If you wanted to talk to me, you could have just walked up to me on the street. You didn't have to break in here like James freakin' Bond."

Liam made another abortive attempt to get off the stool before Snowflake punched him hard across the jaw to knock him back. "You're not going anywhere, dirtbag. Sit down if you know what's good for you."

"Jesus Christ, Snowflake!" Liam grunted. "What was that for?"

Snowflake froze with her pistol aimed at his temple. "How do you know my name?"

"I know all your names. I know you're Echo Boxwood, and you're Dead Betty, and you're called Zero. Am I right? I know all about you guys and I know all about the Last Division. I came here to talk to you—to talk to my sister. I'm not your enemy."

"You sure look like our enemy from here," Lily remarked.

"We've been running crawler programs on the internet for seven years," Betty pointed out. "No one knows about us except the highest security clearances in the government. Do you expect us to believe you came from them?"

Liam stole a peek at her before he cast his eyes to the floor. "Yes."

The friends exchanged glances. No one moved for a second. Then, all at once, Snowflake lunged for him.

She caught him by the throat with her left hand, plastered her gun barrel against his nose and squashed it into his face. "Start talking and talk fast. Who are you really working for and what are you doing here? This is your last chance."

Liam raised both hands and clamped his eyes shut tight. "I'm working for the President. Okay? I came here on a mission from the President of the United States. You guys are being called up into active service again."

Lily's eyes popped and Betty gasped. Snowflake's hands shook menacing Liam with the gun. Those words struck terror into Lily's guts. Called into active service? They couldn't be, not after seven years.

Snowflake let her gun drop and she straightened up. Her arms flopped to her sides and she whispered in a husky voice. "What the hell are you talking about?"

Liam swallowed hard. "Listen to me. The President is in danger. He recruited me to come and see you guys. He has a mission for you. I'm here to give you all the details and bring you up to speed so you can complete it."

Snowflake turned around very slowly and her deep brown eyes swept the circle of faces.

The five women regarded each other for one terrible moment. Lily's heart plummeted into her shoes. They couldn't go back into active service after seven years of self-imposed exile. No way.

Betty broke the silence first. "I'm not going. I don't care what anybody says. I'm not going back into service."

Liam gave a heavy sigh. "You don't have to. You can stay here. Only Lily will be going anywhere."

Lily jumped. "You just said the whole team is being called up."

"They are, but you're the only one going anywhere."

"I think you better explain exactly what's going on here," Snowflake barked. "Start from the beginning and don't leave anything out."

Liam slumped on his stool and pressed his wrist to his bloody nose. "Do you mind giving me some ice or something for this first?"

No one moved. The five women stared at him like he had dropped from another planet.

Lily measured her brother. He looked the same as she remembered, but she might as well have never seen him before in her life.

He stood a head taller than everyone in the room. He even dwarfed Snowflake. His angular shoulders and lanky frame distributed his muscle to make him look thin, but he was just as formidable as a man twice his weight.

He wore his sandy brown hair cut close around his ears and his sea-green eyes sent a wave of nostalgia through Lily.

She used to be close to her brother when they were growing up, but she hadn't seen him in over fifteen years. She knew nothing about him or what he'd been doing since she shipped out to Afghanistan.

He wasn't supposed to know what *she'd* been doing, either, but he found out somehow. If he knew about the Last Division, he must have found out a lot more than he could have learned from a simple internet search.

He raised his eyes to her face. One minute, she was looking at the brother she knew and loved better than anyone else in the world. The next instant, she found herself staring at a stranger.

If he was working for the government, if he was working for people high enough to know about the Last Division, she didn't have a clue who or what he was. She had no reason to trust him.

His eyes darted sideways once before coming back to her face. Lily snapped out of her trance and realized that all her friends were watching her and waiting to see what she would do. This was her brother. What happened to him depended on her alone.

She pivoted away and stalked to the large freezer in the corner. She yanked the door open and took out a bag of frozen peas. She held it out to him. When he pressed it to his face, Lily plucked the pistol out of Snowflake's hand.

She settled the weapon in her hand and dropped her thumb onto the safety. When Liam removed the bag, he found her pointing the gun at his head. "Now start talking. Tell us everything and make it fast or I'll kill you myself."

Liam let his hand drop into his lap. The peas made a crunching noise on his thigh. "All right. Here goes. The government has been experimenting for years to find a way to make time travel possible. About six years ago, they finally found a way to do it."

Echo snorted. "You lying sack of...."

"It's true. They kept it a secret for obvious reasons, but they're always working on stuff like that. They have whole labs dedicated to telekinesis and advanced healing powers and all kinds of crazy crap. You wouldn't believe half the stuff they're experimenting with. They've been doing it for decades and they finally cracked the time travel code. They sent a guy back in time to prehistoric Europe and he brought back a living *Archicebus*, a prehistoric primate that's been extinct for thousands of years. They've got it stuffed in a silo somewhere in Nebraska."

The women gaped at him in blank disbelief. "You're making this up," Snowflake muttered.

He shook his head fast. "They didn't plan to use it for much. They were just going to sit on the technology until they really needed it, but then they found out that rogue elements had developed another way to time travel. They were using black magic and they sent one of their people through the portal to somewhere in Scotland three hundred years ago."

"Scotland!" Echo exclaimed. "What the hell for?"

"The CIA tracked down enough intelligence on the operation to find out the enemy is targeting one of the President's ancestors. This wizard plans to kill her to alter the course of time. If they succeed, they'll wipe out the American President. They'll make it so the war never happened. Your team will never go to Afghanistan. You won't complete your mission. Everything you guys went through will have been for nothing."

He stopped to let his words sink in. Lily looked sideways to find her friends exchanging glances. Zero's mouth fell open. "Are you freaking serious? You want us to believe that rogue elements are using black magic? That's nuts."

"It's true," Liam went on. "We confirmed it all. The President sent me here. He wants me and you, Lily, to go through the portal to stop this wizard guy. He's going after a woman named Lady Rhona Armstrong and he's got the jump on us by about three months. We have to get back there right away. If he succeeds, he could change everything.

He could maybe win the war or even one of the World Wars. He could change the whole course of history."

Snowflake stepped forward and raised her hand. "Hold it right there, Mister. You're not taking one of my team. I don't care if you came from the President himself. This is ridiculous. You can't expect us to believe all that nonsense about time travel and whatever else."

"You haven't even told us who these supposed rouge elements are," Echo pointed out. "You have to admit it sounds pretty flimsy."

"We have only your word that you even come from the government," Betty chimed in. "You could be making it all up."

Liam started to get off his stool. He raised his arms to make his point. "You have to listen to me. There's no time to stand around arguing."

"You still haven't explained why you broke in here instead of just talking to us like an ordinary person," Snowflake went on. "Where did you get the technology to deflect our monitors?"

"I told you I got it from the government," Liam snapped. "Don't you think a government that has invented time travel can invent a device to mask a simple laser signal? Come on!"

"None of my people are going anywhere with you until we substantiate your claims." Snowflake made a grab for his arm. "Come on. We have a holding cell downstairs. You can stay there until someone higher up the chain of command gives us the word that we're supposed to believe you."

He yanked his arm away from her. "You know they won't substantiate it. They would never acknowledge the Last Division publicly, so what makes you think they'll acknowledge this? This is classified."

"I don't care," Snowflake retorted. "You can sit in the holding cell until we get clarification on our orders or we can execute you right now. It's your choice."

Liam spun around and braced himself to fight. "Get your hands off me! You don't have the authority to hold me against my will."

Snowflake hauled back her fist. Lily saw the encounter degenerating into another full-blown battle. "Stop! I'll do it."

"No, you won't," Snowflake countered. "As long as you're under my command, you'll..."

"I'm not under your command." Lily spoke under her breath, but everyone in the room hung on her every word. "We aren't soldiers anymore. I'll go. It's the only way to prove if he's telling the truth. It's also the only way the four of you can keep doing our work without any interference from higher up. I'll go."

Snowflake held out her hand. "Hold it right there. We don't even know if this time travel stuff is real."

"It is." Liam took something out of his pocket. The team leaned in close to inspect a small copper cube rotating in his fingers.

Strange symbols covered its sides, but Lily couldn't make out any other distinguishing features. She couldn't see a lid or any moving parts.

The women stared at the thing. It looked like a toy. "What is that?" Betty asked.

"This device opens the time portal," Liam replied. "When I activate this, it will transport us to the time and place programmed into it, but it will only transport two people at a time. That's why I can only take Lily and not the rest of you. Besides, more than two people would attract too much attention."

Snowflake smacked her lips and rolled her eyes. "What do you take us for—idiots?"

"It's all right," Lily interrupted. "I might as well try it. If it's all hogwash, I'll find out pretty soon and I'm just as capable of knocking him off as the rest of you."

Liam's head shot up and he scowled at her, but she only smiled at him. If he wanted to play games with her, he would find she was no idiot, either.

She nodded to her friends. "Stand down. I got this."

"You don't have to do this, Lily," Snowflake told her. "We're a team. I'm not gonna turn you over to some lunatic just because he cooked up a crazy story like this."

"Don't worry, Lieutenant," Lily replied. "I'm going to check the database first to confirm the order. Stand down and let me deal with my brother."

"All right. Let us know if you need anything." Snowflake jerked her thumb at the others.

They started to head out of the kitchen when a timer rang above the stove. It was four o'clock and time to hand out the afternoon soup and bread.

Zero looped one potholder around the handle of an enormous kettle while Betty took the other side. They hauled the cauldron to the back door and lugged it outside. Snowflake took a bunch of ladles and bowls while Echo followed them with an armload of bread loaves.

Chapter 3

L ily turned her attention to her brother. "You better clean yourself up. I'll be right back."

She moved to the door, but Liam jumped off his stool and grabbed her arm. "You don't really think you can confirm the order, do you? This is black ops. You'll never find any trace of it."

She rounded on him bristling. She never talked back to him before in her life, but a lot of water had passed under the bridge since they played in the dirt as kids.

"You better hope I do confirm it because if I don't, I'm not going anywhere with you," she hissed. "I'm not your kid sister anymore. If you know about the Last Division, you know I would never agree to this without some confirmation. You want a soldier who has gone behind enemy lines. You want someone who can handle herself when the fur starts flying and that's exactly what you got. Now sit down and put those peas on your face. You damn well better be sitting here when I get back."

She yanked her arm out of his grasp and marched off to the office. She plunked down in the same chair, but this time, she thought long and hard before she touched the keyboard.

Black ops this might be, but some trace of the time travel project and the order to track down the Last Division should still turn up on the team's search program.

She laid her hands on the desk and started typing. She spent twenty minutes searching the crawler before she found a line that told her everything she needed to know.

She typed, *Liam Barnett, movements*. She tracked him back to Washington within the last week. She located his visits to the Pentagon and even the White House.

Whoever Liam was working for, he certainly moved in high circles, but that proved nothing.

She continued her search until she hit pay dirt. She delved into Liam's bank records and followed the source of his income.

It led her to an obscure branch of the military called Felix Margoles, but that name didn't match any individual person. It checked out as a sub-department of the Treasury with more than fifty employees, each with no traceable home addresses, next of kin, or employment records.

The department issued funds not only to its employees but to several other cryptic recipients. When she rummaged through the records, she uncovered a file of emails. It contained dozens of PDF attachments of military orders to Felix Margoles's employees.

None of the orders made any sense, so they must be written in some sort of code. She isolated Liam's orders and found one that read,

Clearance granted to travel to Detroit, recruitment detail for Project 17B. Funds released for recruit equipment and infiltration device. Report to Main Office upon completion of objective.

So it was all true. She didn't have to read the fine print or find any smoking gun.

That email, buried under mountains of bureaucratic red tape and computer encryption, described Liam's mission to come to Ironforge and get her on board for this mission. Lily's instincts from her time in the Army told her it was true.

She leaned back in the chair. No matter how much she thought about it, she already knew she would go. She didn't know what she would find on the other side of that portal, but whatever it was, she had to see it for herself. She never backed down on an order yet and she wasn't about to start now.

She cast one last look around the house. After seven years here, she had no other home on the planet.

No one in the world needed her as much as her teammates and the poor people outside these walls. This was her whole world.

What would it mean to leave it all behind....and for what? For someone or something three hundred years in the past?

Her loyalty to her country overrode her objections. She hadn't served on active duty for seven years, but she was still a soldier at heart. Whatever this mission was, she had to complete it. No one else would do it.

She returned to the kitchen to find Liam still seated on his stool with the peas plastered to his face. He peeked over them at her. "Well? Did you find what you were looking for?"

She nodded. "Yeah. I did."

His eyebrows flew up. "You're lying. You did not."

She waved that away. "So.... what? Do you want me to put on a dress or something?"

He studied her jeans and t-shirt with the zippered hoodie over it. "Do you have anything else to wear?"

"I'll go check in my room. Why don't you come with me? You can tell me what would be most appropriate."

He followed her up the stairs to the second story. The team's bedrooms lined a hallway with a bathroom at the end.

Liam surveyed the pictures on the hallway walls. No one from outside ever entered this house and they certainly never intruded on the team's inner sanctum. Lily and her friends kept this place sacred to themselves.

Here they could display photographs of friends and loved ones they'd lost in their travels. Liam paused by a large group picture. Men and women in camo fatigues waved and smiled and made faces at the camera.

"Look at them all," he murmured. "I never knew you had a picture of the whole Division."

"That's the only picture left in existence." Lily eased over to his side. She hadn't looked at that picture in years. It brought back too many memories. "That was the last picture taken of all of us before we went inside."

"Did they all fall on the mission?"

"Not all. We went in with twenty-seven people. We came out with nine. One got hit by friendly fire when we tried to come back over the border. One died of smoke inhalation within hours of completing the mission. The others died of various problems before they could be repatriated Stateside. One died of food poisoning in Angkor Wat and the last one suffered a subarachnoid hemorrhage on the plane home."

Liam shook his head. "It was such a waste of good people."

"The mission wasn't a waste. We did what we went in there to do. We succeeded. The real waste was never being acknowledged by the country we sacrificed for. The real waste was that none of their families ever found out why or how their loved ones died. They never got any benefits and none of the fallen got any decorations for their bravery or a proper military burial. That was the real waste."

Liam continued the rest of the way down the hall. He inspected more pictures of people he didn't know. "Is that why you're here in exile—to protest the military cover-up of your mission?"

"I'm not in exile, Liam. This is my country. I'm right here where anyone can walk up to me on the street and talk to me about it, even my own brother. If any one of those people outside asked me about my service in the military, I would tell the truth. I never agreed to keep it a secret from anyone."

"But they never do ask, do they?"

Liam stopped in front of a picture cut out of a newspaper. It showed Snowflake, Lily, and Zero helping an old lady out of a burning building.

"They never ask because they don't care about you. Those people outside don't care enough about who you really are to find out the first thing about you. They only care about what you can do for them. They can never understand you. That's why you chose this life, so you would be surrounded by people who never found out the truth."

"I'm surrounded by my teammates," she pointed out. "They're the ones I live with and talk to every day. They know all there is to know."

"So you don't have to talk about it. You can all live in the same silence where you don't have to acknowledge what happened."

"We all acknowledge what happened," she replied. "That's why we're here. We took an oath to protect this country. We did it over there and we're doing it here. We agreed to serve and protect. Those people outside need us a hell of a lot more than some strangers halfway across the world. If we're going to give our lives to save others, we might as well do it here."

"So you all agreed to move to Detroit and dedicate your lives to helping the poor and homeless? You agreed to remain a team with the same military power structure, with Snowflake in charge, and using your old code names and everything? You agreed to turn your backs on society and family and love. Is that it?"

"You got it." She turned away. "At least this way I know my life won't go to waste. Even if no one finds out what I did, I can die knowing I did my duty to my country and my people."

She entered her own bedroom, crossed to the closet, and flicked through her hangers. Her wardrobe consisted of mostly casual work clothes with a few pieces of combat gear thrown in.

Liam's voice floated across the room from the door. "You don't have to live like this, Lily. You could go out into the world. You could meet a guy and have kids. You could rejoin the living. You don't have to sacrifice yourself the way your comrades did. You survived the mission. You deserve to live."

She didn't turn around and clipped her words over her shoulder. "That's pretty rich coming from a guy who has dedicated more years of his life to the Armed Forces than I have. I don't see you married with kids. You work for Felix Margoles. You're in exile as much as I am."

When he didn't answer, she turned around to see him leaning against the door jamb and blushing down at the floor. "You're right. If you know that much, you have me pegged. I'm just as trapped in it as you are—maybe more so. I suppose I shouldn't trash your way of life. I know you and the Last Division are doing good work out here. You're carrying on the work you started in Afghanistan and I can't fault you for that."

Lily waved toward her closet. She was in no particular rush to let him off the hook. She still didn't trust him. Did he come here to talk her out of her chosen lifestyle? He would get a rude shock if he did.

"Do you want to look at my clothes or not? You're the one who said we were in a hurry."

He walked over to the closet and scrutinized her clothes. "Is this all you have?"

"I have one dress." She lifted a hanger off the bar to show him a short mini dress, all black with a narrow waist and plain, short sleeves.

He rolled his eyes. "I think you better go the way you are."

"You said more than two people would attract too much attention. These clothes will attract more attention than anything."

"Our accents will already tell people we aren't from there. Besides, I'm not dressed for the times, either. We'll just have to show up and do the best we can. We'll change our clothes to blend in better if we need to."

She put the dress back on the rail. "When do you want to go?"

"Right away." He took the box out of his pocket.

Lily's hand shot out. "Hold on a minute. I'm not leaving without saying goodbye to the others."

"What for? They already know where you're going."

She compressed her lips and darted around him. "You really are the most insensitive jerk I ever met, Liam. Jesus!"

She trotted downstairs to find her four friends in the bedroom around the table stacked with automatic weapons, grenades, and ammo clips. Snowflake stopped mid-sentence when Lily walked in. "What did you find?"

"It checks out. I didn't find any mention of a time travel experiment, but I found enough to satisfy me that he came from the government. I guess I'll go find out what's on the other side of that portal."

Echo approached her and held out both arms. "Good luck. I don't like you leaving like this. We've lost too many people already, but I can see you have to go. Just be careful over there. We need you back here."

Lily hugged her. "With any luck, I'll be back before you know it. We'll find this Lady Rhona and we'll find the person who's trying to kill her. If this time travel thing works, we'll do our job and no time will have passed by the time I get back."

"I hope you're right." Betty put her arms around Lily. "Be careful."

Snowflake held out her hand. "I wish we could do more to help you. I don't like sending you into harm's way without some kind of backup."

"You're my backup, Lieutenant." Lily shook Snowflake's hand. She never felt particularly close to Snowflake. Snowflake was always in command and held herself at a distance from those under her.

Now Lily wanted to cling to her. She didn't want to let Snowflake go for anything. "You keep this place going while I'm gone. I need Ironforge to come back to when this is all over."

"You got it. If that's what you need, I can definitely handle that."

All at once, Lily couldn't stand parting from Snowflake without a hug. She flung her arms around Snowflake and crushed her in her embrace. She crossed a barrier holding them apart. Of course she had to hug Snowflake.

Snowflake never really showed her feelings for her teammates. The burden of command held her apart, but it didn't have to be that way. Lily pushed her back and looked up into tears standing in Snowflake's eyes. Even that made sense.

The five remaining members of the Last Division stood in a circle around the room. None of them wanted to lose another friend—not for anything. Not even an order from the President himself could justify sacrificing one more life.

Lily pressed Snowflake's hand and drank in the sight of her closest friends. They were more precious to her than her own flesh and blood, but she had to do this.

She nodded to Liam. He eased into the room and placed his box on the floor near Lily. He positioned himself on the other side of it and pressed one of the symbols on its side.

The symbol clicked into the surface and a buzzing whine sounded in Lily's ears. A crushing weight imploded her eardrums.

Vertigo seized her and spun her around. Centrifugal force towed her outward from the box with unstoppable power.

Liam's hand shot out and grabbed hold of her a moment before she felt herself ripped away. He grappled for her fingers and they held onto each other for dear life as the tearing maelstrom blacked out the room. Her friends smeared away into a bottomless void and everything Lily knew and loved vanished forever.

Chapter 4

G rant Ritchie narrowed his eyes to study the rooves spread out below him. The city of Kald blanketed the landscape in all directions as far as he could see.

Buildings and houses hid the streets winding through labyrinthian neighborhoods to the great castle edifice of Tyrekirk on the far horizon.

Grant's brother Elliot muttered in his ear. "This is a bad idea. Ye ken that, I hope."

Grant bit back a wry grin. He couldn't think of a companion he'd rather have at his side right now than his brother. Still, the prospects didn't look all that promising for their situation.

Grant bumped his brother's elbow. "Go along with ye. We arenae getting any closer up here."

Elliot dropped behind Grant on their way down the stairs to the street. Elliot kept casting anxious glances over his shoulder while Grant scanned the walls closing them in on all sides.

Tension racked Grant's nerves the closer they got to the ground. His senses prickled.

The stairway opened into a normal street lined with crumbling tenements and wrecked houses and buildings. Grant sealed his back to the wall and ducked his head out to take a peek. The street was deserted.

He waved Elliot forward and the brothers slipped into the open. They trotted silently past one block and then another. They took turns monitoring the area in front and behind them. They paused at every intersection to double-check that no one saw them.

They ran on until they came to an intersection where seven streets converged. Grant paused to survey the area and Elliot whispered behind him. "Did ye see where they went?"

"It looked like they were headed for the old Kirkwall Theatre."

"Whatever for?" Elliot hissed. "Dinnae tell me they plan to catch the afternoon matinee before they attack the castle."

Grant grinned at his brother over his shoulder. "Who can explain why these Buchanans do ought? Besides, the theatre hasnae been operating for years. Perhaps the Buchanans plan to meet some other infiltrators there to coordinate their attack."

"If they are, we winnae be able to take them on our own. Two against...how many? I dinnae like those odds."

"If they're too many, at least we can report their whereabouts."

Elliot snorted. "They'll be long gone by the time we report it. They'll move somewhere else as soon as they ken they're discovered. It's hit them now or never."

"Keep your kilt on until we see how many of them there are." Grant stole another quick look outside. "Now hold yer tongue and come."

He jumped into view and darted across the intersection. His kilt kicked around his knees as he ran and his disheveled brown hair streamed out behind him. The wind caught it and whipped it across his face where it stuck in his sweat.

He didn't stop until he reached the far side. Elliot bumped into him and the brothers took cover in an alley. Grant raked his loose hair out of his face.

"Where are they?" Elliot whispered. "I'm telling ye, man. I dinnae like this."

Grant checked his brother and saw a mirror image of himself. Both men wore Ritchie tartan kilts strapped around their waists with leather belts.

They wore no jackets over their white linen shirts in the summer heat. No one who saw them would guess they worked on one of the most highly decorated patrols in the city.

Grant made a face. "Ye didnae expect them to be strolling to market out in the open at this time of day, did ye? If they're anywhere, they'll be under cover like everyone else. They winnae be out where we can see them."

Elliot didn't answer. He stared past Grant's shoulder with wide blue eyes. Before Grant finished speaking, Elliot nudged his brother's arm and nodded toward the intersection.

The broad expanse of open street yawned vacant and deserted in the afternoon sun. Elliot's lips moved, but hardly any sound came out. "Is that them?"

Grant turned around, but he didn't expect to see anything. His heart nearly stopped when two men wearing Creighton tartans entered the intersection.

Sabers swung from their hips and they wore dirks jammed into their belts like every other man in Kald. The strangers ambled across the intersection with practiced ease. Nothing about them suggested anything unusual—except one thing.

Grant was a soldier of the Royal House of Creighton and a retainer to Laird Balfour Creighton himself. Grant knew every member of Clan Creighton by name and face and he'd never laid eyes on either of these men before.

His breath caught in his throat. "Well, what do ye ken."

"They're only two," Elliot hissed. "We can take them."

Grant nodded, too surprised and pleased to consider any objections. He waved over his shoulder without turning around. "Flank them, lad. Get around to Kilbirnie Street and cut them off."

Elliot raced away. Grant kept his eyes glued to the two figures. His pulse quickened when they approached the alley on the far side. If they entered it, he would lose sight of them. He and Elliot would probably never find them again in this warren of a city.

At the last possible second, a blur whizzed around the corner where Kilbirnie Street joined the intersection. Grant barely had time to catch sight of his brother rocketing into the open.

Elliot descended on the pair with a deep-throated bellow. He vaulted into the air with his saber brandished on high. He brought it down with a devastating hack at the taller of the two men.

The strangers whirled around to face him. Neither had time to draw their weapons before Elliot slashed his blade across the tall one's collarbone.

The stricken man staggered backward and fell onto his seat with a surprised cry. He raised his forearm to defend himself against Elliot.

Grant didn't wait around. He charged into the intersection, unsheathed his weapon, and came up behind the shorter man. The stranger drew his blade and lunged for Elliot before he realized that Grant was on top of him.

The short one turned out to be a much better fighter than Grant expected. He stabbed at Elliot so fast that Elliot had to parry to deflect the blow. The stranger knocked the weapon out of the way and twirled on his heel to meet Grant coming up behind him.

Both Ritchie brothers closed on the man at the same time, but they were no match for him. He danced rings around them. Anytime one of them poked a weapon at him, he wheeled to meet it before he pranced off to confront the other brother.

They closed him in front and behind, but he still managed to hold them at a distance. He bought his friend enough time to get on his feet.

The tall man jumped up, but he didn't draw his weapons to join the fray. He took a flying leap and transformed in midair.

He streaked across the street and his pale skin changed in the sunlight to a mottled, tortoise-shell pattern. His back arched and his legs bent forward at a crooked angle.

Grant saw the threat coming straight for him, but he couldn't move fast enough to meet it. The man changed in flight and brought his feet forward to hit Grant with all four limbs at once.

He transformed into a large cat and four clawed feet sank into Grant's shoulder. They pierced the skin so the animal stuck to him with magnetic force.

Grant spun around to fight the thing, but the pain tearing his skin apart distracted him. He couldn't use his saber against something this close. The weapon fell out of his hand and he seized the dirk from his belt.

He knew all about these cats. He'd heard all the stories and fought them enough times to know the damage they could do.

The members of Clan Buchanan were Highland tigers, the most bitter and dangerous of Clan Creighton's enemies. Now two of these infernal things had infiltrated Kald.

Grant fought down rising panic and forced himself to think as the cat sank its teeth into his neck. It yowled to wake the dead while it shredded his skin and lunged for his throat. Anger seethed in Grant's soul and he struck out with his dirk.

His fist thumped against the soft body and the cat shrieked in his ear. Grant vented all his fury on the thing and yanked it loose. It tore his shoulder, but he didn't care. He hurled it as far away as hard he could and it hit a nearby wall.

The cat pounced to its feet and flew at him. Grant rounded on the thing with his dirk clenched in one blood-stained fist. He bared his teeth and snarled at the animal in murderous rage.

The cat saw him and slowed to a standstill. The two combatants eyed each other in mutual hostility, but the creature didn't launch again.

Grant heard Elliot roaring above another cat's spine-chilling howls. Grant didn't dare take his eyes off his enemy.

From a few feet away, it looked like an ordinary cat except for its exceptional size. It could have been as big as a medium-sized dog.

It lashed its tail back and forth and the hair on its back stood on end when it hissed at him. It flattened its ears against its head and coiled its legs to spring.

Just then, the cat fighting Elliot gave a shriek. Elliot growled once and a sickening thud made both Grant and his adversary look over.

Elliot wrestled his opponent in the air. He held it at arm's length for an instant before he slammed it down hard on the cobblestones. He pinned it there for a moment and Elliot's fist gripped his dirk embedded in the cat's body.

Elliot gave his dirk handle a vicious twist. The cat screamed in agony and changed before Grant's eyes into the tall man that Elliot attacked.

Elliot pulled the weapon free, sprang to his feet, and gave his fallen enemy a brutal kick in the head. The tall man's skull whipped sideways with a wet crack.

At that moment, the cat Grant had been fighting levitated off the ground. It soared through the air and hit Elliot against the ear. It screeched to High Heaven and started flaying Elliot to ribbons with its teeth and claws.

Grant charged the thing in a desperate race to get it off his brother. Elliot staggered back a few steps, and in the instant before Grant reached him, he didn't see the tall man struggle to his feet.

The minute Grant rushed to Elliot's aid, the cat flew off Elliot's head. It changed in the blink of an eye and the short man landed on his feet next to his comrade. He grabbed his friend by the shoulders and the two ran off into the impenetrable maze of the city.

Grant spun around to find his brother dripping blood and panting hard. Blood dripped from his scalp and ear. "Are ye all right, lad? Did he harm yer eyes?"

"I'm just grand." Elliot dabbed his wrist to his hairline. Now that the fight was over, Grant could see his brother's eyes glistening through the blood and sweat. "I'm just sorry we lost those two. Ye dinnae look so handsome yerself."

Grant didn't feel the pain in his shoulder until Elliot pointed it out to him. Grant glanced down. Blood saturated his shirt from his neck all the way to his wrist.

He shook himself. "It's naught. Come on."

Grant nodded back the way they came, but Elliot glanced behind him. "Dinnae ye want to follow them to the theatre? They're both injured. We can catch up with them and finish the job."

"They winnae go back to the theatre now. They'll find a new hiding place and we've more important business to attend to. Come on. We'll get the job done and then see to these wounds. We cannae go around the town like this."

He headed back into the slum's narrow, crooked streets. He retraced his steps to a collection of broken-down buildings all lined up in a row. A high wall separated them from the tidal estuary beyond.

Women and girls of every age and description clustered around the buildings. They leaned out of the windows and lounged in doorways. They hooted and whistled at the Ritchie brothers.

"Grant, me love," a redhead drawled down at him from her balcony. "When are ye coming back to see me? I've missed ye."

Elliot jabbed Grant with his elbow. "He's missed ye, too, Elsie. He'll be right along to tend to yer needs just as soon as we move the..."

Grant whipped around and slapped his brother's arm away. "Are ye daft? What do ye have to go telling her that for?"

Elliot snickered in Grant's face. "Ye ken all the lassies love ye best. Ye're so handsome and generous and tender and...."

"Stow that tripe, ye mapit!" Grant snarled. "What are ye trying to do to me?"

Elliot chuckled low while he followed Grant inside. They shouldered their way through dozens of women, some fat, some young, some toothless old hags, some middle-aged and showing wrinkles, some skeletal, some barely old enough to shave their legs.

Chapter 5

G rant led the way up the brothel stairs. He ignored screams and curses coming from the bedrooms lining the upper level. He had been here so many times that he didn't even hear them anymore.

He traipsed down the long line of doors to the far end. A few soldiers from Tyrekirk leaned against the walls. They nodded to the brothers but said nothing.

Grant came to the last door on the left and unlocked it with his key. He let himself and his brother into the room and shot the bolt behind him.

Elliot bent over the bed and ripped the blankets off with a sudden flick of his wrist. "Tumble out, laddie. It's breakfast time."

A young man with blazing white-blonde hair bolted upright wearing nothing at all. "What do ye think ye're doing, ye muckle horse? Leave me alone!"

"It's time to move, lad."

Elliot's broad shoulders and powerful arms made the smaller man look frail and puny by comparison.

He took hold of the boy by the back of the neck and manhandled him out of bed stark naked. "Ye've had yer lie-in. It's lucky for ye I didnae find ye in the arms of some lassie or I'd have to get rough with ye."

He flung the boy onto the bare wooden floor where the poor thing's bony limbs banged with a loud clatter. The smaller man jumped up in an instant. "Ye wouldnae dare get rough with me. I'm Ness Creighton, Crown Prince of Tyrekirk."

"I dinnae care if ye're the Archbishop of Canterbury. Ye're moving if I have to march ye down the stairs like that. I'm sure the lassies would be most amused." Elliot dragged his suggestive gaze down Ness's scant frame to linger meaningfully around his privates. A cruel smirk contorted Elliot's lips into a sneer.

Ness cringed before that smirk and Grant intervened. "It's after four o'clock and it's time we moved. Get dressed and step lively about it. We dinnae have all day."

He migrated to the window and looked out. The girls' muffled voices floated to his ear from below.

He couldn't see any sign of danger out there and no one would come this close to their safe house with so many witnesses standing around to see.

Ness grabbed his tartan from a nearby chair. His eyes darted back and forth between the brothers while he buckled on his kilt. He puffed his chest out and stood taller once he got his clothes on. "Ye're both covered in blood. How do I ken it's safe out there?"

"How do ye think we got covered in blood?" Elliot fired back. "We got these clearing the streets to make it safe for ye. Now quit yer gassing and come on."

Ness pulled his shirt over his head. "How do ye ken they winnae come back while ye're moving me?"

"That's our job," Grant replied. "We dealt to them once already. If they come back, we'll deal to them again."

Ness shook his head. "Ye're both pretenders. Ye dinnae ken what the devil ye're doing out here. Ye just make it up as ye go."

"That's right." Elliot clamped his burly fist around Ness's elbow and marched him to the door. "We make it up as we go and we're the only thing standing between ye and the Buchanan assassins sent to cut yer throat. Be glad ye have us for ye'd be dead already if ye didnae. Now move."

Ness barely had time to snatch his dark blue jacket off the chair before Elliot shoved him away. Ness raked his fingers through his curly hair and cradled his saber and dirk in his elbow while he buttoned his shirt.

Grant unbolted the door. He and Elliot hid behind the door while Grant eased it back. He peeked outside and caught the eye of one of the soldiers standing there. He nodded to the man and closed the door again leaving it open just a crack.

The soldier turned away. He took a single step and he fell on his nearest comrade with fists flying. He punched his friend in the jaw and the two soldiers collapsed scrapping and kicking and bellowing curses at each other. They tumbled across the corridor. In seconds, the whole brothel exploded in a massive fight.

Grant waited until the din reached an epic pitch before he pulled the door open. He signaled Elliot, who pushed Ness out of the room. Grant swiveled to the left where another door led to a dim, rickety stairway to the ground.

The Ritchie brothers flanked Ness in front and behind. Grant never looked behind him. That was Elliot's job.

Grant scanned the dark stairs until he came to yet another door. He laid one hand on the latch while he drew his saber.

Ness and Elliot pressed up close behind Grant's back and he held his breath. He felt Elliot's tension, but Grant couldn't hesitate now. He pulled the door tight and depressed the latch. It released.

All at once, he flung it wide and sprang into the blazing sunlight. His eyes took a fraction of an instant to adjust before he satisfied himself there was no one around. He hustled across a deserted alley between the brothel and the estuary wall.

Ness crowded behind him with Elliot on his tail and Grant set off at a run down the alley. The three men ran single file to the far end of the building before Grant poked his head around a different corner. Beyond the brothel, the slum streets offered a haven from any attack.

They darted from one corner to the next, but Grant saw no sign of the Buchanans. Of course not. They would be long gone by now. They would have gone to ground to nurse their wounds before they made another attempt on Ness's life.

The trio crossed two miles of slums before Grant let himself relax. Just a few more blocks and he would reach the next safe house on the list. They could rest there and clean up their wounds before they had to move Ness again.

After seven weeks of sneaking and hiding the prince in the slums, Grant was ready for a break. He and Elliot had to stay on constant watch for the Buchanans ever since their first assassination attempt. The brothers got into more skirmishes in the last seven weeks than in all Grant's years as one of the Laird's soldiers.

He halted at another large square with several streets leading into it. Carts, wheelbarrows, and piles of garbage dotted the intersection, but no people.

At least no one could spring out at the brothers unawares without being seen. Grant and Elliot chose this time of day to move Ness. It was safer than moving him at night.

Grant measured the square before he waved the others forward. He and Elliot swiveled this way and that to scan their surroundings on all sides while Ness dashed to the far corner. Elliot steered the prince into the last street where the safe house waited for them at the end.

Grant hung back to cover their backs. At the last moment before he ran after them, he happened to glance down one of the side avenues and he stopped dead in his tracks.

Elliot hissed from behind the wall. "Come on, lad! Just a few more yards and we're there."

Grant waved his saber at his brother. "Ye go on. I'll meet ye over there."

"Come on, lad!" Elliot cried. "Ye cannae stay out here covered in blood. Come on!"

Grant didn't answer. He fixed his eyes on something several paces down the avenue. It struck him as so out of the ordinary that he couldn't ignore it.

A moment later, he heard Ness and Elliot running away. They wouldn't encounter any trouble between here and the safe house. Grant sidled into the avenue and advanced on his object with slow, tentative steps.

Grant knew hundreds of people in this city, but these two people stood out like no others. They stood right out in plain view for anyone to see. They turned this way and that surveying the buildings and walls and courtyards with unmistakable confusion. They were lost.

They looked like no other people Grant had ever seen in his life. The man had sandy brown hair cut close to his scalp. His sparse, bony frame towered over the woman, but no one could mistake him for a stripling. He carried a good amount of muscle spread over that large skeleton of his.

He stood close to the woman with a protective air—not that she needed it. She might be shorter than her companion, but she carried herself with an easy confidence that infused all her movements.

Their clothes attracted Grant's attention more than anything else. They both wore trousers. The man wore plain khaki slacks with leather walking shoes and a blue shirt with buttons down the front.

The woman wore pale blue canvas pants with a curious hooded jacket over her curvy torso. Her rounded back end formed a magnificent globe of inviting flesh just asking for someone to touch it.

Wisps of light brown hair framed a full, moon-round face. Glints of gold and red shimmered in her hair. Most of it gathered into a messy knot behind her head, but a few stray waves undulated in the breeze when she turned to meet Grant's gaze.

Grant stalked down the street with his saber in front of him. Whoever these people were, they certainly didn't come from Kald. Neither wore a scrap of tartan. Their actions told him that they didn't have any idea where they were or how they got here.

He narrowed his eyes the closer he got to them, but he could see as plain as paint they didn't pose any threat to him or the prince. They obviously weren't Buchanans.

They both faced him as he approached. The man frowned and the woman smiled. Grant jerked his chin at her. "What are ye doing here? State yer business."

She shot a sidelong glance at her companion. Grant observed the various ideas flickering through her mind as she tried to come up with some plausible excuse to take the place of her real reason for being here.

"We just...you know...we just got to town." She looked around her. "We were trying to find somewhere to stay for the night."

Grant knew enough about interrogating suspects to recognize when someone was telling him a partial truth. "Where did ye come from? How did ye get to this part of the city?"

She shifted her weight to her other foot. She did it subtly enough to try to hide it, but he saw it anyway. "We walked. We came up the river there...." She pointed behind her toward the estuary. "We came through the forest."

Now that was the truth without a doubt. They walked into town and they didn't know where they were going so they blundered into the slums.

Grant cocked his ear when he heard her accent. He didn't recognize it. "Where did ye come from—originally, I mean? You arenae Scottish."

A flash of color washed over her cheeks and she lowered her eyelashes. "No, we aren't. We're from America."

"America!" Grant's eyes popped out of his head. "What brings ye here, then? Ye still havenae stated yer business."

The man raised his hand to interject. "We're just visiting. We heard we might find someone we know here, so we came to try to find her."

Grant pursed his lips. He had to get back to the safe house. He didn't have time to stand around listening to these two run circles around him.

"I'm a soldier for the Royal House tasked with protecting the Crown Prince's life," he snapped. "There are assassins roaming this neighborhood in search of him right now. If ye dinnae tell me what ye're doing here in clear and precise terms, I winnae have any choice but to arrest ye both as Buchanan spies. Now, for the last time, state yer business. What are ye doing in Kald?"

The two strangers looked at each other one more time and the woman's shoulders sank. "All right. We'll tell you. We came here to investigate a threat against Lady Rhona Armstrong. We have reason to believe some of her enemies traveled here to assassinate her. If you work for the Royal House, maybe we can work together to protect them. Can you help us? I'm Lily...Lily Dindle and this is my brother, Liam Barnett." She held out her hand to Grant.

He found himself shaking her hand. "Me name's Grant Ritchie."

"We only want to help the Royal Family," Lily told him. "That's the God's honest truth."

Grant inclined his head the other way to examine her. He recognized the whole truth when he heard it, but this woman's words made no sense to him at all. "There isnae any Lady Rhona Armstrong."

Lily jolted. "Are you sure? That's not what we heard."

"Armstrong is just a title." Grant pointed toward Tyrekirk. The castle's spires rose above the city. Flags flew from the turrets where anyone could see them. "Clan Creighton uses that name for the ruling Laird. His name is Balfour Creighton and he doesnae have a lady. If he did, she would be the only other person who would use the name Armstrong. There isnae any Lady Rhona or I would ken about it."

Liam smacked his lips. "That's impossible. You must be mistaken. Maybe Lady Rhona is someone you don't know."

Grant rounded on him. He tightened his grip on his saber, but he stuffed his irritation down under an iron heel. He couldn't lose his temper with these strangers. If they were right about another threat against the Royal House, Grant had to find out about it.

"I've been a soldier for the Clan since I was fifteen. I ken every member of Clan Creighton and all their retainers and servants and guards. I ken everyone in that castle and I'm telling ye once and for all there isnae any Lady Rhona."

"I believe you," Lily murmured. "I hope you believe us, too. We only want what's best for the Royal House. We came here because we had a credible report of a threat against the Armstrongs—or the Creightons—whichever they are. We're on the same side. Is there any way we can come with you to find out?"

"Ye cannae come with me," Grant replied. "I'm on a sensitive mission meself."

Lily surveyed the square one more time. "What do you suggest we do? Could we go to the castle? How should we approach the Laird with our information?"

Grant hesitated. That was a problem he hadn't considered.

He had every reason to believe these people were telling the truth. He couldn't ignore their intelligence. He had to either act on it himself or report it to Tyrekirk as soon as possible.

His mind darted back to Elliot. Grant had to tell his brother what was going on. Whatever else he did, he couldn't leave Elliot to guard the prince alone.

On the other hand, he couldn't just send these strangers off on their own. He could get disciplined for leaving them unattended when he knew they might be carrying crucial information about the Laird's safety.

He scanned the pair up and down. The man didn't strike him as particularly noteworthy, especially not after Liam told Grant to his face he didn't know what he was talking about. Grant could have slapped Liam's pin head for that.

Lily made him pause, though. As strange as she appeared, he couldn't deny the sense and direct nature of her words. She knew exactly what she was talking about and she hid nothing from him.

He believed everything she said. Every point she made told Grant they were already working together toward a common goal. "All right. Ye can come with me. We'll find a way to get yer report to the castle, but we cannae do ought tonight."

"Why not?" Liam asked.

Grant ignored him. He turned on his heel and strode off toward the safe house. He didn't check to see if the pair followed him. Their heels scuffed the cobblestones behind him. He didn't need to see or hear anything else.

Chapter 6

Grant gave a rhythmic knock on the safe house door. Elliot peeked out and opened it the rest of the way when he recognized Grant.

Elliot leaped back when Lily and Liam walked through the door behind Grant. "What the blazes is this?"

"I found them out on the street. They've got a report of another threat against the Royal House of Creighton. I couldnae leave them wandering about the town. We have to report this to the castle, so here they are."

Elliot threw up his hands in despair and spun away. "Och, for the love of God, man!"

Ness jumped to his feet. "Are you off yer nut? They could be Buchanans and ye'd bring them here, under our very roof!"

Grant let his sturdy frame fall into a chair. He waved his hand up and down in front of the strangers. "Use yer head, lad. That's what God gave it to ye for. Ye can see for yerself they arenae Buchanans."

Elliot studied the pair more closely. "Ye're right. The Buchanans all have a unique pattern to their eyes. Anyone can recognize them if ye look closely."

"If they're telling the truth, we could be facing a new threat against the Laird," Grant went on. "We must take them to the castle to make sure and I couldnae exactly go on me own, could I? I couldnae leave ye to guard the lad by yerself."

"Even so, what are ye thinking bringing them here, of all places?" Elliot countered. "If ye couldnae leave them outside, ye could have put them in another house, at least, and come back here to tell me. The prince is in enough danger as it is without two unknowns around to complicate matters."

Grant hung his head. Now that he and Elliot got the prince behind protective walls, Grant's mind started to clear. "Ye're right, man. I didnae think of that. It would have been the better course. I admit that now."

"So ye'd play games with me life?" Ness yelled. "What kind of guards are ye?"

Both brothers rounded on him at the same time. "Stuff it, lad," Grant snapped. "This is naught to do with ye."

"Naught to do with me!" Ness bellowed. "Naught to do with me! It's ALL to do with me."

"Put a sock in it," Elliot growled. "Cannae ye see we're trying to work this out to be best for ye? Ye arenae helping at all."

Lily looked back and forth between the parties. "We never meant to cause you guys any trouble. Are you okay? You're both bleeding."

The three men fell silent instantly. Grant and Elliot both stared at her for an instant and then they both looked at the floor.

"We're all right," Grant murmured. "It hasnae been the most stellar day on the books, but it's naught to do with ye. Ye arenae causing us any trouble we arenae already in."

"What's going on?" Lily asked. "If you explain it to me, I might be able to help you."

"No one can help us," Elliot snapped, "least of all ye."

"Dinnae bother about him," Grant added. "He always gets surly when he's in pain. Go get the soap and water, lad, and see if Sarah will bring us some clean clothes."

Elliot scowled at the strangers. He gritted his teeth and then wheeled away to storm out of the room.

Grant let his head fall back against the chair. Elliot wasn't the only one nearing the end of his tether after everything that happened today.

The fight against the Highland tigers flooded back into Grant's mind. He experienced all over again the heart-stopping panic of fighting those cats.

Lily's voice came from right in front of him to make his fears and anxieties even more real. "Who are the Buchanans?"

He shuddered in spite of himself. "They're another Clan across the water. They've been at war against the Creightons for generations and they likely always will be. What ye call the river, the one ye said ye walked along to get into the city, it's a tidal estuary called the Boundless."

"What do ye think ye're doing?" Ness cried. "Ye cannae sit there and tell them all! Ye could be the death of us."

Grant rolled his eyes. He'd heard enough out of this poppet for one day. "Cannae ye see they're strangers from another country? Wheesht, lad, how do ye hope to become Laird if ye cannae recognize the simplest evidence of yer own eyes? They dinnae speak the same as us nor dress the same as us. They arenae Buchanans. They're foreigners and they wouldnae be here at all if they werenae concerned with saving yer worthless hide. Now sit down and shut yer mouth before I shut it for ye."

Ness glared at him for a moment before he wilted into another chair. He kept shooting menacing glances at the strangers.

Grant let out a heavy sigh and turned to Lily. "Now where was I?"

"You said the river was a tidal estuary called the Boundless."

"Och, aye." He passed his hand across his eyes, but he already felt his energy draining away. His head hurt. "The city of Kald sits on a peninsula that separates us from the mainland. Did ye see the mountains across the water?"

Lily nodded.

"That's Buchanan country. They live in the mountains beyond."

"But that's right across the water," Lily remarked. "It must be thirty feet to the other side."

"Aye, and shallow, too," Grant replied. "Anyone can walk across the Boundless without getting his knees wet. That's the crux of the problem. It's so easy for one Clan to attack the other. One or the other is always attacking over the Boundless. It's been going on since the dawn of time with one Clan invading the other and then the other Clan turning around and doing the same thing back. If ye're right and someone is threatening Clan Creighton, it must be the Buchanans."

Lily glanced at her brother. "Maybe not. Our intelligence says the people we're looking for used black magic to send someone here. The enemy we're looking for would be a magician of some kind." She blushed and lowered her eyes. "You probably don't believe in magic. I'm not sure I do, either."

Elliot reentered the room with a basin of water, two towels, and a pair of fresh shirts draped over his arm. He caught the end of Lily's comments while he set down the basin. "There's wizards running all over the place. The threat coming from a wizard doesnae tell us which Clan it's from. Both Clans use magic, so that means nothing."

Liam stepped forward. "This is stupid. Come on, Lily. These guys don't know anything we don't already know. We can find our own way to the castle long before they finish trimming their fingernails."

Elliot leveled him with smoldering blue eyes. "Perhaps ye'd like me to trim that tongue out of yer head for ye. Ye'll get on better at the castle without it."

Grant snarled through locked teeth. "Ye two will get nowhere near the castle without us. Go on and try it if ye fancy yer luck. If ye make it past the front gate, ye'll be taking a wee excursion to the dungeons for the next thirty years. How does that strike ye?"

Elliot snorted with grim laughter and his hand drifted to his saber hilt. Lily opened her mouth to say something, but Ness cut her off. "Are ye finished yet? Can ye throw these two out now? Ye're meant to be guarding me, not communing with spirits."

Lily faced him. "We're all on the same side here. We care about protecting you as much as they do and we're very grateful for the chance to go to the castle with you. You have my word you won't regret it. I only wish we could do something for you in return to show our appreciation."

Her words diffused the hostility. All four men pulled their heads in and Grant looked at the floor. None of the men could stay angry when she talked like that.

Elliot bent over the basin. He stripped off his shirt and lifted handfuls of water to his face. He roared in pain when he scrubbed the blood off his forehead.

Lily turned to Ness. "Tell me about your family. I would really like to know as much about your House as possible. You're the Crown Prince, aren't you? That must mean you stand to inherit the Lairdship from your father."

Ness's expression changed in a flash. A ray of sunshine broke across his pale features. "The Laird isnae me father. He's me grandfather. My father Camdyn was killed by the Buchanans. The Buchanans are the most bloodthirsty...."

"Camdyn Carmichael was killed in open warfare that was started by the Creightons," Grant cut in. "He wasnae murdered in his bed as the popular story would have us believe."

Ness rounded on him baring his teeth. "Ye dinnae ken ought about it. Ye're a dullard from the guardroom. It's ye that'll have yer mouth shut if ye smart off to me like that again."

Grant's temper simmered below the surface, but before he could say anything, Ness hopped to his feet and held out his hand to Lily. "Ye should come up to the roof with me. Ye can see the whole city from up there and I can tell ye all about it. What do ye say, lassie?"

She beamed up at him and slipped her hand into his. "Thank you. I'd like that very much."

He raised her to her feet. She smiled with an angelic light, but she bestowed that glorious beauty on Ness. What Grant wouldn't give to get her to look at him like that.

Ness led her out of the room and Grant's soul revolted against the insult. "Ye cannae go up to the roof," he called out. "It isnae safe for ye up there without a guard."

Ness whipped around to glare at him. "Ye stay down here and guard her brother while I look after her. Ye and Elliot get presentable. Ye arenae fit to set foot outside this house."

Chapter 7

Grant closed his eyes and leaned his head back against his chair. He shut his ears to the sound of his brother splashing in the basin of water. Grant didn't want to get up, not even to wash the blood off his neck and change his shirt.

A new image took the place of that tiger soaring through the air toward his face. He beheld Lily standing in front of him outside. Her moon face shone up at him and her crystal blue eyes drilled effortlessly into his soul.

She spoke to him in such a casual, unassuming way and yet she brought him such crucial information. She changed his whole position with a few words. She showed no sign that he or anything around her affected her the way she affected him.

Then he saw her sitting in front of him in this very room. She talked to him in the same mild-mannered tone, but those eyes! He couldn't get them out of his mind. What was she? Nothing about her made sense, but he couldn't ignore her eyes.

Now she was up on the roof with Ness of all people. Grant couldn't think of any man he disliked more than Ness Creighton or any man that Grant would like less to see her go off alone with.

How could a woman like her see anything in a popinjay like Ness? Grant's blood boiled at the very thought of Ness touching her hand.

Grant didn't dare to do anything close to that. How could Ness suddenly grow the spine to invite her to go off alone with him? Ness didn't have the stones to go to the privy alone, much less monopolize the one woman of quality that stumbled on their party.

A voice startled Grant out of his thoughts. "These Buchanans you told us about—how did they threaten the prince?"

Grant's eyes snapped open to see Liam sitting in Ness's old chair. Liam's eyes told Grant a different story and not one Grant liked very much.

Grant was just trying to decide whether to answer Liam or not when Elliot spoke up. "They've tried to kill him five times. If that isnae threatening him, I dinnae ken what is."

"How did they do it?" Liam asked.

"How did they do it!" Elliot guffawed in his face. "Why, man, they sent their agents into the city. They broke into the castle itself. Wheesht! What difference does it make how they did it?"

Liam turned back to Grant. "Did you see them inside the castle? Did you see them with your own eyes?"

Grant arched an eyebrow at him. What in the world was this man trying to imply?

Grant took his time coming up with an answer. Liam was trying to hedge him into a trap of some kind, though Grant couldn't figure out what that might be. "What difference does it make if I saw them with me own eyes? I'm under orders to protect his life."

"So you didn't see them with your own eyes?" Liam nodded, more to himself than to anyone else.

"We didnae need to see them with our own eyes," Elliot chimed in. "They were on the opposite side of the castle at the time. We didnae even hear it had happened until the following morning when the Laird called us to receive our commission."

Grant cringed. He wished he could tell Elliot to keep quiet.

Liam ignored Elliot and addressed Grant instead. "Where do you plan to take the prince after this? Do you have another safe house lined up?"

Grant closed his eyes again and let out a shaky breath. "Now I ken ye're prying me for information. If I have another safe house lined up, it isnae any concern of yers. We'll deal to ye and yer sister. Then we'll move the prince somewhere ye'll never ken. We cannae chance ye finding him again."

"I was just wondering because..."

Grant shut the voice out of his brain. He didn't want to hear another word Liam said. He didn't want Liam in the same room with him. He wanted to wipe Liam off the map.

What was Ness doing upstairs with Lily right now? Was she smiling in his face with that open, beaming expression of delight and acceptance she gave him when he first invited her to the roof?

Grant's stomach twisted into knots imagining it. Ness Creighton! The worm!

Grant should have prepared for this. He should have hidden Ness in another room where Lily would never see his face. Grant should have concocted a story about the dangerous strangers and how Ness better stay hidden until they were gone.

Grant didn't realize he wanted to keep Lily away from Ness until it was too late. That was the real problem. He didn't realize until he sat down in this chair and she sat down opposite him that he wanted....

What did he want? He would have liked to talk to her alone. He would have liked to earn her trust and find out more about where she came from and what she was doing here. She fascinated him in a way he couldn't explain.

Now he would never get that chance. Ness stole her from him when Grant could hardly claim to have gotten her in the first place.

He had to sit here and stew over his lot. What did he have that could induce a woman like Lily to sit alone and confide in him? He was no prince.

He turned his thoughts to fantasies of torturing and destroying Ness when, out of nowhere, Liam's voice weaseled into his mind again. "The Creightons must have all the advantage over the Buchanans when they go to war. They can fly over the Boundless whenever they want and get farther up the mountains while the Buchanans are stuck on the ground."

Grant's head shot up in a hurry. He tore his heavy eyelids open and glared at Liam. How in the world could Liam know about that? How could he know the Creightons could fly?

He came face to face with his adversary and Liam locked his eyes on Grant. In that moment, Grant understood this man better than he dared to admit. Liam knew. He knew a lot more than he let on. He probably knew everything he claimed not to know.

Grant cast a sidelong glance at his brother. Elliot stood rooted to the floor. His wet hair draped over his stunned face and Grant read the same surprise and alarm on his brother's features.

Elliot looked over at him and a spark of understanding passed between them. They both underestimated Liam. What if Liam turned out to be a real threat to the prince or the Royal House?

Grant did his best to deflect Liam's comments and to hide his discomfort. He couldn't let Liam see how much this threw him off his footing.

Grant shut his eyes and reclined in his chair. "It doesnae matter much to me. I cannae fly anywhere. I'm naught but a lowly foot soldier."

"You can't be all that lowly," Liam remarked. "You're responsible for the Crown Prince's life."

Grant cracked one eye open to study the stranger. "Does yer sister ken?"

"There were certain things she didn't need to know. Getting her to agree to come on this mission was hard enough."

"Ye told her about Lady Rhona."

"I had to. She needed to know our objective or she wouldn't have agreed to come with me."

Grant studied Liam closer. For the first time since Liam started questioning him, Grant recognized a flaw in Liam's armor. Some hidden part of his expression changed when he talked about Lady Rhona.

Grant went onto the offensive. "Ye still havenae told me where ye came from."

"We told you outside," Liam replied. "We came from America."

Grant shook his head. "America it may have been, but that isnae the whole story. What's the rest? Where did ye really come from? Why do ye and Lily have different family names? If ye're brother and sister, ye should be the same."

Liam laughed out loud and got to his feet. "Wherever we came from, it must be somewhere with good information. I think I'll go find her. I'd like to see the layout of the city, too."

Grant leaped to his feet. "Wait a moment!"

"What's the matter?" Liam sneered. "Are you worried your Crown Prince won't like me horning in on him while he's putting the moves on a lady? Is that what you're worried about?"

Grant paused. Why did he think Liam would fail to notice a man putting the moves on his sister? Of course Liam knew what Ness was up to.

Grant wilted into his chair. Why should he stop Liam from interrupting Ness? Liam headed for the stairs and disappeared. Grant let gravity suck him into the chair again, but he couldn't relax.

He looked to his side to find Elliot studying him. "That man will cause us no end of trouble. Ye'll see I'm right, man."

Grant sighed. "I ken it me own self. He's a viper in disguise, I'd say." He raised his hand to comb his hair back and he winced when pain shot through his shoulder.

"Come over and get yerself cleaned up, lad," Elliot told him. "Ye'll feel better, and if those two turn out to be as much trouble as I suspect, we'll need ye on yer feet before long."

Grant heaved himself out of the chair. He didn't want to show his brother just how much his shoulder hurt.

He shuffled to the basin and stripped off his ruined shirt. He dropped it to the floor, but he couldn't exactly take a bath in a basin.

Before he could move, Elliot stepped forward. "Here. Let me do it."

Grant stood still while Elliot pushed the ruined shirt into the water. He saturated it and used it as a rag to clean the blood off Grant's shoulder.

Grant turned his head away so his brother wouldn't see him flinch. He couldn't summon the strength to protest or to do the job himself.

Elliot whistled between his teeth. "These are deeper than I realized. We'll have to bandage them up and put some medicine on them."

"Dinnae ye dare," Grant snarled between locked jaws. "It's naught but a scratch."

"It's a mite more than that, lad." Elliot wrung the bloody water out of the shirt. "Ye've got four bad punctures on yer neck and these scratches cut through the flesh. Ye're lucky he didnae hit the muscle."

"I dinnae need ye to draw me a map," Grant snapped.

Elliot dropped the sodden shirt on the floor. "Stay here. I'll be right back."

Elliot strode out of the room and left Grant simmering in resentment. Why did he have to get hurt now of all times? He hated his brother playing nursemaid to him, but at least no one else was around to see this.

Elliot returned with a small jar of ointment. He smeared it on the scratches and dabbed it on Grant's neck.

Grant kept his eyes closed while Elliot bandaged his whole shoulder. Grant sent up a silent prayer of gratitude to Elliot for keeping silent through the whole excruciating process.

Something touched Grant's hand and his brother murmured in his ear. "Put yer shirt on, lad, before they come down."

Grant slipped the new shirt over his head and tucked it into his kilt. The shirt covered his body so no one could see the bandage. When he looked up, he saw Elliot studying him from across the room.

His brother gave all the appearance of not knowing about the injuries, either. He knew how to preserve Grant's pride in front of strangers. Grant could live with his brother knowing that Grant wasn't in perfect working order so long as no one else found out.

Thank Heaven the cat ripped up his left shoulder instead of his right. He could still hold a saber. He could still fight if he needed to.

Elliot leaned back in his chair and adjusted his shirt cuffs. "We'll have to keep an eye on those two."

"Which two?"

"All of them. It's the lassie I dinnae trust. She's hiding something."

Grant made a show of sitting down opposite his brother. "Where do ye suppose the brother got his information about the Creightons? I cannae sort out where he can have gotten it if he didnae get it from the Buchanans."

"Are ye certain he *didnae* get it from the Buchanans?"

"The Buchanans wouldnae tell it to anyone but one of their own and ye saw yerself these two werenae Buchanans. They're outsiders. I only wish I kenned where they came from."

"They came from America, they say."

Grant shook his head. "Then what are they doing here? Ye cannae tell me they walked out of the forest with that story about Lady Rhona Armstrong. It's poppycock."

Elliot cracked a broad grin. "They've got some imagination to them, at least."

Grant couldn't enjoy the joke. "They believed it. They both did. Ye saw that yerself. They both believe in this Lady Rhona and they both kenned the name Armstrong."

"Then why didnae the brother share his information about the Creightons with his sister? Why would he hide something like that?"

"I dinnae ken, but if she spends any time around Ness, she's bound to find out sooner rather than later."

Elliot's head shot up. "Dinnae tell me ye fancy her. Dinnae tell me ye trust her further than ye can throw her."

"How can I fancy her when Ness fancies her?" Grant grumbled. "What lassie would want a soldier when she can have a prince?"

Elliot gaped at him. "Ye cannae trust her, lad. She's a wild card."

Grant let his head fall back and his eyes sank closed. "She's that, all right, but she's here to protect the Royal House. I'd bet me right arm on that. I dinnae ken about her brother, but when it comes to her, I'm certain of it."

Chapter 8

L ily leaned over the parapet and peered down at the ground. "Wow. This is amazing. Thank you for bringing me up here."

Prince Ness Creighton placed his hands on either side of the parapet by her sides and draped his body against her back. He brushed his mouth close to her ear. "The pleasure is all mine, lass. Ye're worth it."

She didn't respond, but she didn't push him away, either. As long as he was trying to get into her good graces, he was her ticket to the Royal Family.

He rubbed his pelvis against her hip. Who was she trying to kid? He wasn't trying to get into her good graces. He was trying to get into her pants and no mistake.

She did her best not to cringe at the ripple of excitement taking hold of her. She and her friends took a vow seven years ago to swear off love to serve humanity. She hadn't looked sideways at a man in all that time.

When was the last time she got this close to a member of the opposite sex? She could barely remember her high school boyfriend or their late-night make-out sessions in his car. That was before she joined the military and the rest was history.

She didn't tell Ness that, though. The closer she got to him and the more he took her into his confidence, the closer she would get to the Laird and the Royal Family. Ness didn't need to know he would never get anywhere with her.

Ness crushed her against the parapet while he pointed across the city. "That's the Boundless and those are the mountains where the Buchanans live. See? They're nearly close enough to touch."

Lily turned her head away from him. "Is that Tyrekirk over there?"

She already knew the answer, but that wasn't what really bothered her. She knew enough about Scotland to know there never had been a city named Kald or a river called the Boundless or any of the other features of the landscape Ness had been pointing out to her.

She also knew enough about Scottish history to know that Clan Buchanan and Clan Creighton had never engaged in any war in any landscape like this one. There was no Tyrekirk Castle, so where the heck was she? It sure wasn't Scotland—not the Scotland she knew about.

Liam said that box would transport him and Lily back through time, but she was starting to put the pieces together into a much more complete picture. What if he transported her to another dimension.....or a different version of Scotland in the past—a version not connected with the same historical timeline or even on the same planet?

That box could have transported them anywhere. If the US government really had been playing around with time travel, they could have been playing around with anything, including traveling to other dimensions.

This version of Scotland had wizards in it. That seemed to settle it. This was no Scotland connected to the world she knew. A dark wizard traveling back here through time had to come from somewhere.

Liam said the dark wizard in question came from modern-day America. Therefore, there must be wizards in modern-day America, too.

She shook those thoughts out of her head. She had to concentrate on dealing with Ness. He certainly demanded all her attention. She would have to work out the details later. She would have to grill Liam on exactly where he'd transported her, but she couldn't do that until she got him alone.

The castle of Tyrekirk dominated the landscape before her. Houses and buildings packed around the castle in a carpet of urban habitat ending in slums. The sun dipped low and reflected off the castle's towers. The dim light cast the castle in a golden glow.

"It's a beautiful castle," she exclaimed.

Ness drew himself up as tall as he could when he pointed at the castle and he swelled out his chest. "I live there. It'll be mine one day after the Laird dies."

"It looks so stunning," Lily gushed. "I'd love to go there someday."

He eased in close to her face. "So ye shall. Ye shall come there with me, lass. I could make ye a lady."

She blushed and lowered her eyelashes. All this romantic flattery made her uncomfortable, but it also stroked her ego. Maybe she wasn't a used-up hag after all if this handsome young prince took an interest in her.

He lifted one hand to stroke a lock of her hair out of her eyes. He eased close and his mouth quivered like he wanted to kiss her. "Would ye like that, lass? Would ye like to be me lady?"

She hesitated and glanced down at his mouth. He had a nice mouth. Everything about him looked good, but she didn't feel right about lying to him. She shouldn't string him along when she had no plans of letting this go anywhere.

She started to say something, but instead of kissing her, he jumped clear with a laugh. "Watch this! I'll show ye something that will really seal the deal."

He leaped into the air before she could say a word. He stretched one arm to the sky, and in front of her shocked eyes, that arm extended farther and farther. The fingers arched into long, curved talons.

The prince's body blurred. It elongated in a rippling mass of gleaming gold burnished by the setting sun. The indistinct shape grew to an unimaginable length spreading across the whole landscape.

The next minute, the apparition congealed in the sky over Lily's head. Parts of it angled to the sides to become wings while another piece whip-coiled into a scaly tail.

Lily blinked up at an enormous dragon beating its wings against the soft hues of the clouds.

The creature let out a fearsome shriek and arched its long neck to glare down at her. The sun reflected off pointed spikes running down its spine to its tail tip.

It pumped its wings, soared across the Boundless, banked, and flew back. It stalled above the roof, dropped onto its clawed feet, and shifted again as it came to rest.

Ness landed in a crouch. He straightened up and dusted off his hands with a smug grin plastered across his face. "There ye go, lass."

Lily opened her mouth and closed it again. "What did you.... what the....?"

He chuckled and sidled up to her gloating. "Didnae ye ken? The Royal House of Creighton are all dragon shifters, the same way the Buchanans are all Highland tiger shifters. Only the royal Creightons can shift, not like those pests across the water. All the Buchanans can shift."

She couldn't tear her eyes off him. The whole sequence of events played out before her eyes. Liam showed up at Ironforge with that time travel device of his. He said their enemy used black magic and the Ritchie brothers confirmed it.

Now she found out the Creightons and the Buchanans weren't human at all, but two warring Clans of shifters. She understood everything in a flash of insight. Liam must have known all along. He knew and he didn't tell her.

At that moment, the stairwell door burst open and Liam himself sauntered onto the roof. He grinned at Ness and Lily. "How are you two getting along?"

The minute the words escaped his mouth, Grant and Elliot charged out behind him. They rushed Ness and seized him by both arms. "Are ye out of yer mind?" Grant roared. "Anyone could have seen ye. We must move ye now."

"What?" Ness struggled to free himself from their clutches, but the brothers dragged him away. "I winnae leave, not now. Get yer hands off me!"

Grant yanked him off his feet. "Move, lad, before I throw ye over me shoulder and carry ye."

Lily spun around. "What's going on?"

Grant didn't answer. He bowed his head and concentrated all his attention on marching Ness off the roof.

She stepped forward to follow them and Elliot dodged into her path. He held out his arm to block her way. "Dinnae ye move, lassie. Dinnae make me have to stop ye."

Lily froze watching her only lead slip through her fingers. "At least let us come with you. You said you would take us to the castle."

"I kenned ye were bad news the first moment I laid eyes on the pair of ye," Elliot fired back. "Ye arenae going anywhere near the prince again so long as I have ought to say about it. Ye can stay here until we leave. Then ye're on yer own. If I see yer faces anywhere near the prince again, I winnae have any choice but to treat ye as our enemies."

He started to back away. He still held out his hand to keep her at bay. She stretched out her arm. "Grant...."

He wouldn't even look at her. He took a fistful of the prince's sleeve and gave Ness one more tug. They ducked through the door and disappeared from sight.

Chapter 9

Ness struggled against Grant's hold, but Grant only tightened his grip and bent his great strength to kick the prince into the street. They made it as far as the edge of the slum before Ness's temper got the better of him.

The prince wheeled around and gave an almighty yank to free himself from Grant's grasp. "How dare you interfere when I was having a private conversation with a lady?"

Elliot barged up behind Ness, slammed both hands into the prince's back, and sent Ness stumbling farther down the street. "Move, ye raging dobber, or yer head's down the cludgie. We've had enough of yer glaikit gobble."

He gave Ness one more cruel shove that spun the prince nearly off his feet. Grant caught Ness and shook him hard before he set the prince on his feet, but Grant didn't let him go.

He wrestled Ness upright by his jacket. "Look here, lad. Ye've done this time. Understand? Anybody could have seen ye up there showing off for all the world to see. Seven weeks we've wasted scurrying about like mice to keep ye hidden and ye throw all that away in an instant. For what? For a lassie ye've barely laid eyes on."

"Ye said yerself she couldnae be a Buchanan," Ness argued. "She was naught."

"She could have been a witch," Grant countered. "Didnae ye ever think on that? She could have shot ye out of the sky in a moment, and thanks to yer dozy pride, we'd have been nowhere about to stop her. Now we havenae any choice but to haul yer stinking carcass back to Tyrekirk to answer to yer grandfather."

Ness froze. "No, lad. No."

Grant lost his composure for a second. He wound back his hand and slapped the prince across the cheek with all his strength. "Dinnae ye dare to call me a lad! Dinnae ye stand there and insult me on top of everything ye've done!"

Ness cowered under his raised arms. "I'm sorry! I didnae mean to. Only please.... dinnae take me back to me grandfather."

"What choice have ye left us?" Grant thundered down at him. "Do ye think I cherish the prospect of explaining this to the Laird? Ye arenae the sharpest tack in the box, are ye?"

Ness whimpered in despair. He didn't dare put his hands down.

Grant pulled himself together with an effort. He took hold of the prince's jacket and forced Ness to stand up. "That's enough of that, lad. Be quiet and be a man for once in yer life. Come along. We havenae far to go and there'll be hot food and a bath waiting for ye on the other end."

He turned and walked away, too infuriated to waste any more time on this idiot. He didn't trust himself not to hurt Ness badly for what he'd done.

Ness flung out a hand and stammered, "Grant...."

Elliot came up behind him and pushed him forward. "Shut up, ye trollop. Now get marching."

Grant didn't turn around for the rest of the hike back to Tyrekirk. Elliot cursed Ness in between rough blows and the unmistakable sound of Ness whining in misery when he tripped and stumbled on the cobblestones.

Grant reveled in Ness's suffering. The Ritchie brothers devoted countless hours of hardship, lost sleep, and skirmishes against the Buchanans to keep the prince safe all these weeks and this was how he repaid them. Grant could smash the dandy's head in for this.

Full dark descended over the city and Grant walked faster the closer they got to the castle. He didn't want to get caught on the open street after dark with a whimpering pathetic excuse for a grown man.

The guard at the drawbridge raised his eyebrows when the trio appeared out of the gloom, but at least he knew better than to question. He let the brothers through the gate and Grant entered the castle he knew so well.

Even the Chamberlain raised his eyebrows when Grant and Elliot dragged the cowering prince to the Laird's audience hall. Grant hardly dared look the Chamberlain in the eye. "Is he still awake, Maxwell?"

"Aye, he's awake," the Chamberlain piped. "Ye're in luck. Some late-night business with the teamsters took longer than expected. He should be finished in a moment. Then he can see ye."

Grant passed his hand across his eyes. "That's a mercy. Do ye hear that, Ness? Ye winnae have to get yer grandfather out of bed at this hour after all."

Ness refused to raise his head. Maxwell's lips quivered when he studied the boy, but he was too polite to smile.

Maxwell entered the audience hall and left the three men alone and silent outside the door. Grant averted his eyes from the other two. He couldn't even look at his brother. Heaven only knew what he could expect from the Laird after this disaster.

Maxwell returned a few minutes later. "He'll see ye lads now."

He stood back and held the door open for them. Grant led the way into the hall to face whatever came. Elliot's clipped footsteps followed Grant's while Ness dropped back and dragged his heels.

Dark and quiet hung over the audience hall. An oppressive stillness shadowed the deserted throne at the far end of the room.

Grant didn't see anybody at first. Maxwell closed the door on them. The latch struck home with an ominous click that echoed through the hall.

Grant stopped in the center of the hall to look around and saw an old man standing alone by the big windows behind the throne.

The Laird's long white hair draped to his shoulders and his frayed dressing gown brushed the floor above his carpet slippers. His cheeks and eyes sagged under the weight of years.

He gazed across the moon-bright city to the light glistening on the Boundless. The mountains loomed black on black over the landscape. "I hear ye suffered a bit of a mishap, Mr. Ritchie."

Grant bowed his head. So the Laird knew all about it. One of the lookouts at the castle's highest spires must have seen Ness exactly the way Grant feared.

There was no point in lying about it or trying to cover it up, not that Grant ever planned to. "Aye, me Laird."

"And the Buchanan spies?" The Laird's gruff voice cut the silence with an edge of menace. "Ye didnae capture them alive as I ordered ye to, did ye?"

Grant tensed for the inevitable confrontation. The hammer would drop any second now. "No, me Laird."

The Laird turned around with impossible slowness. Why did he have to look like such a harmless old man? Why couldn't he look as dangerous and deadly as he really was?

Grant would have felt better if he did. He would know how to deal with a man like that.

"What happened to them?" the Laird asked. "Where are they?"

Grant fixed his eyes on the floor. He swallowed hard to get his voice to work. "They got away, me Laird."

The Laird ambled a few steps down the floor to where Elliot bowed his head in shame, too. "And ye, Mr. Ritchie? I suppose ye let them get away, too, did ye?"

Grant could will his brother to act contrite and submissive, but he knew Elliot too well. The Laird knew Elliot well enough, too. He chose his words to get exactly the response he wanted.

Elliot's head shot up. "We didnae *let* them do ought, me Laird. We engaged with them and they both shifted into tigers. We wounded them both and we both took wounds fighting them. My apologies for saying so, me Laird, but no one's going to stand there and say we let them get away. We would have gone after them and caught them just the same, but we had to mind the prince."

Grant cringed waiting for the Laird's backlash, but to Grant's surprise, the Laird only turned away. He strolled along the large windows at the back of the hall.

He nodded to himself while he admired the view. "I saw the fight. They're still in the city. Ye two will go back out and track them down."

Grant spun around to find his brother gaping at him. Did he hear right? The Laird didn't chew them out for Ness's blunder. He barely even mentioned Grant and Elliot letting the Buchanans escape.

The Laird sauntered over to the men. He halted a few paces in front of them, raised both hands, and circled them through the air in a rubbing motion before his own face.

The space between his palms shimmered and rippled with a watery light. A bluish glow sparkled on the widening undulations until the whole pool radiated shades of blue and white and deep purple-black.

The circles spiraled faster matching the Laird's movements until a shining mirror of vaporous mystery hovered between the Laird and his three onlookers.

Grant gazed into the magical pool as a scene from the city streets materialized before his eyes.

"There they are," the Laird murmured. "They're heading east along Kilbirnie Street."

Grant blinked at two figures emerging from a building. They turned to face the pool and his heart contracted when he recognized Liam and Lily leaving the safe house where the Ritchie brothers just evacuated Ness.

"Ye two will hunt them down and eliminate them," the Laird continued. "The next time I see ye two in this room, I expect to hear that the Buchanans are no longer in this city."

Grant up picked his jaw off the floor. "Eliminate them! Ye said ye wanted them alive."

"That was before. Get rid of them."

Grant shot another alarmed glance at his brother. Ness stared back and forth between the brothers flanking him and his grandfather's conjured apparition. Grant opened his mouth and closed it more than once in a confusion of conflicting emotions.

How could he tell the Laird that Liam and Lily weren't the Buchanans they were looking for? One look at the Laird's wrinkled face told him the Laird already knew that.

The Laird had seen the fight in his magical pool. Nothing happened in this city—at least not anything important—that the Laird didn't see.

He must have seen the Buchanans. He must have seen the short man and the tall man who shifted into cats.

The Laird knew perfectly well that Liam and Lily weren't Buchanans. So why was he sending Grant and Elliot out to kill them?

The Laird himself ordered Grant to bring the Buchanans back alive so he could interrogate them for information about their Clan's activities. Now he changed that order to assassinate Liam and Lily.

A shiver ran up Grant's spine. Whoever Liam and Lily were, they posed a much greater threat to the Laird than the Buchanans. How was that possible when Liam and Lily claimed to be protecting the Laird's family?

Grant read the same truth written on his comrades' faces. Ness and Elliot understood the same tangled mystery, but none of them dared to say a word.

Grant turned around again and found the Laird regarding him with those cold, deadly eyes of his. "Do I make meself understood, Mr. Ritchie?"

Grant and Elliot both blurted out, "Yes, me Laird," at the same moment.

The Laird turned his back on them and shuffled back to the windows. "Find them. Dinnae ye come back until they're finished. Ness, ye may return to the Fourth Tower."

Ness took a few rapid steps forward. "But, me Laird...."

The Laird's head snapped sideways. He didn't turn around. He rotated his chin as far as his shoulder before he stopped. That slight movement was enough to silence Ness in a heartbeat.

Ness froze on the spot and the Laird went back to surveying the landscape. "I'll assign ye new guards within the hour. I'm sure they'll be less likely to cock up a recruit's job like guarding ye. We'll keep ye safe here until the repercussions of yer exploit die down. Goodnight, gentlemen."

Grant slumped against the wall outside the audience chamber and covered his eyes. "Dear Lord in Heaven!"

"What the Christ was that?" Ness hissed. "He wants ye to track down and kill Liam and Lily."

Elliot propped his hands on his hips and paced up and down. He kept shaking his head and biting his lips. "So much the better. At least we winnae be stuck nursing ye."

Ness rounded on him with his hands balled into fists. "Ye cannae kill them. Ye cannae stand there and tell me ye plan to kill Lily."

"Listen to ye!" Elliot shot back. "All ye care about is that lassie. Did ye hear him? Ye're confined to the Fourth Tower. Ye're in disgrace and ye're more concerned with the lassie that got ye into this pickle. Wheesht, laddie! Ye're softer in the head than I realized."

"Ye can tease me all ye like, Elliot," Ness returned. "Ye ken as well as I that Liam and Lily arenae Buchanans."

Elliot didn't reply. He stopped pacing and lowered his gaze to his shoes. "We ken they werenae Buchanans," Grant murmured, "and the Laird kens it, too."

Ness whirled around to confront him. "Ye winnae kill Lily, Grant. I ken ye winnae."

Grant couldn't meet his gaze. "I dinnae ken what I'll do. I only ken I cannae come back until I do kill her."

"Ye bloodthirsty bastard!" Ness launched himself at Grant snarling and spitting. Grant didn't bother to push himself off the wall. Ness didn't scare him. Grant could pummel the prince into next week with one arm tied behind his back.

Elliot caught the prince in his powerful arms and wrestled him back. "Easy, laddie."

"Ye son of a cow!" Ness spat the whispered words through gritted teeth to keep his voice low. "I swear I'll kill ye. Let me go! Dinnae ye dare go anywhere near her. I swear if ye harm a hair on her head, I'll...."

"Ye'll what?" Elliot fired back. "What will ye do? Ye'll sob in yer teacup? Hold yer wheesht, ye bloody bairn. Ye're impossible."

Grant heaved an almighty sigh. "I ken as well as ye that she wasnae any Buchanan, but we cannae go against the Laird's order. It could mean death for us both if we did."

Ness shrugged Elliot off, but his features still contorted with barely suppressed rage. "I'm going with ye. I'm going with ye to track them down. I have to satisfy meself ye dinnae mean to do as he says."

"Ye arenae going anywhere," Elliot snapped. "Ye'll stay right here in yer precious Fourth Tower and mind yer manners."

Ness puffed out his chest at Elliot. Grant had never seen the prince so resolved on anything. "Who'll make me stay—ye? Ye're gutless, the pair of ye, if ye go through with this. To think I respected ye! Ye're naught but hired killers."

Elliot clenched his jaw and glared at Ness, but Grant only blew out another broken sigh. "We havenae killed anyone yet, lad."

Ness spun around to face him, but at least he lowered his voice to a hoarse whisper. "Do ye really plan to kill her?"

Grant hung his head. "I dinnae ken, lad. I dinnae ken what to think. I dinnae dare to think what it really means."

"It means they're spies," Elliot chimed in. "They mightnae be Buchanans, but they're spies from somewhere. He didnae care about the two that got away. He didnae even really care about Ness showing himself like that. He cares more to remove these two than anything else. They must be truly dangerous."

"Lily isnae dangerous!" Ness exclaimed.

Grant shook his head. "I dinnae dare believe that. He's got some other reason to get rid of them, but I dinnae think they're spies. Are ye telling me they made up that Lady Rhona story for a lark? I'm telling ye they both believed it. They were telling the truth when they said they came here to protect her."

Elliot went back to pacing. Ness eased closer to Grant and his voice cracked low. "Give me yer solemn oath ye winnae kill her."

"I cannae promise ye that," Grant replied. "It's me own life or hers. I'll only promise ye I'll track her down. I havenae any choice but to do that much. What I do when I find her, I dinnae ken."

"Let me go with ye, Grant," Ness urged. "I can help ye. Ye ken I can."

Grant let his chin fall onto his chest. "I cannae do that, lad. I wish I could, but I cannae. If the Laird found ye gone—which he's bound to do before long—we'd all be revealed for traitors. We'd all be executed or forced to flee as fugitives."

Ness's shoulders collapsed in defeat.

"Stay here, laddie," Grant whispered. "Stay here and stay safe. That's the best ye can do now."

"Promise me," Ness rasped. "Promise me ye winnae kill her."

Grant couldn't help laying his hand on the prince's shoulder. "Ye ken I dinnae want to kill her any more than ye want me to. I'll do what I can."

"Are ye out of yer mind?" Elliot interjected. "Ye heard the Laird's order. Do ye want to ruin us all? How can ye even think to go along with this madness?"

Grant forced himself upright. "He's trying to trap us. Ye ken this yer own self, laddie. He's trying to trick us by sending us after people he kens are innocent. I winnae play his game. I'll track them down. Then we'll see what's what. I'm not an ox he can steer about by the reins. I'm still me own man."

"What do ye plan to do?" Elliot asked. "Ye must admit they were strange. They clearly came from a foreign land and they wouldnae tell us straight out where they came from or how they got here. Ye saw that yerself. They may have been telling the truth about Lady Rhona, but they were hiding something. I ken it."

"I ken it, too," Grant replied. "I dinnae trust their story and they left too many questions unanswered. The only way to find out is to track them down and that's what I mean to do. We would have to find them anyway to follow the Laird's order."

"They werenae Buchanans," Ness grumbled. "I cannae believe that about Lily."

"Then how did her brother ken about ye and the Creightons?" Grant returned. "He kenned ye were dragons before he ever set foot in Kald. How do ye explain that?"

Ness wilted in resentful silence. Grant read all the signs of agitation and frustration in his brother's face, but nothing remained but to follow the course before them.

A small noise from Ness attracted Grant's attention back to the prince. The younger man kept his head down, but he didn't look anywhere near hangdog enough at being left behind.

Grant studied him for a second before he turned away. He nodded to Elliot, but before he left, he leaned close to Ness's ear. "Stay here, and for the love of God, stay out of trouble. Dinnae ye give him any reason to think ye dinnae accept his order. Understand?"

Ness nodded, but he refused to meet Grant's gaze. Elliot traipsed off down the corridor somewhere and left Grant no choice but to follow.

Grant walked several paces away from Ness before he looked back. The prince stood in the same spot with his head bent. He gave every outward appearance that he accepted his fate, but an air of defiance and energy still lingered around him.

Elliot touched Grant's sleeve. "Are ye coming, lad?"

"I'm coming." Grant trailed his brother back to the castle gate where the guard let them back out into the starry night.

Elliot moved off into the streets, but Grant hesitated to leave. He gave Tyrekirk one last heartfelt glance.

"What's on yer mind?" Elliot asked in his ear. "Is it the lassie ye're thinking on?"

Grant shook his head. "It's that lad. He's up to something. I dinnae ken what it is, but he's bound to blow it sooner or later."

"He's a scabby minge." Elliot turned on his heel to walk away. "I hope he gets the chop. It'd be an improvement on his intellect."

Grant grinned and plunged into the dark city behind his brother. Whatever mischief Ness had hidden up his sleeve, he no longer concerned the Ritchies. Ness would have to learn to take care of himself one of these days, so why not today?

Chapter 10

Lily winced when the safe house door creaked. It sounded too loud in the silence. Nothing moved darkness outside, so she slipped out of the building into the deserted street. Liam stepped out behind her.

Lily ducked around a corner into an alley where the streetlamps didn't reach. The shadows hid her while she caught her breath. "There's no one around to follow us, but we'll have to find somewhere else to spend the night."

"We should head for the castle," Liam suggested.

Lily shook her head. "Not yet. Damn, I wish we hadn't lost those guys. They were our best lead at getting close to the Royal Family."

Liam's teeth showed in the shadows when he grinned. "You're just disappointed because you lost your Prince Charming."

Lily rolled her eyes to Heaven, but at least he couldn't see her cheeks burning.

When she thought about the three men, she didn't remember Ness's scales and wings gleaming in the setting sun. No, she remembered Grant more than the other two.

He was just as tall and solidly built as his brother, but with slightly lighter brown hair tied in the customary ponytail behind his neck. His blue eyes radiated a more greyish hue than Elliot's bright sapphire eyes.

Grant carried himself with something closer to delicacy than his brother. Nothing in his muscular body or his movements made him seem weak or less capable than Elliot. Lily couldn't explain it to herself, but Grant's actions made her think he might be more introverted, more cautious, more circumspect.

Liam mentioning Ness made her relive the moment when she first met Grant in the avenue. He examined her so closely and read her innermost being. She couldn't hide anything from him and his gaze tempted her to reveal everything to him in return.

She had to accompany Ness to the roof when she really wanted to stay and talk to Grant. If only he had protested Ness's intrusion, who knows how far their connection might have gone? He couldn't exactly stop his Crown Prince from leading her away, though, could he?

Liam interrupted her thoughts. "I'm telling you we should go to the castle. We should talk to this Laird Balfour, whoever he is."

"You heard what Grant said. Laird Balfour doesn't have a lady. Are you sure your information is right about Lady Rhona?"

"How could it not be right? It came from the President of the United States. Are you saying he sent us here on a wild goose chase?"

"I'm not saying anything. I'm saying there is no Lady Rhona."

"That's what those men want us to believe," Liam argued. "We don't know if it's true. They could have been lying."

She replayed the look of puzzlement and confusion on Grant's face when she told him that she and Liam came to investigate a threat against Lady Rhona's life. Grant wasn't lying. He never heard of any Lady Rhona. Lily was certain of it.

"There is no Lady Rhona," Lily murmured, "and there's no wizard threatening the Royal House, either. If there was, those men would have said so straight out instead of concocting some elaborate ruse about there not being any Lady Rhona. Either the President is lying to you or you're lying to me. Which is it?"

"I don't know what you're talking about." Liam stole a peek out of the alley. "I told you everything I know about this mission."

"That's absolute crap, Liam." Lily lowered her voice to a threatening snarl. "You knew all along that the Creightons were dragons, but you never told me. Did you know about the Buchanans being Highland tigers, too? Oh, what the hell am I asking for? Of course you knew. How am I supposed to trust you if you keep lying to me about everything?"

He spun around with a gasp. "Okay! I was under orders not to tell you about them being shifters. Felix Margoles knew the Last Division would never believe the order if I told you, but I swear to you the Lady Rhona thing is real. We're here to stop the assassin who came to kill her. What do you think we're doing here if not that?"

"How should I know, Liam?" Lily shot back. "Maybe Felix Margoles made up the story about Lady Rhona to get us back here. Maybe they had some other reason to send us here. How should I know?"

Liam bent close to her so his nose came within inches of her face. "Listen to me, Lily. I understand you don't want to trust me right now and I don't blame you, but I'm telling you the truth. When I was at the Pentagon, I saw the President's family tree. Lady

Rhona Armstrong is right there on it. I don't know who she is or where she is or why the Creightons haven't heard of her, but I'm telling you the God's honest truth. Lady Rhona is real."

Lily stared at her brother in the dark. She couldn't see his eyes, but she heard the strain of urgency in his voice. She still didn't want to trust him.

She leaned back against the cold stone wall. "All right, Liam. I'm going to let it go this once, but if I find out you lied to me about anything else, we're finished. Understand? I swear to God I'll go back to Detroit and you can stay here and hunt after ghosts. Life is too short and I already did my duty to my country."

Liam bowed his head. "All right. I can accept that."

She studied his profile for a moment. Then she walked around him and set off through the streets. She didn't turn around or speak to him. She headed east along the street they originally took to enter this city.

After almost an hour of walking, Liam rushed up next to her. "What are you going to do, Lily?"

"I have no idea. Maybe the Buchanans had something to do with threatening Lady Rhona."

"It couldn't have been the Buchanans. The magician came from our time."

"You heard what Grant and Elliot said," Lily countered. "Both Clans use magicians."

"Then who was it that came through from our time?"

Lily spun around and stopped. "How the hell should I know? How do you know anyone came through from our time besides us—because Felix Margoles told you so? Excuse me if I don't put much stock in that. Unless we see some evidence that some black magician is after Lady Rhona, my money is on the Buchanans."

"Well, how are you going to track them down?" Liam asked. "They're across the Boundless and we're in Kald."

Lily froze and blinked at him. A dozen ideas wrestled in her head. "Grant and Elliot had just gotten finished fighting a pair of Buchanans. That must mean the Buchanans are still in the city. We can find them. Maybe we can get some information out of them."

Liam snorted. "You're banking a lot on what Grant and Elliot said."

"I put a lot more stock in what Grant and Elliot told me than anything *you've* told me, Liam, so I wouldn't push my luck if I was you."

She turned away still seething with resentment. How could her own brother deceive her like this? How could he deliberately mislead her when he knew her history in combat zones? How could he ask her—her! —to go on a dangerous mission in an unknown place without all the facts to keep herself alive?

She might never be able to forgive him for this. If he was anyone else in the world, she would have dumped him then and there. She would have knocked him out, stolen his time portal device, and gone straight home. That's what a real soldier would have done. She would have treated him like the traitor he really was.

She couldn't do that to her own brother. She cursed Felix Margoles or whoever planned this stinking mission. They must have known she wouldn't abandon her brother. Of course not. That must be why they chose her.

They could have picked a few Special Ops people better qualified for this mission than a retired pilot who'd been out of the service for seven years. Why didn't she see this coming? She never should have left Ironforge.

She stormed down the street trying to get her temper under control. She entered one of the many intersections where multiple streets converged into an open space.

A door opened across the square and firelight shone out of it. People crowded around tables inside. Their laughter and the clink of dishes drifted into the night.

A hulking man staggered into view and slammed the door behind him. The inviting scene vanished and the stranger teetered across the square toward Liam and Lily.

Lily saw her chance. She strode up to the man and did her best to smile. A blast of stale alcohol fumes hit her in the nostrils and her stomach turned. "Excuse me, but was that an inn you just came out of?"

He gave a deafening belch right in her face and clapped his massive hand on her shoulder. The impact made her knees buckle. "Aye, lassie. Ye tell the landlord Big Blair Gibbs sent ye and he'll give ye an extra dram on me."

Lily did her best not to recoil from the man's stench. She only wanted to get herself and Liam under some roof for the night. She didn't care where.

Liam came up to her side. "What's going on?"

Big Blair doubled over and vomited a stunning torrent of colored spew on the cobblestones at Lily's feet. She flung up her hands and walked away. "Come on, Liam. Let's get inside."

She entered the inn and left Big Blair in his misery on the pavement outside. Heat enveloped her and dispelled the uncertainty and tension of their predicament—for now, at least.

To her amazement, Liam pulled out enough money from this time period to pay for a hot meal and a room for the night.

Raucous laughter and shouted conversation fired back and forth across the main room. Lily couldn't make out half of what the guests said, but she didn't really care. She enjoyed their company and their crude sense of humor.

Her mind drifted back to Grant while she ate. He looked more like a man than anyone she'd ever met even with blood staining his shirt, muck clinging to his kilt, and sweat plastering his hair across his forehead.

What was it about him that attracted her so much? He didn't even excite as much of a sexual response in her as she expected. His masculine presence caught her attention more than anything.

He interested her at a level deeper than the physical. She wanted to know him, to understand him, to confide in him, and to have him confide in her. She hadn't felt this way since.... well, since Afghanistan.

She hadn't wanted to get really close to anyone even before she enlisted. Not even trusting her teammates and putting her life in their hands could come close to this.

She wanted all that and more from Grant. She wanted him as her comrade, her brother-in-arms, but she wanted something deeper, too.

She wanted to be the only one he trusted like that. She didn't want to be his comrade-in-arms. She wanted to be the only person he trusted with secrets he wouldn't share with his own brother.

For the first time since she left the military, she secretly wished someone knew the ultimate truth about her.

Her teammates back at Ironforge knew all about the Last Division. They were there for the worst of it. Lily didn't have to confide in them and they didn't have to confide in her.

In that way, Liam had been right about her need to stick by them. They kept each other's secrets, but they also made certain none of them ever had to talk about what happened. Not even Liam or any other government sticks who read the classified file knew the real, hideous truth.

Now she found herself craving someone she could talk to about it. She never realized the secret had been eating her up on the inside like this. She ached to tell someone, someone important, someone she could trust.

At the same time, she dreaded Grant finding out. What if he recoiled in horror? What if he never wanted to have anything to do with her again?

He wouldn't do that. She knew that in her gut. He was a soldier. He would understand. He would care.

She had never met anyone she cared so much about and she had only talked to him for a matter of minutes.

How did that happen? How could she yearn so deeply to unburden herself to someone she just met? If she had been alone with him only a few minutes longer, she would have told him everything.

Chapter 11

A shaggy Highlander bumped into Lily when he sat down next to her on the bench. His whiskey glass jostled when he banged it on the tabletop and some of the liquor sploshed out.

"Oops!" He bent forward and sucked up the whiskey between his lips. He gave a loud slurp and sighed in contentment. He looked around and noticed Lily watching him.

He immediately changed his expression to a jocular grin. "Good evening to ye, lass. Dougie McFadden's me name. How's the pork?"

Lily spiked a piece on her fork and put it in her mouth. "It's first rate and I'm Lily Dindle. How's the whiskey?"

He burst out laughing. "It's top of the mark, too. Thanks for asking. What brings ye out at this time of night? Shouldnae ye be home with yer man and yer bairns?" He peeked around her, saw Liam, and pulled his head down. "Och! Excuse me!"

"Don't worry," Lily told him. "He's my brother."

"Och! Well, then! Yer brother! Where did ye say ye're headed? Ye arenae from Kald, I suppose."

"No, I'm not and I don't really know where I'm going. We just stopped in here to try to figure that out. Big Blair Gibbs recommended this place, so we figured what the heck, right?"

The man's face went white as a sheet. "Big Blair Gibbs! Is he here?"

"He went home a little while ago. How about you? Are you from Kald?"

He slammed his fist against his chest. "Born and bred! Wouldnae have it any other way, neither."

Lily sized him up while she chose her next words. "And I suppose you're loyal to Clan Creighton, too. I suppose that makes Laird Balfour a pretty good ruler."

The smile evaporated off his face. His eyes darted around the room before he bent low and murmured into his beard. "I wouldnae go as far as that."

"I hear there are some rogue Buchanans in town," she went on. "I hear they've made a few attempts on Prince Ness's life."

Dougie relaxed and rested his elbow on the table between sips of his drink. "If there are any Buchanans in town, they'll be hiding out in Damerell."

"What's that?"

He jerked his thumb over his shoulder. "The slums on the west end of town, of course. All the unsavory types gather over there. Some even say the lowest of the low go on about cooking up a revolution against the Creightons, but ye cannae believe everything ye hear."

Lily pricked up her ears. "Really? That sounds like people are pretty unhappy with the Laird."

"Och, they can be as unhappy with him as they like. There wasnae ever any ruler born who didnae have some bloody goat after his head. It's almost a badge of honor, like."

Lily shrugged. "That's very true. Still, do you really think there are Buchanans hiding out over there? You'd think the Creightons would be pretty set on hunting them out and getting rid of them."

"Och, they're set on it, all right. The Laird is always sending people out to hunt up Buchanans. Then again, maybe he only says that to hunt up the rebels and makes it out they're the Buchanans instead."

Lily's eyes widened. "Do you really think so?"

Dougie spread his palms where she could see them. "I didnae say I think so, but some do. I'm only saying it. Anyway, if there's any Buchanans to be found, they'll be in Damerell. They couldnae last long in this town if they stayed anywhere else."

Lily nodded over her food. Grant and Elliot got into that fight against the Buchanans in the slums. It made sense that the Buchanans would still be there if they were anywhere.

Dougie ducked his head to sneak a peek at her face. "Ye dinnae want to go hunting any Buchanans, lass. Ye stay out of Damerell. Do ye hear?"

"I'm not hunting any Buchanans," she replied. "I'm just passing through. I was just curious. That's all."

Dougie snorted. Just then, Liam elbowed her in the ribs. "What are you doing? You shouldn't be talking to him."

"How else do you expect to collect any information on our position? We can't exactly walk up to the castle and knock on the front door."

"*Why* can't we walk up to the castle and knock on the front door? What's the point of wandering around out here in the boondocks when our objective is at the castle?"

She rotated in her seat to confront him. "Do you hear how ridiculous that sounds? You heard from the horse's mouth that there's no Lady Rhona in the castle and none of the Royal House has even heard of her. I say we track down any Buchanans if we can. Either way, we'll find more people sympathetic to our cause out here than we will at the castle."

He shook his head. "This is a bad idea."

"I'll be the judge of that."

"This is my mission, Lily. I'll make the decisions."

She raised her eyes to his face and her eyelids snapped. "Tell me something. How many times in your life have you gone behind enemy lines? How many times have you taken enemy fire or been blown out of your vehicle by land mines? Hmm? Tell me that."

He averted his gaze and compressed his lips.

Lily humphed. "That's what I thought." She turned back to Dougie. "Have you ever seen one of the Buchanans in their cat form?"

His eyes popped out of his head. "Seen 'em? Och, no! I dinnae even ken anyone who's seen them. They're elusive, see. They keep to their mountain."

"Except the ones who come into the city, right? Why do you think they do that?"

"How should I ken? Perhaps the whiskey's better over here." He guffawed with laughter and brayed to three other men on his other side.

Lily had to smile at him. "You're probably right."

Dougie got involved in a heated conversation with someone else at the table. Lily took the opportunity to slide her plate away and stand up. She inclined her head to Liam and slipped upstairs to the room they had rented.

Liam eased the latch closed behind her. "You might have more experience in situations like this, Lily, but you still have to listen to me. You can't just pull rank and shut my ideas down."

"Last I checked, Liam, you haven't had one idea since we showed up here. If you can think of any other way to find out who might be threatening Lady Rhona—if she even exists—I'm all ears."

She wandered to the window and looked out. The city spread before her as far as the eye could see. A rim of dark forest surrounded the town on its southern and western sides.

Kald lay becalmed between the forest and the mountains across the Boundless. They cut off any sight to the north. The city might as well be on a planet by itself.

Somewhere out there, across time, modern-day America kept living its life. Lily's friends kept feeding the homeless and helping the poor make better lives for themselves while Lily was stuck in this no man's land between worlds. She might as well be dreaming a dream in her room back at Ironforge. This whole situation hardly seemed real to her right now.

Liam collapsed onto the bed. "I guess we won't be making any progress before morning anyway."

"Don't get too comfortable. We're leaving in a few hours."

His head shot up. "What?"

"You didn't really think we were going to lie around here and wait for the sun to come up before we followed up that lead Dougie gave us, did you?"

"Lead? Dougie? What are you talking about?"

She smacked her lips in annoyance. "Jesus, Liam! What school of espionage did you graduate from? Didn't you hear a word I said to that guy downstairs?"

"I heard you blathering our business all over the inn. That's what I heard."

Lily walked over to the bed. She plunged her hand into his pocket and pulled out a handful of money. He lunged upright, but she got away before he could stop her. "What the....?"

Lily crossed to the door and opened it.

"Hey!" Liam yelled. "Where do you think you're going? Come back here with my money!"

"I've got some business to attend to. Stay here. I'll be right back."

She ducked out of the room and came back in a few minutes. She sat down in a chair under the lamp, laid two pistols on the table, and started checking them over.

Liam glared at her from the bed. "Just exactly what do you think you're doing?"

"I'm arming myself. Only a moron like you would come to a place like this unarmed."

"I suppose that makes you a moron, too, then, for coming with me."

"I suppose it does." She lowered the hammer on one of the guns and started loading the other.

She never used flintlock weapons before, but she'd seen enough movies and read enough *Little House on the Prairie* books to understand the basics.

She got the guns loaded before she reclined back in her chair. She didn't care what Liam said. She couldn't afford to let her guard down on this mission again. She let him trick her into this mess. Now she had to get herself out of it in one piece.

This was no tea party. She could thank Grant for showing her that. She wouldn't get back home without some conflict and she didn't plan to get caught in it with her pants down.

She watched from the window and listened until the noise in the rest of the house died down. The other guests trooped to their rooms one after the other. The inn didn't fall completely silent until the eastern sky lightened with streaks of grey.

Lily shook Liam awake. He jumped up. "Huh?"

"Get up," she whispered. "We're leaving."

She jammed the two pistols into her waistband and tiptoed out of the room. The pair snuck downstairs and through the empty inn to the streets.

The city yawned as silently as the grave all around them. Lily turned her steps back the way they came, back toward Damerell. She did her best to take different routes while keeping to a general westward direction.

Liam shadowed her all the way, but she didn't check his progress. She no longer cared if he kept up or not. He had made himself irrelevant to her mission. She couldn't rely on him for much, so she ignored him.

She paused to check her bearings at the intersection where she first met Grant. Now she would be entering a part of the slums she didn't know.

She weighed her options when Liam sidled up behind her. "So how do you plan to find any Buchanans in this maze?"

She didn't get a chance to answer before something hit her in the head. She heard one ear-splitting screech and then what felt like dozens of needles punctured her neck and shoulders and scalp. They tore her to shreds before she could react.

She struggled out of confusion and alarm when she realized that something furry was grappling at her head. She raised both hands to wrestle it away, but it stuck tight.

She pried her eyes open to find a cat the size of a retriever gripping her with all its might. It yowled and spat while it kicked its hind legs into her chest.

She fought down panic trying to remember what Ness had told her. The Buchanans were Highland tigers. How did they find her? That hardly mattered now. One of them was attacking her and she had to fight back.

Her mind flew to her guns, but she couldn't get her hands off the creature. She clenched her fists into its fur and tried to peel it off, but it overpowered her. How did it get so big?

She wheeled right and left. She couldn't see a thing beyond the tabby belly covering her face.

She peeked to one side and saw Liam fighting another cat. It hugged its forelimbs around his neck while its hind feet scored his legs and cut his pants to ribbons.

Lily took one hand off the creature to reach for her gun, but the cat wrenched its head around and sank its corner fangs into her scalp. She roared in pain and threw up her arm again to force the creature back.

She gripped two handfuls of the animal's loose skin, jerked it free with an almighty effort, and hurled it away in a rage. The cat slammed into a wooden barrel propped outside someone's door. The cask cracked in half and the cat grunted when it hit the ground.

It bounded up in an instant and rocketed straight at Lily. She pulled one of her guns and planted her feet to take aim. The cat streaked through the air and changed before Lily's eyes.

Lily squeezed the trigger, but the cat rotated in mid-flight. Long reddish-brown hair waved out from its head and its pointed face changed into the delicate features of a stately and beautiful woman.

Lily was so surprised she almost forgot to shoot—almost. At the last second, she fired.

The bullet exploded from the muzzle. A cloud of blue smoke blocked Lily's view of her enemy. The next instant, the woman hit her full tilt and rode her to the ground.

The two women tumbled over each other. The strange cat woman seized Lily's gun and tried to wrestle it out of her hand.

Adrenaline kicked in and Lily felt the familiar surge of power coursing through her. No one would take that gun away until they pried it from her cold dead fingers.

Lily saw the woman up close in the heat of battle. Lily's heightened senses read the woman's fine skin and the deep, penetrating intensity of her eyes.

Yellow stripes radiated out from the pupils to a rim of bright orange around the perimeter. That must be the pattern that Elliot mentioned.

The woman startled Lily out of her thoughts by hauling back her fist. She smashed Lily across the jaw and backhanded her swinging the other way.

Explosions burst in Lily's brain. She had to get this woman off her, but when Lily tried to reach her other gun, the woman pinned her wrist to the ground.

Lily's mind went into a tailspin. Liam staggered against buildings and barrels a few paces away trying to free himself from his attacker.

Lily glanced his way in time to see the cat tilt its head to one side and make a dive for Liam's throat. The creature bit into Liam's neck.

This couldn't go on. Lily had to stop the fight before these two strangers killed her and Liam. Their mission would die with them and no one would know why.

She slithered her left hand between the woman's body and her own. She thrust her palm forward with unnatural force and knocked the woman's grip off her wrist.

The minute she got her hand free, she rotated her chest and corkscrewed off the ground to smash her gun across the woman's face.

The woman's head whipped sideways, but the blow didn't affect her much. She could sure take a punch, whoever she was. Lily adjusted her strategy now that she knew who she was dealing with.

In the fleeting instant before the woman could react, Lily lunged off the ground. The woman still held Lily's left hand down, but Lily heaved her torso off the cobblestones and attacked the woman's face and head with her pistol butt. She rained one blow after another on the woman's skull going both ways.

She sensed the woman's strength weakening and Lily doubled down on her attack. She grabbed a handful of the woman's hair, piked at the waist, and slammed her forehead into the woman's nose.

That did the trick. The woman's hold on Lily's other hand went slack. Lily hauled the woman's head back and tackled her flat. She pounced on top of the woman and yanked her other pistol to blow the woman's brains out.

Out of nowhere, the other cat launched off Liam, hit Lily square in the chest, and ripped her off the woman. In a split second, Lily found herself tussling with this other cat, but it didn't hold her down. It bowled her over and over across the rough cobblestones.

The collision knocked the gun out of Lily's hand. The cat leaped free and batted Lily with its claws. It hooked her clothes and flipped her onto her stomach before it jumped on top of her. Its mouth closed around her neck and she felt the razor teeth prick her skin to bite.

Lily's blood thundered in her ears. She couldn't die like this. Her brain screamed for her to do something.

Liam yelled from nearby, "Lily!" but she couldn't do anything. She couldn't even see him.

She craned her head around and saw that strange woman rise slowly to her feet. Blood poured from her nose and her flaming hair crowned her head in a blaze of wild glory. She sauntered across the intersection and picked up Lily's gun.

The woman stalked over to where Lily lay on her stomach pinned in the cat's jaws.

The woman aimed the gun at Lily's head and smirked through her blood-stained teeth. "A nice try, but pathetically useless in the end. Goodbye to ye, lassie."

Chapter 12

Grant halted in front of the safe house and Elliot surveyed the city just beginning to stir with the rising sun. "Well? Where will we look now?"

Grant shrugged. "I'm not a wizard. Ye'd think the Laird would at least have told us where to find them."

"They'll head for the castle, I suppose—if that was in fact their mission—which I doubt."

Grant shook his head. One direction was as good as another to him.

Elliot sucked air through his teeth and hissed. "Sssht! Do ye hear that?"

The brothers held their breath to listen and the small hairs stood up on Grant's neck when he heard the scream of a cat.

He and Elliot bolted in that direction at top speed. They raced through a zigzag course of interconnected streets until they skidded to a stop in one of Kald's many intersections.

Grant's heart plummeted into his shoes when he saw the last of Lily's fight against the cats. He ran to intervene, but by the time he got there, she lay face down on the paving stones with a huge cat perched on her back. It sank its jaws into her neck for the killing stroke, but it didn't bite.

A tall woman in a plain dress towered over her with a gun aimed at Lily's head. Blood, sweat, and grime transfigured the woman into a demon.

Liam rushed the woman to stop her from shooting Lily, but the woman only straight-armed him away.

The woman's knuckles tightened on the trigger grip. Her jaw tensed and the hammer cocked back.

At that moment, Lily flung her arms above her head. She grabbed both of the cat's ears and pitched it sideways. The hammer came down and she pulled the cat's head into the path of the bullet.

The gun exploded and the cat's head splintered in a mess of pulp and brain.

Before the woman could react, Lily hurled the cat's body the rest of the way over. Its weight struck the woman's legs and made her stumble.

Lily launched herself to her feet and Grant didn't wait to see any more. He charged into the square and drew his saber on the run. Elliot flanked him with a blade in each hand.

Lily didn't see them. She locked her gaze on the woman and advanced with both hands flexed to grab her opponent. The woman, on the other hand, stood facing the oncoming brothers and Liam came up behind her.

The woman scanned the party closing her in on all sides. She still gripped the pistol in her hand, but it wasn't loaded anymore.

Grant raised his saber and aimed the tip at her. They could capture her and interrogate her to get her to tell them where the other Buchanans were hiding. She would be a prize worth taking back to the Laird.

The woman cast one more desperate glance around. She looked over her shoulder for any way out, but Liam blocked her path. The Ritchie brothers spread out to flank her.

Lily spotted them when they came to her side, but she didn't bat an eyelash. She trained all her attention on the woman. Capturing this fugitive meant everything.

Lily copied the brothers and spaced herself to form the circle. Grant started to relax. It was all over. They had the woman boxed in. She couldn't get away and she knew it.

At that moment, a deafening bellow boomed across the intersection. Grant barely had time to look over his shoulder when a wheelbarrow came hurtling out of the shadows. It whistled past his ear and smashed to matchwood against the wall by Liam's head.

Everyone whipped around at once to see a monstrous giant crash into view. It lumbered out of an alley and scooped up a water trough sitting in the gutter.

The giant pitched the trough at the party and the projectile sailed straight over Liam's head. It shattered several feet away and spilled water all over the street.

The giant thumped into the intersection. Its every step shook the Earth. The rising sun shone over the houses and lit up the giant's hideous features. One ear stuck out of the top of its head along with a few tufts of sparse hair. The other ear protruded from somewhere near where the corner of its jaw would have been if its jaw had been the normal shape.

One eye boggled at an angle toward the sky. The other drooped to look at the ground on the other side of the giant's feet.

One arm came out of its shoulder at the usual angle while the other grew out of its front ribs. The mouth opened on one side to show a few scattered, mangy teeth. The other side stayed closed when the creature roared in fury at nothing in particular.

Grant spun around to face the oncoming menace and spotted something moving behind its back. A tall, thin young man emerged from the same alley and moved his fingers in curious patterns.

Grant recognized the boy from the Laird's court. Bluish-white shimmers jetted from his fingertips to surround the giant and he moved it around on puppet strings. He was a wizard and he used magic to manipulate the monster.

The gleaming tendrils flowed down the giant's arms to its hands. The wizard's magic infused the monster with energy that burst out of it in explosive movements.

The giant flailed its massive arms to one side and smashed its fist into the nearest wall. Blocks came loose and scattered at the giant's feet, but it already was turning its attention to the party staring at it in horror.

Grant moved a step back to let the thing through. The wizard came from the Laird, so he must have sent the giant after the Buchanans.

Elliot sidestepped to give the creature access to the woman, but the thing didn't go after her at all. It wheeled to the right and hooked its misshapen arm around Lily. It hoisted her off the ground and brandished her on high.

She yelled and kicked and punched the giant's arms, but it only clenched her tighter. Grant lunged forward to intervene, but another young wizard stepped out of the same alley and took his place next to his companion. He curved his fingers into a fist and flicked them at the party.

A rotating ball of greenish fire erupted from his fingertips, passed the giant, and changed into a twisting, tumbling, knotted ball of rope.

It rolled past Grant's head and flew straight for Liam. The rope hit him in the stomach and a hundred tendrils slithered all over him. They wound him in their coils until he couldn't move.

Liam and Lily fought back with all they had, but the wizards' magical spells held them captive. Grant spun one way and then the other, unsure which to help first. He hardly dared tackle the giant, but he couldn't leave Lily unprotected.

The Buchanan woman took in the whole sight and backed away. She checked the giant and the ropes binding Liam. She looked back at the wizards, but they never gave her a second glance.

She eased back one step at a time until she came to the edge of the intersection. Elliot spotted her and sprang forward to cut off her retreat. "Hey! Stop, ye!"

At that moment, one of the ropes holding Liam broke free and shot across the street. It whipped around Elliot's ankle to pull him back. The woman saw and made her last break for freedom.

Grant dove for Elliot and severed the rope holding him. It cracked back and snaked around to attack Grant, but he had already leapt clear.

He rushed the giant and plunged his saber into the creature's tree trunk thigh even though he already knew that wouldn't do any good.

The creature thundered to the skies, but no blood came from the wound. It wasn't alive. It was another magic spell.

The giant lumbered toward Grant and swung its other arm to pulverize him. Lily aimed a pointed kick at its head and the monster missed by inches to give Grant a chance to jump out of the way.

Just then, a torrential blast of icy wind screeched past Grant's temple. It ruffled the giant's hair, blew around its head, and hit the young man manipulating the thing from behind. It struck him hard and the man's kilt flew forward when he staggered under the blow.

The giant let out another stricken bellow. It stopped trying to hit Grant and searched for the source of the attack. Grant, Elliot, and Lily all did the same and saw Liam.

Licks of fire crawled up his legs and incinerated the ropes holding him a prisoner. Before he got free, he grabbed the loose end and twisted it around his arm. He massaged it between his fingers and hurled it at the giant.

The line stretched out of his hand into a long whip. Dozens of ropes twisted and contorted over each other twining across the intersection. They streaked past the giant to attack the wizard who created the ropes in the first place.

The man couldn't get his hands up fast enough to protect himself. The fibers surrounded him in an insoluble mass. He couldn't escape. His comrade spun around to stare and then he whirled the other way to confront Liam.

Liam didn't give either of them a chance to counterattack. He curled his fingers and yanked his magical ropes to jerk the wizard off his feet. The man flew forward and collided with his friend.

The giant shuffled its feet in confusion. Its eyes boggled in all directions, but it didn't move or attack so long as Liam distracted the wizards.

Lily gaped at her brother with her mouth open, but Liam didn't notice. He advanced on the giant while he focused all his attention on the two wizards.

The taller wizard in charge of the giant snapped his fingers. The giant wavered for a moment and then put out its foot to sidestep. A second giant identical to the first materialized out of the apparition to take its place in the square.

Grant shrank back and raised his saber ready to fight for his life. The second giant mirrored the first in every detail except that it wasn't holding Lily in its fist. The wizard snapped again and a third giant appeared.

Elliot bumped into Grant as they both inched away. Only Liam advanced. He marched right up to the three giants, but he didn't even look at them. He acted like they didn't exist, which they probably didn't.

Liam strutted between the giants' legs and stopped face to face with his enemies. The smaller wizard jumped to his feet, drew in a deep breath, and puffed out his cheeks.

All the rope Liam used to bind him exploded off the wizard in tufts of shredded hemp. The fragments fluttered to the ground and the two wizards confronted Liam side by side.

Lily burst into a frenzy. She kicked and scratched at the giant holding her. She sank her fingernails into its eyes and kicked it in the teeth. The creature roared in fury, but that left two more giants to come after Grant and Elliot.

Grant measured the battle. He and Elliot couldn't take the wizards and he could only defeat the giants by defeating the wizards. Grant eased back one more step and bumped against a solid brick wall.

One glance at Elliot told him his brother sensed the same impending doom. They couldn't fight these giants and they couldn't get away.

The taller wizard arched his back and raised both arms out from his sides. He inhaled a deep breath and lifted off the ground.

That curious bluish glow animating the giant sparkled out of the wizard's chest and rippled down his arms. It flowed wider to form two wings on either side of his body.

He grew bigger and bigger until the shining image all around him covered his features. He took the shape of an enormous ghost woman gleaming and floating in the air above Liam's head.

All of a sudden, the thing shot forward and the ghost extended its arms toward Liam. The beautiful face transfigured into a gaping, grinning skull baring ugly teeth to bite him.

Liam shot out a hand and fired some vaporous energy at the figure, but it blasted straight through the thing and had no effect.

The smaller wizard darted in front of his friend and dropped down on one knee. He lifted his arms above his head and his comrade took hold of his wrists. The two combined their power into one gargantuan shade looming over Liam.

Liam punched one hand in front of him followed by the other. A ball of fire erupted out of one palm. Then he unleashed a streak of lightning from the other. None of his tricks made a dent in the ghost.

The shade swelled to twice its size, three times its size, and kept on growing. It curved forward to surround Liam. The two giants menacing Grant and Elliot marched another shuddering step forward. One of them bent down to grab Grant, but he slashed its hand with his saber.

Tension crackled in the air. The bigger the ghost got, the more threatening and oppressive the atmosphere became. It threatened to blow at any second.

The giants made another swipe for Grant and Elliot. The brothers hacked their sabers back and forth, but they couldn't hold the creatures off much longer.

At that moment, the simmering pressure building around Grant's head detonated in a catastrophic boom. The ghost burst in a flaming concussion of light, sound, and heat.

The shockwave sent Liam spinning away. His arms and legs flew forward. He soared past the giants and landed flat on his back on the cobblestones.

Lily screamed his name as the giant holding her turned its attention to Liam's lifeless body.

The creature stomped across the intersection and straddled Liam. It picked him up and turned the floppy remains over and over in front of its ridiculous eyes.

"Liam!" Lily shrieked. "Liam, wake up!"

Grant's heart sank. Liam alone stopped those wizards from annihilating all four of them. The Laird never cared about the Buchanans. He was after Liam and Lily.

The Laird must have sensed that Grant couldn't go through with killing the pair the way the Laird ordered him to, so he sent these two wizards to do the job instead.

Now the wizards would use their giant puppets to execute the Ritchie brothers along with Liam and Lily. Whatever threat Liam and Lily posed to the Laird would die with them. No one would ever know about it once the Laird eliminated all the witnesses.

The giant dropped Liam's body to the ground and lifted his foot to stomp Liam to a pancake. The giants standing in front of Grant and Elliot leaned forward, too.

They spread their meaty hands to grab the brothers. Grant braced himself to go down fighting. He couldn't do anything to kill these giants.

The two wizards stood back against a building well out of danger to watch the giants do their work for them.

The giant in front of Grant made a grab to snatch him off the ground. Grant lunged with his saber, but instead of cutting the monster's hand, he impaled it through the palm. The thing bellowed to shake the city and reared back in alarm.

Grant tried to pull his weapon free, but the giant moved too fast. It jerked the blade out of Grant's hand and left him unarmed.

The giant balled its other hand into a fist and raised it high to flatten Grant when, out of nowhere, a blistering jet of fire woofed across the square. It thumped around both giants and scorched their hair off their scalps.

Everyone turned at the same moment and Grant's eyes nearly fell out of his head when a huge golden dragon strutted around the corner. The rising sun angled between the buildings and lit up the creature's scales.

The dragon lowered its head close to the ground, opened its mouth, and spat another inferno of flame, not at the giants, but at the two wizards.

Both men raised their hands to protect themselves, but they were too late. The fire caught them and scorched them to ash in seconds.

The two wizards screamed and writhed in their death throes, but the dragon didn't let up. It unloaded a vicious barrage until two men twisted into knots and vaporized in smoke.

The giants vanished the instant the fire destroyed the wizards. Grant's saber clattered to the pavement in front of him. Lily dropped like a stone and landed on her feet next to her brother.

Chapter 13

Lily dropped on her knees next to her brother and cradled his head in her arms. "Liam! Liam!"

Why, oh why did this have to happen? Why did he have to die like this? She picked him up and rocked him in her arms. He startled her out of her mind by coughing and convulsing out of her grasp.

She pressed his head to her chest. "Oh, Liam! I thought you were dead!"

Grant rushed the dragon and waved his saber at it. "What the devil do ye think ye're doing? How many times do I have to tell ye to keep out of sight?"

The dragon shrank in on itself. It imploded to a fraction of its size and changed into Ness Creighton.

The prince propped his hands on his hips and bobbed his head at Grant. "Ye're welcome for saving yer stinking backside. If ye'd let me come with ye in the first place, none of this would have happened."

"If we'd let ye come with us in the first place, we'd all be in the dungeon right now—or worse," Grant fired back. "Do ye realize what ye've done? Ye've condemned all of us to death. The Laird will ken we betrayed our orders—all of us—ye, too, lad."

"What orders?" Lily asked.

Grant compressed his lips and Elliot answered for him. "The Laird ordered us to kill ye—both of ye. He must have guessed we couldnae go through with it, so he sent his wizards to make sure."

"Why would he want to kill us?"

"Ye tell me," Elliot returned. "Why would he want to kill ye? What are ye doing here that threatens him?"

"I don't know anything about that," she returned. "I told you everything I know. We're here to help him, not to threaten him."

"None of that means ought," Grant interrupted. "We have to get out of the city before he sends another team to bring us down."

Ness waved to the right and the left. "Excuse me! Is anyone even slightly grateful that I just saved all yer lives? I havenae heard one word of thanks."

"Thank ye," Grant snapped. "Now will ye hold yer noise and get the hell out of here?"

"Where are we supposed to go?" Lily helped Liam to his feet, but he wobbled and leaned on her for support.

"There's only one place to go and that's the forest west of Kald. Come on. We havenae much time and it's near broad daylight. Anyone coming after us will see us plain as day."

Lily staggered under Liam's weight, but they only made it a few blocks before Liam rallied. He straightened up and supported himself on his own feet. The party moved much quicker after that.

Grant and Elliot guided the party through slums that became more squalid and run-down the farther they went. Lily glanced behind her toward Tyrekirk dwindling into the background.

How could she be running away from her objective instead of toward it? Maybe she should have listened to Liam and gone to the castle when she had the chance. Now she might never accomplish her mission.

Then again, if the Laird wanted her dead, going to the castle would get her killed. Now she was running for her life to get away from the very man she came here to help.

The party ran for a long time before they came to the last sparse buildings dotting the city's edge. In a moment, the party passed through the city wall and plunged into deep woods lining the estuary.

Grant and Elliot kept up a punishing pace. Liam and Lily stayed with them, but Ness kept falling behind. The four of them had to stop too often to let him catch up.

Grant said nothing, but the fifth time this happened, Elliot took hold of the prince's fancy jacket and gave him a cruel yank. "Keep pace with us, lad, if ye dinnae want to be left behind."

Ness sweated and puffed. Lily's heart went out to him, but she kept quiet. This was a matter of life and death. None of them could sacrifice themselves for Ness's comfort. If he couldn't keep up, he would probably get captured or killed.

The sun went down behind the trees. The forest grew dark long before the stars came out, but the Ritchie brothers maintained their grueling drive until long after nightfall. Ness whimpered at practically every step and stumbled over the slightest obstacle.

Lily hardened herself against him the longer this went on. He was a baby. He had never faced any hardship in his life and he would become a liability if he couldn't put up with this.

Grant halted on the brow of a low hill where they could see over the woods. The lights of Kald shone in a pool of beauty lining the estuary. The forest surrounded this vantage point in an endless sea of black.

Grant pointed down the hill on the other side. "We'll make camp down there. It's as good a place as any, but we winnae risk a fire. We're still close enough to Kald to be seen."

No one argued. Ness limped at the rear on the last torturous steps down the hill. The group halted in a small clearing among the thick trees and Ness collapsed to the ground.

Grant and Elliot completely ignored him. Grant took a turn around the clearing and peered into the darkness, but there was nothing to see. "We'll set up a watch and take it in turns to get some sleep."

"I winnae stand watch," Ness grumbled. "I'm too exhausted to see straight and I cannae walk another step."

Lily rolled her eyes. She didn't mean for anyone to see her, but she caught a hint of a smile twitching the corners of Grant's mouth when he noticed.

"We'll take our turns with you," she told him.

"I'll stand the first watch," Liam replied. "My head hurts too much to sleep anyway."

"I'll stand with ye," Elliot added. "The rest of ye lot get some sleep. We'll wake ye at midnight to take yer turns."

"Aye." Grant squatted down.

"I'm cold," Ness whined. "Why cannae we light a fire? No one can see us. The hill blocks us from town."

Grant sat the rest of the way down on the ground. "Go to sleep and rest yer feet. Ye've another long march in the morning."

"I asked ye a question. Why cannae we have a fire?"

Grant's voice cut the stillness with a much sharper edge. "Because I say so. That's why. Now do ye want to sleep or do ye want to moan all night, for I winnae sit around and listen to ye."

Ness rubbed his arms with his hands. "It's too cold to sleep out here on the ground."

Grant snorted and propped his back against a nearby trunk. "It feels all right to me."

Lily watched the interplay between the two men. Grant's subtle authority shone through everything he did. No one could argue with him, not even the Crown Prince. Grant's word was law, even to his own brother, and what he said went no matter what.

Lily's old attraction took hold and she sat down a few feet away from him. She wanted to talk to him, to figure him out, but she didn't know where to start.

Elliot batted Liam's shoulder. "Come along, lad. We'll take a wander about the park."

The two men strolled off into the dark and Grant turned to Lily. "Where did ye learn to fight like that?"

She blushed and lowered her eyes. At least he couldn't see her cheeks burning in the shadows.

Before she could answer, Ness scooted over next to her. "Come to me, lassie. Let's keep each other warm tonight."

He put out his arms to embrace her, but she only laughed. "You just said you were too exhausted to keep watch, so you must be too exhausted for anything else. Lie down and rest."

"It's too cold," he insisted. "How can I sleep when I keep dreaming of ye?"

Lily shot another sidelong glance at Grant. This time, he smiled with all his teeth showing. The expression encouraged her.

"Here," she told Ness. "Lie down here with your head near me. I'll stroke your hair until you fall asleep. Maybe once you're asleep, you won't think about me anymore."

"I'll never stop thinking about ye, lassie. Ye're me one true love."

Lily laughed it off, but she couldn't stop blushing, especially with Grant watching. She guided Ness down on the ground at her side. He folded one arm under his head and she ran her fingers through his hair until his breathing lengthened in the easy tide of slumber.

She looked up to find Grant studying her. "Ye're a sorceress, lassie. Ye ken ye are."

"Not me. I think you have me confused with someone else."

"I didnae mean that kind of sorceress. I only meant ye used yer charms to deflect him from courting ye."

She tried to make his comments into a joke. "Don't tell me you're jealous of him."

"I was at first. I didnae see it before, but now I realize a woman like ye could never really have anything in common with him."

"What do you mean—anything in common with him? He's a prince. I'm...."

He waited for her to finish. "Ye're what? What exactly are ye and yer brother?"

Lily colored again. She watched her hand caressing Ness's head so she wouldn't see Grant scrutinizing her. "I don't know what *he* is. Whatever he is, I'm not. I could never do.... what he did back there."

"He's a wizard," Grant replied. "That's plain."

"I don't know anything about that. If he is, it's news to me."

Grant cocked his head. "Tell me where ye came from. Tell me the truth this time. Ye're a fighter. I havenae seen a woman fight like that before. Where did ye learn it?"

She shrugged the question away. She didn't want to talk about that. "Don't tell me you were really jealous of him."

"Is it so hard to believe?" Out of nowhere, he put out his hand and rested it on top of hers where it lay on her knee. "I havenae met any woman that captivates me the way ye do. I want to understand all. Dinnae ye ken ye can trust me by now?"

Lily froze at his touch. Did she make a mistake? Did she make him think she wanted more than she did? Who was she fooling? She *did* want it, but now that it happened, she didn't know what to do or how to act.

"How couldnae ye ken yer own brother's a wizard?" he asked. "How could the Laird go after ye like that if ye didnae ken? I must ken, lass. Ye must tell me if we're to join together like this."

A spark of alarm coursed up her arm and down her leg from his hand. "Join together! No one said anything about joining together!" She pulled her hand free and scooted away from him.

"I didnae mean that! I meant traveling together, no...." He broke off, too flustered to continue. "Och, never mind. Ye've got yer prince. Ye dinnae care ought for a common soldier."

"Do you think I care about him being a prince? How could you think that? Do you think all his flattery means anything to me? You should know better."

"How can I ken when ye winnae tell me ought about yerself? Ye dinnae trust me. I can see that much."

Lily sank back down on the ground. She wanted to tell him. She really did. If he was going to get offended at her pulling away from him, he better know the real reason why. "It's not that. I do trust you. It's just .... things happened to me....in the past. I...."

He sat impossibly still. He made no sound. He didn't move. If she was going to understand him and confide in him, it was now or never.

"I was in a war," she murmured. "I was in the Army and I got caught in a dangerous situation. My Division was assigned a mission behind enemy lines. We went in to evacuate a group of civilians that got trapped by the enemy. They would all have been wiped out and we went in to get them to safety. I was the pilot...."

"Och, aye," he replied. "What class of boat was it?"

She took a deep breath. She couldn't lose her composure, now when she perched on the brink of revealing her innermost self to him.

"It wasn't a boat. Anyway, we lost a lot of good people on that mission, but we got all the civilians out. We didn't lose a single one, but it got ugly for a while. It looked like none of us would make it out alive. It took all of us fighting and a lot of us giving our lives before we succeeded."

He didn't say anything. She found herself shaking from the effort of getting the words out. She never dreamed telling someone would be this hard.

"In the end, there were only five of us left alive. We made a pact to turn away from the world and dedicate our lives to serving humanity. We swore off love and family and everything. We've worked for seven years to help the poor and the needy before I got called up to go on this mission with Liam. That's the only reason why...."

He stared straight ahead of him into the dark. "I see."

"I'm sorry, Grant." She found herself talking faster in a desperate race to convince him of something she wasn't sure of herself. "If I was going to get with anybody, it would be someone like you. You're.... well, I guess it doesn't matter. I made a promise, and even if I hadn't, I'm not the sort of person you or anybody else would want to get involved with."

He whipped around to stare at her. His eyes glittered in the dark. "What makes ye say that?"

"I'm messed up. I've been in combat. I've seen my comrades blown to pieces before my eyes. I've dragged their dismembered bodies to safety, even when I knew there was no chance that I could save them. I've seen the worst humanity can dish out. I'm.... I'm haunted."

"I've been in combat, too," he hissed. "Did it ever cross yer mind I might want someone who had been in combat, someone haunted? Did ye ever think on that?"

She blinked at him. That possibility never did cross her mind.

She never once considered that someone who had been in combat, someone who had seen his comrades die before his eyes, might want the company of someone like himself.

She always thought she was too damaged to be attractive to anyone. She thought she was poisoned on the inside. She thought anyone who found out the truth about her would understand why she had to stay isolated and alone for the rest of her life.

Her teammates in the Last Division understood because they carried the same poison inside them. They helped each other confine their contagion to Ironforge where they wouldn't corrupt normal people trying to live decent lives.

She sized up Grant as if for the first time. If he was telling the truth that he was haunted like she was, maybe he could help her isolate it, too.

Maybe, between the two of them, they didn't have to keep it isolated anymore. Maybe they canceled out each other's poison so it wouldn't contaminate anything ever again.

"So why do ye and yer brother have different family names?" he asked. "Do ye have different fathers or some such mix-up?"

"Dindle was my code name during the operation. We had to keep our identities a secret from the civilians. The authorities wanted to be able to deny that they sent any military personnel into the area if any of us got captured or if the enemy captured the civilians and tortured them to find out who helped them. We all used different names. After we repatriated back home, we decided to keep our command structure and to keep using our codenames. Don't ask me why. It doesn't make any sense when I look back on it, but it seemed like the right thing to do at the time. It just seemed like that was the best way to continue what we started on the mission."

He nodded, but he didn't answer. What was he thinking? He sat so still that she couldn't read his reaction. An air of silent attention hovered around him.

He finally turned away, leaned back on his elbow, and pillowed his arm under his head. "We'd best get some sleep, lass. Liam and Elliot will be back in a few hours to wake us up. Go to sleep. Ye've done some hard miles today and ye'll be doing some more tomorrow if I'm not mistaken."

He closed his eyes, but Lily remained awake for a long time after he fell asleep. She gazed down at his face.

What if Liam was right? What if there was a chance for her to come back from the living dead? What if she wasn't locked in a tomb of past nightmares? What if a time came for her to break the vow she made to the Last Division?

Chapter 14

G rant stood in the silent forest and studied Lily's sleeping face. She lay curled up on the cold, hard ground next to Ness.

The prince tossed and turned in fitful agitation, but Lily slept without disturbance. A peaceful expression played on her face and her eyes darted back and forth under her eyelids.

She presented such a mysterious puzzle. Even that story she told him last night brought up more questions than it answered.

What war could she possibly have fought in that matched the details she described? He couldn't think of any war in recent history where a woman pilot would have gone behind enemy lines to save a bunch of trapped civilians.

She wasn't lying, though. He was certain of that. No one would claim to be haunted by combat who wasn't. Her skills and her presence of mind fighting the cats and the giants proved that. She learned to fight somewhere. Where else could she learn than in the Army fighting a war?

His stomach flipped gazing down at her. The secret smile she gave him when Ness moaned about the cold gave Grant the thrill of his life. Ness could never understand about being haunted by combat. Maybe Grant had a chance with her after all.

Ness's pathetic efforts to win her over deflected right off her tough exterior and now Grant understood why. She swore off life and love and happiness after her experience in the war. If Grant couldn't have her, Ness didn't stand a chance.

Liam sauntered over and settled himself on the ground nearby. His presence disturbed Grant out of his thoughts and he shook Lily by the shoulder. "Time to wake up, lassie. It's time to go on watch."

She bolted upright. She stared around her with wild eyes before she frowned up at Grant. "It's midnight, lass. Time to change the watch."

She rubbed her forehead before she nodded and stood up. The more she moved around, the more her features cleared.

She moved with deliberate, purposeful movements that told him she was ready for anything. She got to her feet, brushed the dirt off her trousers, and got busy pulling her hair into a tidier knot behind her head.

She made a circuit of the clearing before she came back to squat next to her brother. "Did you see anything out there?"

"Nothing," Liam replied. "It's all quiet."

"Did you go back up that hill between here and town? Did you see anything moving between here and Kald?"

Elliot sat down on the other side of Ness and started unwinding his tartan to use as a blanket. "We've been up there three times. There's naught over there—no pursuit, no lights, naught."

"They wouldnae send a ground pursuit, either way," Grant cut in. "The Laird wouldnae bother with that when he could magic us back to the castle with the flick of his wrist."

Lily faced him. "Those guys who tried to kill us used magic and you said they came from the Laird."

"Aye. The Laird's the most powerful wizard of them all. What of it?"

"Our intelligence says a wizard is threatening Lady Rhona. That's who we came here to stop. Maybe the Laird is the wizard we're looking for."

"There isnae any Lady Rhona," Grant insisted, "and why would the Laird threaten one of his own? It doesnae makes any sense. Besides, the Laird isnae any black magician. The Buchanans are the only ones who would try to assassinate a member of the Royal House and they have wizards, too."

"Will ye two kindly take it outside so the rest of us can sleep?" Elliot rolled over and wrapped his tartan around himself. "If ye solve the world's problems, ye can tell us all about it in the morning."

Grant nudged Lily. "Come along. Let's see the sights and we can talk about it on the way."

She fell in at his side and they headed off into the dark forest. He caught her checking their position as they went. She really was a soldier and she never balked at the hardships of this life. She was used to it. She was even used to the crude talk of men in the same position.

He took a while to broach the subject that was on his mind. "How much do ye ken about that brother of yers?"

"Hardly anything. I haven't seen him in nearly fifteen years. Then he showed up a few days ago to recruit me for this mission. I hadn't spoken to him or seen his face in all that time. I have no idea what he's been doing except that he was working for the government. Now that I think about it, I can see he's been into all kinds of stuff I might not like to know about. What about you and Elliot? You guys seem pretty close."

"Aye. I havenae been out of his sight once since I can remember. We've spent every day together growing up and we've worked and fought and bled together every day since we went into the Laird's service."

"That sounds like a pretty nice way to work," she replied. "It's nice having people near you that you can rely on."

"Do ye? Do ye have people near ye that ye can rely on that way?"

"I have my old teammates, the last surviving members of my Division. We stayed together after we left the service. We've lived together ever since. I don't know what I would have done without them. They're my family now. I sure miss them. I trust them a lot more than I trust Liam."

He nodded to himself. "Och, aye, but he's here and they arenae."

"Yeah, and I'm stuck with him. He's my only ticket back home."

He cocked his head to study her. "Back home—to America?"

She looked away. He touched a sore spot there, so he changed the subject.

"What will ye do, now that ye cannae return to Kald? How will ye go about finding this Lady Rhona?"

"I have no idea. I suppose it's more a question of staying alive at this point. We can't keep running through these woods forever and neither can you."

"Ye're right about that."

She looked behind her. "Let's get up to the top of that hill and take a look around."

"There winnae be any pursuit. If they're coming after us, we'll never see them coming."

"I know. I just want to look around. Maybe we'll see a way out of this and I want to get a bearing on the land."

They hiked up the hill and Grant pointed west. "Ye can see the mountains where the forest ends. Ye'd have to cross them to get to the next district. Even then, the locals would probably return ye to the Laird if he asked them to. He's got more influence than ye think."

"What about beyond those mountains?" She pointed north.

"Ye arenae going over there. That's Buchanan land."

"I know, but I'm just wondering what's beyond them. If the Laird is out to kill us, maybe the Buchanans are our best chance to escape. The enemy of my enemy is my friend."

He shrugged. "Maybe, but I wouldnae like to cross Buchanan territory even to get clear of the Laird. They're vicious, those people."

"What's so vicious about them? They looked pretty normal to me—besides being cats, I mean."

"They're brutal. They've lived on that mountain for generations. They're hardened warriors and the harsh climate makes them tougher than any Creighton ye can throw a stick at. The Buchanans thumb their noses at the dragons. They consider the dragons weak and affected and the tigers have all the advantage on the ground. The Creightons dinnae dare engage them without a squadron of dragons in the air to protect themselves. The Creightons wouldnae stand a chance in any war against the Buchanans without that."

Lily scanned the surroundings. "Hmm. They sound like interesting people."

Grant snorted. "Did that woman who attacked ye seem all that interesting? She seemed deadly to me."

"Why do you think they attacked us in the first place? They had no reason to think we were coming after them."

"But ye *were* coming after them," he pointed out. "Why?"

"After what you said at the safe house, I got thinking maybe they were the ones threatening Lady Rhona. You said they made attempts on Ness's life, so why shouldn't they make attempts on Lady Rhona's life? Maybe they even know who she is. Anyway, I thought I'd give it a shot and a guy at an inn told me they would be hanging out in Damerell if they were anywhere."

He arched his eyebrow. "Ye were talking about it at an inn?"

"I made it a casual part of the conversation. I mentioned to the guy sitting next to me that I heard there were Buchanans at large in the city. This was after I met you and you and Elliot had just gotten in a fight with them. The guy told me they would be hiding in Damerell. That's as far as the conversation went.... except for the part where he told me there are elements in Damerell that want to unseat the Laird."

"Well, there ye go, lass," he remarked. "That explains all."

"What does? I don't understand your meaning."

"Someone at the inn must have heard ye. Either the Buchanans were there and ye didnae notice them or someone told them ye were looking for them. That's the only reason why they would attack ye out of nowhere like that. They must have thought ye were hunting them—which ye were."

"Yeah, but...." She stopped. "I guess you're right. I wouldn't have noticed them if they had been there. They would have looked like ordinary people and there were too many guests to see everybody."

"So what do ye suppose about getting out of this?" He waved at the forest.

"I have no idea. It doesn't look like...."

All at once, his arm shot out. He grabbed her and pulled her flat on the ground.

She cried out once, "What the...Hey!"

He held his finger to his lips and pressed her down flat on the hilltop. He pointed across the Boundless to where the mountain swooped low to the water's edge.

The stars gave just enough light to make a cluster of indistinct shapes gliding along the rocky beach. The moonlight caught them as they came closer and Grant counted seven cats.

Lily raised her head to gape at the creatures. They darted forward before they paused to prick their ears at the slightest sound. Grant held his breath watching them.

A bunch of trees jutted toward the estuary a few paces down the beach. Rustling sounds echoed across the water. In a flash, the cats streaked forward and dashed across the gravel on silent paws.

The next instant, a young buck broke cover and made a wild leap for the open beach. He took one huge bound to get away, but the cats burst into a sprint and ran him down. They swirled up his legs, bounded onto his back, and hauled him to the ground.

The buck roared in pain and fear, and in a moment, the sound cut off with a choking cough. It ended with the primal growls and tearing noises of the cats devouring their prey.

Grant cast a glance at Lily. Her wide, staring eyes reflected the moonlight taking in the whole scene. The cats buried their faces in the carcass, and for a few minutes, nothing disturbed the stillness.

After a tense moment, one of the cats leaped clear, straightened up, and its limbs unbent to become human arms and legs. The cat changed into a man and he burst into raucous laughter.

That deep voice filled the whole night and it produced a similar effect on the other cats. They tore themselves away from their meal, and in a minute, they all transformed into big, strapping, muscular men.

They slapped each other on their backs and walked away down the beach talking and laughing.

Grant collapsed on the ground, laid his cheek against the soil, and waited for the Buchanans to leave before he dared to move.

Lily slipped back down the other side of the hill. "Wow," she whispered. "They really are amazing. I can't believe I actually got in a fight against those things."

"It's lucky they were only out hunting," Grant replied. "If they tried to cross the estuary, I wouldnae have any choice but to report it to the Laird."

"How could you do that when he's trying to hunt you down?"

"Exactly." He pulled her to cover before they both stood up and headed back to camp.

Chapter 15

The sun rose grey and dim by the time Grant and Lily got back to camp. They found Liam and Elliot on their feet.

Ness cowered in black despair in the same spot where he spent the night. He hugged his arms over his chest and kept his face turned away.

"Let's be on our way, lads," Grant began. "We've a long way to go to put a few choice miles between us and Kald."

"Where exactly are we going to go?" Elliot asked. "We've nowhere to run."

"We cannae leave Kald," Ness blurted out. "Where would we go? Where would we live? What would we eat?"

The others ignored him. The Ritchies and Lily and Liam drifted into a loose circle to discuss their situation.

"I say we keep heading west beyond the mountains," Elliot suggested. "It's the only direction away from Kald and it's our best chance to get clear of the Laird's influence."

"We cannae go there," Ness interrupted. "They dinnae ken the Laird. If I went there, I'd be lost."

"Ye're lost as it is," Elliot countered. "Ye winnae be less a prince there than ye are here, so suck it up and be a man."

Ness's head shot up. "Dinnae tell me I'm not a prince. I'm still a prince. I'll always be a prince."

Elliot smacked his lips and threw up his hands. "Will someone muffle this whore's flume? I cannae listen to any more of this."

Grant glared at Ness. "Ye werenae ever a prince, lad, so eat it. No one told ye to leave Tyrekirk. Come to think on it, I seem to recall specifically ordering ye to stay put, so dinnae go pissing up me kilt now."

"Ordered me, did ye?" Ness rose to his feet smoldering with fury. "*Ye* ordered *me*! I think no."

"Will you three shut up for a second?" Liam interjected. "What difference does it make if you're a prince or not? We're all in the same situation here."

"I'm a prince," Ness muttered. "I'm still a prince."

Lily patted his arm. "Okay. You're a prince. Now can we talk about the position? Grant and I went up that hill and had a look last night. There are only two options: go west or go north."

"We arenae going north," Elliot snarled. "We're going west. It's the only option."

"It isnae any option for me," Ness chimed in. "Do ye get that?"

"The Laird may have influence in the west," Elliot went on, "but that's all it is: influence. We can work our way through the area to the western coast. Perhaps we can book passage to the colonies or some such place. We can get out of Scotland with our lives."

"I winnae be going west!" Ness shrieked. "Do ye hear me?"

"We could consider going north," Grant suggested. "I was of yer mind, lad, until Lily mentioned it last night. The enemy of my enemy is my friend. If the Laird is out to kill us, that puts us in line with the Buchanans."

Elliot leveled him with a hateful stare. "Ye cannae be thinking to lay in with the Buchanans. Not a bit of it, lad."

"Ye were sneaking around last night in the dark with Lily?" Ness bellowed at Grant. "I should have kenned! In all that talk about going to sleep and being ready to march this morning, ye were aiming to get between us. Ye plotted the whole thing to steal her away from me."

Before anyone could speak, he launched himself at Grant. He got as far as jamming his hands into Grant's throat and forcing Grant back a few steps before the other three caught hold of Ness.

Lily plunged into the mix angrier than anyone. She forced her way between the men and shoved Ness away. When he made another grab for Grant, she slammed her hands on Ness's chest and sent him staggering. "Get off of him, Ness! What do you think you're doing?"

"He's a coward and a sneak," the prince spat. "He's a traitorous, murderous, conniving, dirty...."

"I am not your property," Lily thundered. "Get that through your head right now, both of you." She whipped around to glare at Grant when she said it. Then she confronted Ness fuming to the point of violence. "I am nobody's property. I am not some prize up for grabs for you two to fight over. I decide what I do and who I do it with. Do you understand that?"

She waited for someone to answer her, but no one said a word. Ness shrugged his jacket into place and tugged it down to straighten it. When he refused to look at her, she stuck her face right up against his nose and roared at him at full volume. "I said do you understand that?"

He bowed his head and nodded. She spun around to face Grant. "Do you understand that?"

He nodded without looking away.

She drew in a shaky breath to get herself under control. She hadn't lost her cool like that in years, but these men drove her to it.

"None of us can afford to fight like this. We're all in fear for our lives and fighting amongst ourselves won't help us at all. I don't want to hear another word from any of you about anybody taking me away from anybody else. I'll make my own decisions about where I go and who I talk to. The very next person who implies otherwise better be ready to back it up in a fight. Got that?"

Everybody nodded. Ness looked at the ground. Grant stared straight into Lily's eyes and never flinched once.

Lily felt herself shaking. She clenched her fists to stop herself from falling apart. "After what happened the other night, I can understand why none of us wants to go north, so let's table that idea for now. It was just an idea. That leaves going west, so let's do that."

Liam spoke up. "There is one other option, Lily. You and I could go back to Kald."

She whipped around to stare at him. "Go back to Kald? Are you nuts?"

"Our mission is there. We won't find any answers to the west or to the north. It's Kald or nowhere for us."

"We'd be taking our lives in our hands," she pointed out. "The Laird already tried to kill us once."

"That's because he doesn't know we're here to help him. If we went to the castle and explained our mission, we could make him understand we're not his enemies."

"You're assuming a lot. He's the most powerful wizard we've encountered thus far. How do you know he isn't the one we're trying to stop?"

"How could he be?" Liam asked. "He couldn't have just arrived."

"What do ye mean, just arrived?" Elliot asked. "He's been Laird of Kald for nearly seventy years."

Lily didn't say anything. She couldn't exactly tell these men that she and Liam were looking for a time traveler from the future. Liam was right about that. The Laird might be a wizard, but he couldn't be any black magician from modern times.

"We have to go back to Kald to get near the Royal Family," Liam went on.

"How?" Lily demanded. "We had a chance with Ness. Now that chance is gone and we have no idea who Lady Rhona is."

"We could ask the Laird," Liam replied. "We can get him to help us find her."

"There isnae any Lady Rhona," Ness insisted. "What's more, there never has been. I ought to ken. I've spent me life studying the histories and genealogies of our Clan."

Liam lowered his eyes to look at the ground. "I still say we go back to the city."

"*Ye* can go back to the city—both of ye," Grant replied. "We're going west. The sooner we get beyond the mountains, the better our chances. Ye'd both do better to come with us."

"I'll be the one to decide where we go," Ness snapped. "I'm still Crown Prince of Clan Creighton. Me own guards cannae tell me what to do."

Elliot rounded on him with smoke billowing out of his ears. "Ye arenae Crown Prince of the sewer any longer, lad, so pull yer head in before I punch it in."

Grant laid a hand on his brother's arm. "Easy, lad."

"Holy Christ, I'd like to bloody his snotty little nose!" Elliot boomed. "Ye cannae even spend a night on the ground without sobbing for yer mother's teat, much less take charge of four people who've walked that road a hundred times before ye. Do ye hear the sniveling rot coming out of yer gob, ye toff-nosed..."

Lily bit back a grin. "Okay, okay. That's enough. You aren't taking charge of anything, Ness, so just let us decide what we're going to do."

"What is there to decide?" Ness countered. "The Laird saw ye in his magic seeing pool, so he can see us here. The minute ye decide ought, he'll ken about it and he'll come after us. He kens where we are right now." His voice broke and he slumped into a heap on the ground. "It's only a matter of time before he finds us and...."

Lily blinked down at him. Then she raised her eyes to Grant's face. "Is that true? Did the Laird use magic to locate us? Is that how his wizards found us?"

"Aye. When we got back to Tyrekirk, he showed us the two of ye leaving the safe house. That's how we kenned where to find ye."

"How is that possible? How could he know we were in the city?"

Grant shrugged. "He kens all. He sees all. He's got any number of devices he can use."

Lily spun around scan the forest. She saw faces watching her from behind every tree. "If that's true, we have to get out of here now. We have to move." She wrestled Ness to his feet. "Come on. Move out."

Ness dragged his heels. "What are ye doing, lass? We havenae any idea where we're going."

"None of us does." She gave him another pull to get him walking. "We can't stay here. Come on. Quit stalling."

The Ritchie brothers didn't argue. They set off west with her. Liam didn't. He raised both arms and let them slap down against his sides. "Aw, come on, Lily. You're going the wrong way. Why won't you listen to reason?"

She didn't answer. She was done talking. If the Laird could use magic to locate them in the city, then Grant must be right.

A wizard with that kind of power could track them anywhere. Their only hope was to keep moving and to change location as often as possible to avoid detection.

The party hiked through the forest heading west, always west. No one said much. Lily would have tightened her belt against the hunger gnawing away at her insides, but she didn't have a belt.

Instead, she rolled the waistband of her jeans over to make them tighter, but that didn't do any good.

The hunger faded after a while, and every now and then, the group crossed a stream where they scooped water into their mouths to ease their thirst.

Lily pushed herself to keep up with the Ritchies. Her training at Ironforge didn't prepare her for this ordeal. She'd gotten soft and out of shape in civilian life.

Ness shuffled through the dry leaves as though his feet weighed a thousand pounds. Lily spent most of the day behind him at the far end of the line alternately encouraging and threatening him. She held his hand and sometimes pushed him from behind.

She got tired of that game by noon and marched ahead with the others. If that didn't send Ness a message that he needed to man up, nothing would.

Grant and Elliot took turns leading the way even though none of the friends really knew for certain where they were going.

The brothers followed the moss growing on the tree trunks. Every now and then, one of them ran his fingers over it to make sure it pointed behind them. That was the best way to keep their direction in this forest where the canopy hid the sky.

Lily stumbled in a hazy half-dream of confused thoughts. She drifted between her old life at Ironforge and this weird labyrinth of magic and competing forces. The men around her started to remind her of mythical characters in some otherworldly epic that caught her in its path.

Grant led the party with his quiet dominance and level-headed intelligence. He was the only one who would hold eye contact with her when she lost her temper and yelled at him and Ness for fighting over her. He heard her and saw her for what she was. He was the only one of the whole group who acted like her outburst was normal and natural under the circumstances.

His brother Elliot matched him in power and intelligence, but with a hint of unpredictability so typical of a younger brother. Elliot never held back on expressing his annoyance at Ness.

Then there was Ness, the pampered prince so full of his own shallow importance. He couldn't even function outside his precious castle.

Liam snapped her out of her thoughts by sidling up to her and murmuring in her ear. "I meant what I said, Lily. We could still go back to Kald."

Lily's head shot up. She checked ahead and behind her. Grant and Elliot were far enough ahead and Ness was far enough behind. None one could overhear their conversation.

"And I meant what I said, Liam," she returned. "We can't go back to Kald. It's too dangerous."

"You know that isn't true. We'd be just fine in Kald. We don't need these guys. Let them keep going west. We have a job to do back in the city."

Lily clamped a lid shut to stop herself from going off on him, too. "I can't believe you would even consider abandoning these men in their hour of need. They saved our lives, remember? Besides, Ness is a prince and he's our best shot to get near the Royal Family."

Liam kept his voice low. "If I remember rightly, it was me who saved *their* lives."

Lily stopped dead in her tracks and rounded on him. "As a matter of fact, it was Ness who saved all our lives, including yours. It's our duty to help protect him and he can't go back to Kald."

"We could take him with us. We could take him back to his grandfather. He could explain to the Laird that we're...."

"No, Liam," she barked. "We're not going back—not yet. I don't want to hear any more about it until we can find a way to do it safely for everyone."

Liam stole a sidelong peek at her face. "Are you sure that's the real reason you don't want to go back?"

"I don't know what you're talking about. I said it was. What else do you need to know?"

"Are you sure you don't want to stay for some other reason? I can see the way you act around Grant. It's obvious you two have some serious chemistry going on."

Lily threw up both hands, as much from embarrassment when he mentioned Grant. "You're imagining things. There's nothing going on between me and Grant."

"Whether there is or there isn't, you've got the attention of at least two men in this group. That's got to be pretty flattering for a beautiful woman like you."

"Oh, please, Liam," she chided. "You know I'm not interested in any of these men."

"I'm not saying you're interested. I'm saying you're too swayed by their flattery and attention to think straight about this mission. You don't see the most obvious solution to our problem when it's staring you in the face. You don't want to leave to go back to Kald because you don't want to give up their attention."

She turned away and forced a laugh. "You're imagining things."

"Am I?"

She snorted and marched forward faster to leave him behind. She left him behind along with all his insidious remarks. She hustled forward until she came up behind Elliot. Liam wouldn't dare talk like that where the brothers could hear him.

She stayed in that position for the rest of the day, but Liam's words had a way of sneaking into her mind. She didn't want to think about Grant that way. She could blow off Ness as a dandy and a peacock, but not Grant.

She didn't want to get involved with anybody. She committed herself to the isolation and simplicity of her life with her teammates. With any luck, she would solve this Lady Rhona mystery and get back to Ironforge.

She didn't want to leave any lingering feelings behind her for a man she barely knew. Nothing would ever happen between her and Grant, but Liam's suggestions couldn't help but make her wonder.

What if....? No, that wasn't possible. She couldn't reopen old wounds to let herself feel that pain all over again.

She watched Grant walking ahead of her. The hairs on the back of his neck ran down to the cut of muscle between his shoulder blades. His body spoke to her in ways she didn't understand. His nature spoke to her in forgotten ways so that she understood him at a root level.

He was a man. His masculinity colored everything he did. It seeped from his pores and energized every movement.

She had known hundreds of men in the military and afterward, but Grant's masculinity somehow meant so much more to her now than it ever did before. No man had ever struck her as so significant or important to her until now.

Chapter 16

Grant called a halt at sundown. Ness buckled to the ground in despair. Liam sat down next to him, still smiling and cheerful. That expression didn't sit well with Grant.

Liam didn't approach this situation with the right attitude. His overly positive attitude was just as dangerous or more so the Ness's negative one.

Grant said nothing, though, especially not when Liam tried to cheer up Ness by chatting to him about life back in Kald.

Grant squatted down near them and rummaged in his sporran. He had a flint and a few tattered scraps of paper in there. He could start a fire if he wanted to, but he still didn't think it wise.

Aw, what was he thinking? The Laird and his men would find the party by magic whether Grant started a fire or not. Why shouldn't he and his companions enjoy some comfort in the meantime?

Lily interrupted his thoughts. "I'm going to climb that hill over there and see if I can spot any break in the terrain. I'll be back soon."

Grant glanced over his shoulder as she walked away, but he couldn't exactly gawk at her with Ness, Liam, and Elliot all sitting near him. He went back to fiddling with his things until he judged that enough time had passed.

He got to his feet. "I'm going to see if I can find any game in this forest. I'm peckish."

He made it a few paces before Elliot jumped up to follow him. "I'll come with ye."

Grant nodded at Ness and Liam and whispered to his brother. "Keep an eye on those two, will ye? Dinnae let His Royal Majesty wander off or do anything silly."

Elliot cracked a grin and went back to his post. Grant's heart skipped a beat as he slipped off into the forest. As hungry as he was, he had no plans to search for something to hunt. He wanted to catch up with Lily.

He trusted her the most of all their party second only to his brother. He knew now that his instincts about her were correct. He had one other person in this group he could rely on and he needed her ear right now.

He walked east for a few minutes before he circled south to flank her. He came upon her walking through the trees.

She jumped away before she recognized him. "What's going on? Is everything all right back at camp?"

"They're all grand—all except Ness, of course. It's ye I wanted to talk to."

"About what?"

He put out his hand to detain her. "We cannae go on like this, lass. Ye ken that as well as I. We cannae keep blundering through these woods with no plan in mind. Ness cannae keep up the strain. It's only a matter of time before he cracks. He winnae make it over the mountains to the west."

She glanced toward the hill she said she wanted to climb. "Yeah, I know. That's kind of why I wanted to take a look around. I wanted to see how far it is."

"It's too far for the likes of him. If it was only the four of us, we'd cross it with no bother, but I dinnae like to leave the prince behind." She looked away again and he watched her features churn. "What's amiss, lassie? What troubles ye?"

She puffed out her cheeks and bowed her head. "It's Liam. He wants to ditch you guys and take Ness back to Kald." Grant narrowed his eyes at her and she gasped. "I told him I wouldn't go. I told him it was too dangerous, not just for us but for Ness, too. I don't think I convinced him, though."

Grant's head spun. So Liam wanted to take Ness back to Kald. No wonder he was working so hard to butter up the prince. The fool!

Grant pursed his lips and squared his shoulders. "I think ye ken we cannae go back. Elliot and I winnae risk our lives for any imaginary Lady Rhona and we cannae let ye take the prince back."

"I know!" she exclaimed. "I don't want to go back, either. I don't want to split up with you."

He opened his mouth to say something, but he stopped himself in time. He found himself gazing down into her bottomless eyes.

She just said those words. She didn't want to split up. She might have meant she didn't want to risk dividing the group, but he heard only one thing. She didn't want to leave him.

He threw all caution to the wind. "I dinnae want to split from ye, either, lass. Ye're the glue holding this ship together."

She blushed and lowered her eyes. "Hardly. You and Elliot are the ones doing most of the work. We're just along for the ride."

"Ye're wrong, lass. There's naught for me but ye and Elliot. The other two.... well!" He waved them away. "I couldnae imagine going this road without ye."

He felt better now that he got that off his chest. She looked at him differently after he said it out loud. She hovered closer to him.

Colors and emotions flashed over her face and in her eyes when she gazed up at him. What was she thinking right now? Was she thinking the same thing he was? Did she think of him the same way he thought of her?

On an impulse, he darted forward and kissed her. He kept his eyes open to check her reaction. She froze with her eyes fixed open to stare at him. Her gaze bored straight into him.

He planned to dive in, steal a quick peck, and retreat, but her eyes caught him in their mesmerizing power. He stopped there with his mouth locked on her lips and his mind swam in her unflinching stare.

He held himself stiff and tense for a second waiting to see what she would do. The next instant, the tension dissolved and her lips melted against his.

Their lips drew them together and they were kissing, kissing eternally in a delicious warmth that filled Grant's whole being.

Without thinking, he lifted both hands and cradled her face. He guided her to one side and her mouth opened to meet him. Her sweet breath flooded his brain and her skin radiated impossible beauty and warmth.

Her tongue swirled with his in an intoxicating dance of satiny softness. He got lost in that magical sensation that welcomed him into a blissful world he'd never experienced before. He sank into the endless well of her swallowing him whole.

Out of nowhere, an almighty force ripped her off him. His eyes shot open to find Ness slamming Grant and Lily apart with both hands. "Ye rotten traitor! How dare ye!"

Grant stumbled back, too surprised to react. Lily cried out, "Ness!" but Ness dove between the pair and rounded on Grant.

"She's mine!" Ness snarled. "I'll flay ye alive for this. Dinnae let me see ye near her again. How do ye dare to lay yer filthy hands on her?"

Grant snapped back to his senses and backed farther away. His confusion and alarm faded and he stood back k out of range watching the prince fume and splutter in childish rage. The prince wouldn't be nearly so upset if he stood a chance in hell with Lily.

Ness glared at Grant and Ness's eyes flashed. His face contorted in shades of purple and pink waiting for Grant to retaliate or claim that Lily was his.

Her words echoed in Grant's head and he stayed where he was. *I am nobody's property. I am not some prize up for grabs for you to fight over. I decide what I do and who I do it with.*

He didn't need to hear or know anything else. If she kissed him or if she kissed Ness, Grant didn't have to fight anybody to prove it. He didn't tell her what to do and he certainly didn't tell her to love Ness or to not love him. That was none of Grant's business.

Ness smoldered in ferocious passion. Grant still didn't respond and the prince launched himself at Grant and slammed both hands against Grant's chest. "Ye heard what I said! Dinnae ye come near her again or I'll...."

He didn't finish the sentence before Grant saw the unmistakable signs. Ness swelled out his shoulders. His chest muscles broadened and his face darkened.

His eyes narrowed and kept on narrowing. Grant had spent enough time around the Creightons know when one of them was about to shift into his dragon form.

Grant moved his hand to his saber, but it wouldn't do him any good if it came to a fight. If Ness shifted, Grant would be defenseless against a full-grown dragon.

All at once, Lily darted between them. She got in Ness's face talking fast. "It's all right, Ness. Thank you for defending me. Grant kissed me, not the other way around. He surprised me as much as he must have surprised you. It's all right. It's all over now. You got me away from him."

Her words penetrated the prince's rage and his skin started to go back to its usual color. His swelling body shrank to its normal size. Lily steered him away, but she did it slowly and deliberately and kept Ness's eyes locked on hers.

Ness turned his back on Grant and forgot all about him. Lily walked off with Ness leaving Grant standing there by himself.

How could Lily kiss him like that one minute and abandon him the next? He could swear that kiss meant as much to her as it did to him. Now she left him out in the cold to take care of her pet sucker.

Just then, she glanced back over her shoulder, made eye contact with Grant, and a charge of understanding passed between them.

She was still there. The same depth of connection communicated to him through her eyes—the connection that made him kiss her in the first place. She was dealing with Ness to pacify him and placate him. Nothing more.

Grant let out a broken sigh. He couldn't cope with all the warring emotions struggling in his head. He couldn't keep riding this tidal wave of conflicting desires. It would kill him in the end.

A whispered voice answered his own thoughts. "We must get away from those two before they cause some real trouble."

Grant turned away to clap his brother on the back. "They couldnae cause any more trouble than they already have."

Chapter 17

Lily concentrated on her feet moving one in front of the other. She got lost in her own thoughts and let her legs do the walking for her.

One mile after another, one step in front of the other—what difference did it make in the end?

She felt numb except for that one little corner of her heart that leapt and sang and cried and prayed when she thought about Grant.

She kissed him. Grant kissed her and she kissed him back no matter what she told Ness to calm him down. She couldn't deny the truth and she didn't want to.

She couldn't decide how she felt about him when he did it, either. She wanted him to do it last night when they went on watch together. She wanted him to do it in the safe house when they first met. She wanted him to do it in the street when he first walked up to her.

How could she get all fluttery over a man when she made a promise to herself and to her teammates to swear off love for the rest of her life?

She could tell herself that she would never kiss Grant again, that it was a random fluke in a stressful situation.

None of that meant squat right now. She wanted it then. She wanted it now. She would do it again if she ever got the chance.

She shook herself out of her trance and looked around. Liam walked in front of her through the endless trees. The two of them were completely alone.

She stopped dead in her tracks. "Liam!"

He turned around smiling at her. "Yeah?"

"Where is everybody?" She scanned the surroundings struggling to stay calm. "Where are the others? Grant! Ness! Elliot! Where are you?"

She dodged into the trees before she returned to Liam. She kept calling, but no one answered.

Liam stayed where he was and watched her run around in circles. "They aren't here, Lily. They can't hear you."

She spun around fighting to breathe and gaped at him in horror. Was this monster really her brother? "Where are they?"

"I magicked them away, or I should say I magicked us away from them. I transported us to a different part of the forest."

She stared at him in stunned horror. Then the dam burst. She rushed him and pounded her fists into his chest. "What did you do to them? What did you do to them?"

He fought her off and shoved her away. "They're perfectly safe. They're in another part of the forest. They'll keep traveling west and we'll go back to Kald where we belong."

She stumbled backward and her eyes bulged. She didn't recognize the man standing in front of her. "How could you do this? Do you realize what you've done?"

"I didn't do anything. You were the one who did it. I saw you kissing Grant and just look at the way you're acting now. You're way too wrapped up in your feelings to think clearly. Our whole mission is back in Kald and you're too involved with these men to see that."

"So what?" she demanded. "You just took it upon yourself to send them away—or us away—without even asking me?"

"That's right. I had to do it for the sake of the mission. Now they're gone. They'll go their own way and we'll go ours, so get used to it. I did it so you would have no choice but to go back to Kald instead of farting around out here."

He turned away and kept on walking the way he'd been going when she first came to her senses. She watched him walk a few paces into the trees, pause, and call back, "Are you coming or not?"

She didn't answer. This could only mean one thing. Not only did he use his magic to separate her from the guys, but he also turned himself and Lily around without her even noticing it. They were no longer headed west, but back east toward Kald.

She seethed over what he had done, but at the same time, a nagging hint of fear ate into her heart. She came from a world where magic didn't exist, and here she was, trapped alone in a forest with a man more powerful than anything she could imagine.

How did Liam become a wizard? Where did he get his training that he could pull off a stunt like this?

He didn't turn around again. He would tramp out of her sight if she didn't hurry to catch up with him. What choice did she have? She could never find her way back to Kald without him—or anywhere else, for that matter.

She made sure to stay behind him. She couldn't stand the sight of his face. He terrified her more than anything. He made a decision to change their course. He did it, not only without her consent, but without her even being aware that he did it.

If he did that much, he must be in charge of this mission instead of her. She kidded herself into thinking she was in command here. She was the one with military experience after all. Why else would the government recruit her for this mission?

All that must have been a mistake, a trick of her own vanity. Liam had been in command the whole time. He let her believe she was making the decisions. He did it to massage her ego while he pulled the puppet strings behind her back.

She didn't talk to him for the rest of the day. At dusk, he led her to a cave in an embankment. Lily didn't know how he found it, but she long since gave up trying to figure out how he did any of this.

The cave cut off the last remaining light coming from outside. "Let's get a fire going," Liam suggested. "You gather some wood and I'll see about finding something for us to eat."

She didn't answer. She went back outside, got busy gathering sticks and branches, and hauled them back to the cave.

When she finished arranging the tinder and twigs into a log-cabin shape, Liam touched his finger to the dry leaves. They ignited and flames flickered around the wood.

Lily blinked down at it in a daze. Why did this surprise her? She already knew he had magical power. He admitted it himself. She should have expected this.

Liam sat down on the other side of the blaze and took two cans out of his pocket along with two stainless steel forks. He passed one can and one fork to Lily. "Here. Eat this."

She turned the can over in her hand and read the label. *Hormel Corned Beef Hash.*

She didn't ask where he got them. She also didn't ask why he didn't share his abilities with the other men when he had the chance.

He could have saved them days of hunger and discomfort, but he didn't do that. He deliberately let them suffer in hunger for days rather than making it easier for them.

She looked up to see him prying the lid off his can, sticking in his fork, and shoveling the food into his mouth. She smelled it from here.

Saliva squirted under her tongue and her hunger overcame her objections. She snapped back the lid and started eating.

Liam finished first and set his can and fork aside. He picked up a handful of dirt from the cave floor and tossed it into the fire.

A shower of sparks scattered in the flames. They swirled into a map of the forest with a glowing red line showing the way back to Kald.

"There you go," he mused. "The way back is pretty straightforward. I should have expected that from those guys. They kept a straight route west. They didn't deviate from it at all. I'm impressed."

Lily told herself to keep quiet, but her curiosity got the better of her. "Did you think they didn't know what they were doing? They seemed pretty capable to me—all except Ness."

Liam chuckled to himself. "Maybe. Now let's see if we can locate Lady Rhona."

He puckered up his lips and spat at the shining bright map. His spit sent a ripple of light through the map before it settled into the same glowing pattern.

Liam frowned. "That's weird. She should show up on here somewhere. See? The map even includes the mountains where the Buchanans live. We should be able to see her if she was there."

"Where did you learn all this magic, Liam? I didn't know you were so heavily involved in the government."

He didn't look up. "There's a lot you don't know about me. I learned it from Felix Margoles. The government has teams of wizards, witches, and spellbinders. They've been experimenting with magic for years. They would be stupid not to use it."

"Is Felix Margoles a person or a secret branch of the government?"

"It's hard to say exactly. It's a very private entity. That's all I know about it, to tell you the truth. I deal with my superiors. They give me orders and I carry them out."

"How did you get involved with it?"

"I spent about five years training in a special division of the experimental services. You were in the Army at the time. Then you deployed to Afghanistan. I've been on assignment ever since and you've been locked up in that convent of yours."

"It isn't a convent!"

"Call it what you want. It amounts to the same thing in the end. Anyway, I couldn't really communicate with family while I was on assignment, so I wouldn't have been able to tell you what I was doing even if we had seen or talked to each other. Felix Margoles is strictly classified, but I will tell you that I was deployed overseas around the same time you were. We might even have had something to do with ending the war when we did."

Lily studied him more closely. Who was this man? He might as well be a total stranger for all she knew about his experiences, his skills, and his capabilities.

If she knew their mission would come to this, she never would have agreed to travel back in time with him. He was a complete unknown to her.

He bent his head and did something near the ground. When he straightened up, he held something in the palm of his hand. He extended it toward the map and blew a puff of powder into the image.

"What is that?" Lily asked.

"It's a certain type of seed. I collected it outside. Do you see these pinpricks of light showing up? They're wizards. Cripes, look at them all!"

Lily gazed into the map. Dozens of glowing white specks showed up all over the map. They clustered in Kald and scattered up the mountainside toward Buchanan territory.

Liam leaned back against the cave wall. "Well, that didn't help us any. I thought maybe I could find the wizard we're looking for, but there are too many of them. We'll have to locate him some other way."

"How do you know the wizard is a male? Did Felix Margoles tell you that, too?"

"No, he didn't. It could be a female. I only assumed it was a male. Anyway, we can't do anything more tonight. Tomorrow we'll go back to Kald and pick up where we left off before we got diverted out here."

The fire lit up the cave, and after a few minutes, the map faded and disappeared. The flames warmed Lily's aching bones, but nothing could dispel this sinking feeling that Liam was anything but what she thought.

She didn't understand him, and worse, she didn't trust him. She couldn't rely on him not to undermine her or thwart her efforts the minute it suited him. He told her as much in no uncertain terms. She couldn't even feel grateful to him for the food and the fire that he so generously provided.

They relaxed on either side of the fire without saying anything. After a while, Liam stretched out on the floor and went to sleep. Lily stayed awake a long time thinking everything over.

What could she do about Liam? She couldn't match his power in a hundred years. She had no choice but to accept this situation and go along with his plans.

Chapter 18

E lliot shoved Ness from behind. "Keep moving, laddie."

Ness stumbled forward and nearly toppled off his feet. "Will ye leave me alone?"

He shuffled forward a few steps before he slowed to a crawl again. Elliot veered around him and strode ahead. "Fine, then. Stop here if ye must. We could have been over the mountains by now if we didnae have to carry ye along."

"No one's carrying me," Ness mumbled.

Elliot didn't turn around. He passed Grant and strode around the next bend out of sight.

Grant didn't turn around, either. He kept up his steady pace, but he no longer cared to escape the Laird's wrath ever since he and Elliot discovered Liam and Lily gone.

He would even have been happy to go back to Kald to face the consequences if it meant he could just find Lily again. How did this happen? How did he get so attached to a woman he only kissed once?

He didn't realize she meant so much to him until she disappeared. He kept catching himself looking around for her.

Ideas popped into his head and his first instinct told him to talk to her about them. Then his heart sank when he remembered that she was gone.

He spent his whole life sharing hardship and danger with his brother. Now along came this strange woman and not even Elliot could fill that void.

Grant didn't want to share hardship and danger with Elliot anymore. He wanted to share them with Lily. He wanted to look up and see her standing there.

Ness woke him from his stupor. "Wait for me, Grant."

Grant turned his head, but not so far that he could see the prince. "We're done waiting on ye, lad. If ye cannae keep up, ye'll be left behind. Now pick up yer feet a bit. We've spent too much time lagging behind for yer sake. If we get taken, it'll be thanks to ye stopping so often."

Ness whimpered and Grant heard a thud. "I dinnae care if I'm left behind. Go on, then. I'll stay here."

Grant rounded on the prince, but Grant was too far beyond caring to lose his temper. He regarded the sunken heap of misery sitting slumped and beaten by the path.

Ness's shoulders hunched and he hugged his arms around his middle. Grant saw the exhaustion, hunger, and despair of Ness losing everything, but at the same time, Grant saw through all that to the spoiled child who always got what he wanted. Grant and Elliot were the first people in Ness's life who stood up to him and wouldn't accept his tantrums and his demands.

Then, on top of all that, Ness bowed his head and burst into tears. His shoulders shook and his hair fell over his face. Grant rolled his eyes to Heaven. Whatever next?

He hesitated to mollycoddle the prince for even one second longer. Ness said he wanted Grant and Elliot to leave him behind. Grant could take the prince at his word and walk away, but the sight of a grown man so wretched tugged at Grant's heartstrings.

He strode over to Ness. He planned to lay his hand on the prince's shoulder, to comfort him somehow before urging him to get up and go on, but he never got there.

He came within ten feet of the prince when a ghostly apparition vaporized out of the ground. The shade made no sound. It didn't even disturb the leaves at Grant's feet.

It floated into view with barely a whisper, formed in front of Grant's face, and blocked his path to Ness.

Grant got one look at a shadowy form hooded in black. Blank eyes stared out at him from an indistinct face, but the rest of the thing had no features—no mouth, no nose, no skull or bones that he could see.

Grant stumbled backward to get away from it and bumped into another one coming up behind him. He jumped the other way in panic when he touched what would have been its body. It felt like no human body he could recognize and made him feel sick to his stomach.

The next instant, dozens of those things floated up out of the ground. They sprouted all around Grant and Ness to surround the two men. Grant seized his saber and lunged for the prince.

Ness leapt to his feet and wheeled backward to press his back against Grant. At least Grant had one solid person to stand with him even if Ness didn't know how to handle the saber at his belt.

The ghost-things moved into a solid wall around the men. Grant spun left and right trying to keep them all in view, but they blocked his sight of anything outside their circle.

His heart pounded and his knees turned to water. "Elliot!" he bellowed. "Elliot!"

He swiped his saber in desperation trying to drive the things away, but the blade slashed right through it. "Elliot!" Grant roared.

At that moment, one of the ghosts stooped over. Something like an arm stuck out from under the robe and a murky pool of shimmering black undulated across the ground. The darkness lapped at Grant's ankles and fixed his foot to the ground so he couldn't move.

Ness squealed in fright and Grant stared at the prince's feet stuck in the same ooze. Ness was trapped, too.

Grant hacked at his enemies in all directions and stabbed his blade into the nearest wraith. The weapon plunged to the hilt in a cloud of nothing. "Elliot!" he screamed.

He pulled his blade back and made one last wild chop for the nearest head. The creature raised its arm.

The hooded robe surrounded the creature's arm so Grant couldn't make out any hand or shape underneath, and in a split second, a crackling sword of light erupted from the upraised limb to block Grant's stroke.

Grant yanked his saber to free it from the creature's grasp, but the ghost's power held it up. Grant couldn't move it no matter how hard he tugged. He tried to uncurl his fingers, but he couldn't let go of the saber hilt, either.

He grabbed for his dirk. Ness whined in terror behind Grant's back and Grant's mind exploded. He had to get out of this. The Laird must have sent these shades to capture the three men. Did these things already take down Elliot, too?

Grant seized his dirk, but he couldn't pull it out of his belt. It stuck fast, and when he tried to take his hand off it, he found that one trapped, too.

Now he couldn't move hand or his feet. He was powerless. He couldn't even call out for Elliot anymore. He couldn't hope that his brother was still alive.

The ghosts started to change. One after another, the faces became more distinct. Their black robes changed to tartan and kilted men that Grant knew from the Laird's service surrounded him. They were all wizards.

The wizard holding Grant's saber thrust one hand toward Grant's torso. Rope slithered from the wizard's fingertips and wound around Grant's ribs. The coils snaked down his hips to bind his legs.

Grant thrashed in every direction to break loose. He had to get free if it was the last thing he did. He exploded in a frenzy trying to tear his hands off his weapons, but nothing worked. The ropes hauled him down into the sticky ooze clotted at his feet.

The wizard attacking him wrenched at his fiery weapon and buckled Grant to his knees. He went down still holding his blade above his head. He couldn't let go of it.

The other wizards moved in on Ness to haul him down and Grant saw his last hope fading before his eyes.

At that moment, a sword flashed through the air and a deafening clang startled Grant into spinning around. In a flash, Elliot smashed his own saber into the magical weapon pinning Grant down.

The impact broke the spell. The wizard's hold snapped and the saber came free in Grant's hand. Elliot rotated the rest of the way into position and slashed at the wizard with all his strength.

His sudden appearance took the enemy by surprise. The wizard brought up his weapon to defend himself, but not fast enough. Elliot's sword smashed down and cleaved the wizard's head all the way to his neck.

Grant didn't hesitate an instant. The black sludge still fixed his knees to the ground, so he hacked the wizards' knees instead. He chopped one man down and slashed his blade across his enemy's throat.

Elliot flew everywhere at once. He stabbed three wizards before the rest recovered from their surprise. Elliot sprang from one foot to the other fighting everyone at once. He hacked another four rushing him from the side when, out of nowhere, an enormous club struck him across the back of the head.

The blow sent him reeling into the black puddle. He pitched onto his face at Grant's side and the inky, sticky ooze closed around Elliot's body.

"ELLIOT!!" Grant roared, but he had bigger problems of his own.

The pool rose around his chest and waist. It soaked his shirt and towed him down into its depths. It swirled over his thighs and crawled higher to his neck.

Elliot lunged upright to break free. His eyes raced around in search of anything he could grab hold of and he shot out his hand to Grant. "Hold onto me, lad!"

"Elliot!" Grant pawed the air to grasp that hand.

The tar bubbled around Elliot's neck and soaked his hair. It inched down his arms and swallowed his legs in its gluey hold. Elliot whined in terror. He flapped his hands to grab Grant, but his fingers slipped.

Grant attacked his brother in a frenzy. He couldn't let that stuff suck his brother down. Grant seized Elliot's forearms and heaved with all his might, but Elliot didn't budge. The black closed over his ears and snuck around his cheekbones.

Elliot's eyes darted everywhere and he gulped mouthfuls of air, but still that horrible mass crept up on him until it touched the corners of his lips. He gave one last hopeless cry, "Lad!" before the puddle dragged him under.

Grant held his brother by the arms. He refused to let go at all costs. The stuff slurped up Grant's wrists. Creeping cold gripped his heart, but he didn't care anymore. He would rather die than let go of Elliot.

He braced himself for the inevitable when a thunderous bellow made him look up. A few feet away, Ness struggled against dozens of ropes holding him a prisoner.

Five wizards converged on him. Magical ropes sprang from the wizards' fingertips to lash Ness's arms and legs to his sides. The prince jerked all over the place, but the ropes bound him too tightly.

Ness gave another roar of anguished rage like no human voice Grant had ever heard. It boomed across the landscape and shook the forest to its roots, and in front of Grant's eyes, Ness erupted out of his human skin to become the golden dragon that saved them in the city.

Ness shifted faster than Grant had ever seen before. The dragon whipped around spitting fire at the wizards. He scorched ten to death in one powerful breath and charred the ropes to cinders.

The wizards couldn't get away from him fast enough. He narrowed his eyes to slits and stalked his prey with deadly certainty.

Just then, Grant felt Elliot's fingers tighten around his forearm. Grant's spirits soared. Elliot was still alive under all that muck.

Ness flicked his long tail and smacked another seven wizards aside. The rest scrambled for cover while others fired magical weapons at Ness to bring him down.

They hurled lightning and shot spears they conjured out of thin air, but all their spells deflected off his tough skin and drove him wild.

One wizard rushed out of the pack and wound back his arm to throw another volley, but he never got a chance. Ness wheeled, his long neck uncoiled, and he snapped the man in his jaws.

The wizard shrieked in agony. Ness flailed his head and shook his victim until the man's arms and legs cracked with the force.

Grant almost pitied the wizard, but at that moment, Grant spotted something in the wizard's hand.

The wizard let out one last tortured groan and a wink of gold sailed through the air. Ness never saw it coming. A gold chain uncurled against the treetops and fell over the dragon's head.

Ness imploded the instant it touched his spikes. He bellowed in pain as his whole glorious body collapsed in on itself and Ness Creighton, the man, fell broken and powerless on the ground.

The wizards rushed him and loaded him with so many ropes that he couldn't rise.

Cold seized Grant's heart, but that cold didn't come from watching Ness's defeat. The slimy ooze traveled up Grant's arm, over his shoulder, around his neck, and eventually sucked his head down into the darkness. It pooled in his lungs and stopped his breath until he lost sight of everything he'd ever known to be real.

Chapter 19

Lily stole a peek around a corner of one of Kald's many buildings. Darkness covered the city and the first stars dotted the sky. "There's the inn. We can stay there tonight."

"We shouldn't go back to the same place," Liam whispered. "You know that as well as I do."

"The Buchanans were here a little while ago," Lily pointed out. "If they aren't here now, we can find someone who knows where they are."

"I keep telling you we ought to go to the castle," Liam countered. "Forget the Buchanans."

"Just imagine how useful Ness would be if we wanted to go to the castle," Lily countered. "It's too bad you didn't think to bring him with us."

He shrugged. "Ness could hardly help us when he can't even take care of himself."

Lily froze against the wall. "Look!"

The inn door opened and cast a square of yellow light into the shadows. Lily stared as the tall woman who almost killed her stepped into view along with a tall man with short grey hair. They set off across the intersection without a care in the world.

"That's them," Lily hissed. "Those are the Buchanans."

"Let's catch them while we have the chance," Liam whispered. "Sneak around in front of them and confront them. I'll come up behind them and catch them while they're distracted."

"And if they attack?"

"If they attack, you can handle them. Now go." Liam disappeared into the shadows.

Lily measured the terrain for a second before she spun away and bolted into the dark. She tiptoed against walls keeping her target in sight.

She veered to her left to cut the Buchanans off. Where was Liam?

She came to a good hiding spot and paused to catch her breath. She didn't want to engage those tigers again, but hopefully this time the Laird's men wouldn't be hanging around to interfere.

The woman's wiry figure came closer and drew level with Lily's position. Lily braced herself and stepped into the street to cut the Buchanans off. The woman pulled up short and scowled at Lily once. Then the woman burst into a crazy grin.

Lily's heart sank. Now she had no choice but to fight this woman all over again and she couldn't hope the woman would do it in her human form. The man murmured something in the woman's ear and the woman shook her head still grinning like mad.

Lily clenched her fists and prepared for the fight of her life. She barely got away from these creatures last time. She no longer entertained any illusions about the Buchanans' power and tenacity.

With no warning, the woman broke into a run and took a flying dive to attack Lily. The woman held out both hands to catch Lily by the throat, but she shifted into a cat before she got there.

Lily's heart stopped and adrenaline flooded her. She switched into fight mode and dropped back on one foot back to absorb the impact. The cat rocketed at her going a mile a minute and its jaws widened to bare its razor fangs.

Lily stood her ground, and at the last second before the cat hit her, Lily seized it in both hands and sank her fingernails into the animal's fur.

She let the cat's momentum carry it past her head and she sent it hurtling headfirst into the nearest wall.

She barely had time to turn around before the second cat launched. An enraged yowl made her wheel to meet the second cat slashing its claws in her face. Lily barely got her hands up in time to block the animal from scratching her eyes out.

He hit her full force and sank his hind feet into her shirt. He kicked at her midsection and swiped his forepaws in her face.

Lily squinted to protect her eyes while she fought to control him. Where was Liam? Where was his magical power now when she really needed it?

For one terrible minute, she actually wondered if he planned this whole stunt to get rid of her. Why else would he send her into unarmed combat against these cats? She was stupid to believe that he would come up behind them and bail her out.

At that moment, something caught the male cat by the hind legs and yanked him off. The cat sailed wide before she saw Liam several paces out of harm's way. The shadows concealed him except for an unearthly light radiating from his hands.

Lily didn't see how he grabbed the cat from so far away until another screech pierced her ear from behind.

Liam flicked his thumb and index finger and a black whip of energy zinged past Lily's eyes. The female cat howled in pain when Liam jerked back his arm and the cat hurtled toward him.

Liam hauled the cat on a collision course for his head. He raised his other hand and the animal crashed into it with a devastating slam. The concussion echoed across the street.

The cat bounced off, but Lily didn't see what happened between them before the male cat pounced on her. She didn't see where he came from. He dropped on her from above while she was busy watching Liam manhandle the female.

A spine-chilling screech set Lily's hair on end, and before she knew what was happening, dozens of spikey claws punctured her scalp. They ripped down her neck when the cat landed on her head and grabbed to hold on.

She whirled to one side, but she couldn't see the thing covering her face. Lily scratched and tore the creature's fur to get the thing off, but it sank its claws into her skin. She couldn't get it loose without hurting herself.

Out of the corner of her eye, she spotted Liam crouched over the other cat. Did he kill it? The thought gave Lily new energy. She peeked around for anything she could use against this creature, but she couldn't see anything.

Her panic turned to rage. She couldn't let these cats beat her. She bowed her head and took a running charge at the nearest building. She smashed her head into it and used the cat's body as a cushion. Her neck bent at an unnatural angle, but the pain only fueled her to destroy this thing before it killed her first.

The cat yelped and its claws loosened. Lily followed up her advantage and yanked it the rest of the way off. She vented her fury on it and flung it around.

The cat recovered just enough to put up a fight. It contorted and floundered in her hands. It took all Lily's effort to keep her hold on it.

The cat did its best to scratch her arms and wrists. It worked itself into a compact ball, but that only worked in Lily's favor.

She clenched her fingers around its ribs and swung it like a bat. She clubbed its head into the wall and felt the satisfying splat of its disintegrating skull.

That feeling drove her into a blind rage and she hurled the thing into the wall again and again. She pulverized its brains to a sodden mess before she realized the cat no longer posed any threat to her.

The cat flopped limp and blood-soaked in her hands. She raised her eyes to find Liam and the female staring at her with wide eyes. The woman lay immobile on the ground at Liam's feet. She had her eyes open, but she didn't struggle anymore.

Lily stumbled over to them with the dead cat still dangling from her hand. Blood dripped down its tail and splashed on the pavement at her feet.

She nodded at the woman. "Aren't you going to kill her?"

"Of course not," Liam fired back. "I'm going to question her. You said you wanted to find out what the Buchanans knew about Lady Rhona. Now we've got one and she won't be much good to us if she's dead."

Lily blinked down at the woman. The rush of battle faded from her mind and left her dazed.

She couldn't bring herself to think of this woman as anything but an enemy. If the woman so much as tried to get to her feet, Lily would have to kill her, too.

Liam nodded behind him. "Go back to the inn and get us a room. Once you do that, I'll bring her along."

"A room?" Lily asked. "One room...for all three of us?"

"Yes, Lily. One room for all three of us. Here." He handed her some money.

She shuffled back to the inn in a trance, walked into the crowded room, and found the landlord. "I'd like a room for the night, please."

He gaped down at her hands and said nothing. He shuddered before he hurried away without saying anything.

She glanced down and saw the cat still hanging there. Its blood soaked her sleeves up to the elbows and blood dripped onto the carpet.

Lily went back outside and pitched the carcass into an alley. She washed her hands in the water trough and rolled up her sleeves so the blood didn't show so much. Then she returned to the inn.

This time, she found the landlady at the bar and repeated her request. The landlady didn't act at all concerned and she gave Lily a room in exchange for the money.

Lily went back outside and gave Liam his change. "I got it."

He grabbed the woman by her dress and hauled her to her feet. "Come on."

He marched the woman into the inn. He didn't look right or left until Lily closed the bedroom door behind them. Liam shoved the woman into a chair.

"What did you do to her?" Lily asked. "Why isn't she fighting back?"

"I bound her with magic," Liam replied. "Now she'll tell us anything we want to know."

Chapter 20

G rant blinked to get the glue out of his eyes, but he still couldn't see anything. Something touched his shoulder. "Are ye there, lad?"

"Aye." Grant coughed to get his throat working. At least Elliot was still with him, wherever they were. "Are ye all right?"

"Aye," Elliot whispered back. "They've taken all our weapons, of course—the bastards."

"Do ye ken where we are?" Grant asked. "I cannae see ought. I've still got that stuff in me eyes."

"There's naught to see," Elliot replied. "We're in the Laird's dungeon as near as I can tell."

Grant sank back with a sigh. He touched the damp stone wall behind him and groped around. Elliot must be right. Where else would they be after getting defeated by the Laird's wizards?

"Any sign of the trollop?" Grant asked.

Elliot chuckled low and wound up coughing. "Dinnae make a joke of it. The lad gave himself defending us. I never thought I'd say it of him, but he showed real courage fighting those men."

"Aye. Do ye ken what happened to him?"

"No. I woke up here the same as ye."

"How long have I been out?"

"I dinnae have any sense of time in this dark. but I was awake for several hours before ye woke up."

Grant didn't say anything else. The brothers could only expect one outcome from being locked up in the Laird's dungeon.

They defied the Laird's order. He ordered them to kill Liam and Lily and Grant and had helped them escape instead. They helped Ness escape.

Where was Ness? Awaiting execution somewhere else in this crypt, no doubt.

Elliot's big frame came to rest against the wall next to Grant. "We made a pretty good run for it. That's about the best of it."

Grant felt himself spinning into despair and he couldn't let that happen. "What's the plan now?"

"Plan? Why, get the hell out of here, of course. That's the plan."

"That's the aim. Aye," Grant returned. "So what's the plan?"

"I dinnae ken. Ye're the one that always comes up with the plan. I'm naught but a soldier."

Grant grinned in the dark. Good old Elliot. Grant could always count on his brother to keep his spirits up.

Grant started to shoot back another joke when a clang of metal interrupted him. A beam of blinding light shot into their cell and both brothers jumped up.

A team of guards flanked the cell door and they waved the brothers out. "Ye're going before the Laird."

Grant and Elliot didn't bother to resist. What was the point? They could joke about escaping, but no one could get out of this dungeon.

The guards steered the brothers to the same waiting area outside the audience hall where they met Maxwell again. The old Chamberlain scratched his nose with the tip of his quill pen and eyed Grant and Elliot over his spectacles. "Well, laddies, I cannae say he's in the most sparkling of moods. I hope ye've a good yarn to spin while ye're in there."

Grant hung his head. He didn't have any yarn to spin apart from the truth. If the Laird didn't accept that, he might as well execute Grant and Elliot right now.

The heavy doors swung open. The Laird sat on his high throne at the far end of the hall wearing all the finery of his office. He couldn't look more different from the old man of the other night if he had sprouted three heads.

Grant squared his shoulders and he and Elliot strode into the hall to take their places at the Laird's feet. Grant kept his eyes down and waited for the axe to fall.

"Well, Mr. Ritchie," the Laird boomed. "Ye disobeyed me orders. Ye didnae kill those spies the way I told ye to. What have ye to say for yerself?"

Grant shook his head. The Laird called both of them 'Mr. Ritchie', but when he spoke like that, Grant always answered first. He was the older brother and he had always been in charge since he and Elliot first entered the Laird's service.

"I cannae excuse disobeying yer orders," he murmured. "I can only say the people ye sent us to kill werenae any spies. They dinnae belong to Clan Buchanan at all."

"What makes ye think that?" The Laird's voice cut Grant to the quick and made him flinch. "I asked ye a question, Mr. Ritchie. What makes ye think they werenae spies?"

"They werenae even Scots." Grant looked up without meaning to. He wound up looking straight into the Laird's face. "They didnae speak or dress as we do. They couldnae be Buchanans. They didnae even ken who the Buchanans were or ought about the wars or the Creightons or ought. They were strangers—foreigners. Just ask...."

He broke off. He dared not tell the Laird to ask Elliot for confirmation.

The Laird glared down on both brothers. Out of the corner of his eye, Grant saw Elliot standing with his head bowed in silent submission. If Grant hoped to convince the Laird of anything, he was on his own.

The Laird sniffed at Grant's outburst. "Ye dinnae ken ought about them. Ye should have done as I bid ye. Then perhaps ye wouldnae be standing here awaiting the gallows."

Grant wilted. So the Laird did plan to execute the brothers after all. If that was the case, what did he have to lose? "I ken they came here to help ye. They say they came here to save the life of some Lady Rhona Armstrong or other. I dinnae ken who that might be, but she must be a member of Clan Creighton. They say they tracked a wizard here who was trying to assassinate her. Those two came here to help ye and protect one of the Royal Family."

"There isnae any Lady Rhona Armstrong," the Laird snarled, "so the tale must be a lie."

"I ken there isnae any Lady Rhona," Grant stammered, "but ye must see these people arenae yer enemies. They've been trying all this time to come here and talk to ye and make ye understand that."

The Laird rose to his feet with a sudden, swift movement that made Grant shut his mouth in a hurry. The old man towered above his head so menacingly that Grant bowed his head again and held his tongue. He'd already said too much.

The Laird stood still for a long, terrible moment and then boomed out louder than ever. "Do ye ken where those two came from? Do ye have any notion who they are or what they're doing here beyond what they told ye themselves?"

Grant kept his eyes down. "No, me Laird."

"They came from the future," the Laird rumbled. "They came back in time from three hundred years into the future to usurp me reign and to remove Clan Creighton from power. Did ye ken that, laddie?"

Grant's head shot up and his eyes popped. The future? How was that possible?

The minute the words crossed his mind, puzzle pieces started slotting into place in his brain.

All the curious, nonsensical things that Lily had told him suddenly made sense. The war, the Army, her experiences in combat—of course they didn't sound right to Grant at the time. They hadn't happened yet.

He blinked and discovered the Laird observing him with keen, piercing eyes. Grant did his best to get his expression under control, but it was too late.

"I see ye ken more than ye're telling me." The Laird sat back down with a sweep of his arm. "Very well. If that's the way ye like it, ye can go back where ye came from and await execution in comfort and satisfaction."

The guards appeared out of nowhere and escorted the brothers back to the dungeon. The guards pushed Grant and Elliot into the same dingy cell and slammed the door shut in their faces.

Darkness blocked out Grant's sight. He couldn't get his eyes to register even the tiniest pinprick of light no matter how hard he strained them to see something.

Despair weighed him down, but the next minute, his mind shifted gears. Oh, well. So much for that.

Elliot bumped his shoulder. "Ye didnae really expect him to listen to ye, did ye, laddie?"

"Not much." Grant slid down the wall to sit on the floor. "At least I tried."

Elliot sat down next to him. "How long do ye suppose we have?"

"Maybe two hours," Grant muttered. "I dinnae care so long as it's quick."

Chapter 21

L iam straightened up in front of his captive. She sat on a wooden chair in the upstairs inn bedroom, but Lily couldn't see anything holding the woman down.

Magical restraints bound the woman's hands at her sides just as if she was tied up with ropes. She jerked against the invisible restraints and tried again and again to get out of the chair.

"Who are you?" Liam asked. "What's your name?"

The woman fixed him with a hateful glare and spat on his shirt. "Go hang yerself."

Liam shook his head. "I thought as much."

He put his hands together and pressed them palm to palm, and when he pulled them apart, a shimmering tangle of glowing threads spread between them.

They grew longer, stretched out, and surrounded the woman. They slithered over her limbs and wrapped around her chest.

She struggled even harder. She searched the room with such a wild, frightened expression that Lily pitied her. "What are you doing to her?"

"Don't worry," Liam answered over his shoulder. "It doesn't hurt. It will only force her to tell the truth. Now what's your name?"

The woman gave another vicious twist, but the magic held her fast.

"What's your name?" Liam repeated louder.

The woman gasped in despair and bared her teeth at him. Her copper-red hair came loose and scattered into her eyes. "Edeena Buchanan."

Liam relaxed, but only a little bit. "All right, Edeena. I'm Liam Barnett and this is Lily Dindle. Now why don't you tell us what the Buchanans are doing in Kald? Why are the Buchanans trying to assassinate Ness Creighton?"

"Do ye think we give a stuff about any Ness Creighton?" Edeena snarled. "He can go spin on a fence post for all I care."

"Why did you try to kill him?" Liam asked. "Grant Ritchie says you and your people broke into Tyrekirk more than once and tried to kill him."

"I tell ye the Buchanans dinnae give a fig for that overstuffed fop. No Buchanan ever tried to kill him. It's Lady Ilisa we care about. She's the only reason there ever was a Buchanan on this side of the Boundless."

Liam raised one eyebrow. "Lady Ilisa? Who's that?"

"She's wife to our Clan Chief, Neill Buchanan, ye dolt!" Edeena bellowed. "The Creightons captured her and they're holding her in the castle as we speak. We came over to rescue her and none other. No one tried to kill the prince, I can tell ye that much."

Liam cast a sidelong glance at Lily. "Maybe it's Lady Rhona."

"I dinnae ken ought about any Lady Rhona," Edeena growled. "It's only Lady Ilisa we care about. They're holding her for ransom in the Black Turret to get the Buchanans to give up fighting. They think they can force us to surrender in return for Lady Ilisa, but we'll never lie down. Never!"

Liam wandered over to Lily and scratched his jaw frowning. "This Lady Ilisa sounds like the closest thing to our mission. We should try to find her."

"How do you explain the name change?" Lily asked.

He shrugged. "Maybe it's a code word for her. Maybe they're using that name to hide her true identity. I don't know. It sounds promising, though."

Lily nodded, but before she could answer, Edeena blurted out, "I'll kill ye both for this. Ye'd best let me go before me own people find out what ye've done."

Liam rounded on her. "You're not going anywhere. You're going to help us get into Tyrekirk."

"I winnae do any such thing!" Edeena jerked and struggled on her chair. "The instant I get free of this, I'll kill ye both with me bare hands."

Liam sighed and murmured under his breath to Lily. "We'll never be able to turn our backs on her. She'll keep threatening us as long as we keep her with us, but we can't let her go."

"Can you do anything about that?" Lily asked. "It seems a shame to waste her, now that we finally got her under control."

Liam sauntered back to the chair and studied Edeena from a safe distance. "I'm going to cast a mate-bonding spell on you. It will...."

"No!" Edeena shrieked. "No! Ye cannae!"

He held up his hand. "It will ensure that you don't do anything to harm me or betray me as long as the spell is in place. Once we get inside the castle and find Lady Rhona, I'll break the spell. Then you'll be free."

"No!" Edeena flew into fresh fits of tearing at her arms and trying to get out of the chair. "Dinnae do that! Ye cannae!"

Liam ignored her. He turned one palm up and traced a curious pattern on it with his index finger. Lily couldn't see what he was doing, but a strange buzzing noise came from his hand the longer he did it.

After a few minutes, he lifted his index finger and touched it to Edeena's forehead. She exploded in turmoil. She whipped her head right and left to get away from him, but nothing she did would break the contact with his finger.

He kept pressing it to her forehead until she stopped thrashing. She collapsed whimpering into her chair. She hung her head and panted in defeat.

Liam dropped both hands and Edeena's arms sagged at her sides. The magic release its hold on her, but Edeena didn't move.

"You can get up now. We'll get you something to eat, but I order you to stay in this room." Liam turned his back on her and walked over to Lily. "There. That's done."

"Did you really have to do that?"

"What else could I do? If I didn't bind her to me, she would have killed us both to get free. Now she won't be able to and she'll have no choice but to help us get into the castle."

Lily walked around him and approached the chair. "Come on, Edeena. You can take the bed tonight and get some sleep. I'll..."

She put out her hand to touch the woman's shoulder, but Edeena jumped away snarling and spitting. "Ye foul witch! Ye killed me cousin Farlan. I'll tear yer eyes out for that."

Edeena made a grab for Lily. Lily barely ducked out of the way in time before Liam slapped Edeena's hand down. "Stop that this minute! You'll protect and defend Lily the same way you would me. Do you understand?"

Edeena gnashed her teeth in his face. She kept casting murderous glances at Lily.

Liam raised his voice and thundered at Edeena. "I said do you understand?"

Edeena shrank away and didn't answer. She backed into a corner and curled into a ball. She turned her face to the wall and didn't move again all night.

Chapter 22

A strange voice startled Grant out of a sound sleep. "Grant! Are ye there?"

Grant struggled to get his brain back into gear and to place the voice. Then he remembered.

He pushed off the wall to sit himself up. "What are ye doing down here, laddie? Ye should be up in the Fourth Tower where ye belong."

"I'm just as much a prisoner in the Fourth Tower as ye are down here," Ness replied. "I'm awaiting execution the same as ye."

"Well, then, be grateful ye're there and no here. At least ye have a soft bed and food and sunlight."

"Stow all that!" Ness hissed. "We're getting out of here."

Elliot's rough voice interjected from Grant's left. "Who's we? I dinnae recall anything about we."

"I ken a way we can get out," Ness whispered. "I can get the keys and I can show ye the way, but ye must promise to take me with ye when ye go. I winnae stay behind to meet me death while the two of ye make off into the sunset."

Grant instinctively turned toward his brother, but they couldn't see each other in the dark. Grant would have given anything to check his brother's reaction to this suggestion. He would have known in an instant whether Elliot wanted to go along with it.

Elliot smacked his lips. "Give me one good reason we should take ye along. Ye caused us naught but trouble the last time. It's thanks to ye and yer dozy antics that we're in this hole to begin with. If ye'd have kept up like I told ye, we'd be over the mountains now."

"If ye dinnae take me with ye, I winnae break ye out," Ness returned. "Ye can stop here if ye'd prefer."

Grant glanced at Elliot again, but he judged by his brother's silence that they had both made their decision. What other choice did they have—stay here and await execution?

Ness must have known the effect his offer would have. "I'll be back tonight with the keys. Be ready to move."

"Wait a moment, lad," Grant called after him. "How do ye ken yer grandfather winnae execute us before ye come?"

"We're all three scheduled for tomorrow morning at sunrise. One of me guards finds it amusing to taunt me by counting down the hours for me and laughing about it. If we get clear tonight, we'll be all right."

Silence fell over the cell. Grant didn't even hear Ness leave, but Grant knew Ness was gone.

Grant and Elliot sat for a long time without saying anything. So Ness Creighton had some pluck after all.

Grant hated to put himself in the prince's debt, but he would do it to get out of here.

Elliot interrupted his thoughts. "Well, that's it, then."

The hours dragged by and Grant passed the time by turning over the scenario in his mind.

If Ness could steal the keys and escape from the castle, why did he need to take Grant and Elliot with him at all? Grant didn't have to think hard to know the answer. Ness needed Grant and Elliot to help him survive afterward. The Laird would recapture and execute Ness within hours or even minutes without Grant and Elliot helping him.

Grant traced the path out of the dungeon again and again, but he couldn't figure out how Ness planned to escape. Without knowing Ness's secret route, Grant couldn't anticipate resistance from the guards or any other obstacle.

The Laird could send up any number of magical booby traps to stop the fugitives. Grant only hoped Ness took them into account.

Grant almost gave up waiting. He started to turn over to lie down and go to back sleep when the cell lock clicked. He rocketed upright in a second. Elliot stiffened at Grant's side.

"Are ye there, Grant?" Ness whispered.

"Aye. So ye've got the keys. Let's go."

Grant got to his feet and started forward, but Ness stopped him with his hand on Grant's chest. "Hold hard a moment."

"What for?" Elliot snapped. "If we're going, we're going now."

"There's another prisoner slated for execution tomorrow morning," Ness told him.

"What's that to us?" Elliot asked. "Ye're the one who said we'd make a break for it tonight and now here ye are."

"She's a lady," Ness returned. "The guards told me about her. We cannae leave her here."

"How do ye even ken who she is?" Grant asked. "She could be anybody."

"That's what I've come to tell ye," Ness replied. "Just wait a few more hours until I find out who she is. If we can take her with us...."

"Ye want to take an unknown lady with us?" Elliot barked. "Forget it."

"Elliot...." Ness began.

"I said no!" Elliot snarled. "It's bad enough we have to take ye along, but a lady? I think no. If we're going, we're going now. Ye've got the keys and a way out. Ye said tonight, so let's go. That's me final word."

Ness swiveling around to face Grant for confirmation. Elliot didn't make these decisions very often. He usually left the hard work to Grant, but Grant knew that tone in his brother's voice even if Ness didn't.

When Grant didn't answer, Ness sighed. "It isnae right."

"Are ye going or no?" Elliot demanded.

Ness turned away. "Follow me, then."

Ness unlocked the door and the brothers followed him out of the cell. Grant dragged his fingertips along the wall to guide himself. Ness's heels rang on the stones in front of him and rose when Ness started climbing the stairs.

Ness took a side turn somewhere that Grant didn't recognize. His eyes strained for any trace of light, any hint of where he was and where he was going.

Just when he thought he couldn't bear the uncertainty a second longer, he bumped into Ness. Ness whispered over his shoulder. "This is it. This door opens into the outer courtyard. From there, it's a short run to the laundry chute leading to Searson Avenue."

Grant did a quick mental calculation. He knew the layout of the whole castle, but he never knew about this passage.

Once the party got into the chute, they could slide down to Searson Avenue. From there, they could run away into the city—so long as the Laird's guards didn't notice them beforehand, that is.

Ness turned his key in a lock and fresh air hit Grant in the face. He squinted out at the courtyard drenched in green and purple. The sun was going down.

At that moment, a squadron of soldiers trooped across Grant's line of sight. They escorted a petite, stately woman in the center of their square.

She wore a full-length black gown that matched her silken dark hair. She kept her eyes down and the sunset lit up her clear skin. She wore no jewelry, but her beauty shone through for all to see.

Ness stiffened. "That's her. That's the other prisoner. We have to free her."

"We winnae do any such thing," Elliot growled into his ear. "Do ye want to risk yer life for her? Do ye want to go to the gallows with her tomorrow morning? That's what ye'll do if ye go out there."

"I winnae leave her to her death." Ness lunged for the door.

Grant grabbed him and hauled him back. "Elliot's right, lad. Ye'd be throwing away our lives along with yer own. We cannae allow ye to go out there. If ye want to save her, do it after we get free."

Ness tried one last time to break Grant's grip, but Grant held firm. He couldn't lose this chance to escape, not for anything or anyone. He pinned the prince against the wall until the soldiers crossed the courtyard and disappeared.

He waited until the coast was clear before he poked his head into the open. Then he stepped outside. "Come."

Elliot crowded against Grant's back to urge him forward and all three men stepped into the courtyard. Grant checked the area for any sign of guards, but he didn't see anything.

The silence racked his nerves. At least some soldiers and retainers from the Laird's court should have been hanging around the courtyard in between guarding the front gate and going off duty for the night. This courtyard should never be completely deserted.

Ness didn't stop. He crossed the courtyard to another wall thirty feet away where a small wooden trapdoor opened into the laundry chute. Grant's pulse quickened. This just might actually work.

A grunt made him glance over his shoulder in time for Elliot to pitch into him from behind. Grant spun around to catch his brother when a posse of wizards rushed the party from across the courtyard.

Elliot stumbled to his feet. Grant floundered to free himself from his brother and then the wizards opened fire. One shot a swarm of bees at the fleeing men. Another launched whizzing arrows from his fingertips.

Grant lost track of all the magical weapons the wizards used. He was too busy getting Elliot off him and diving for cover behind a horse's stall in a corner of the courtyard.

The instant the fight broke out, dozens of guards flooded the courtyard and Grant immediately thought of the Laird.

Grant didn't put it past the Laird to keep all his sentries hidden until Ness and the two brothers showed themselves. The Laird always did things like that. Now the Laird would throw everything he had at them to destroy them entirely.

The bees hit Grant in the face and buried Elliot in a cloud of stinging buzzes. An arrow tore through Grant's hair and cut his ear before he and Elliot ducked behind the wall.

The tethered horse stamped and screamed in the stall, but the wizards just kept on coming. The Laird's forces poured from all directions until guards and soldiers blockaded the courtyard.

Grant lost sight of the chute and he didn't know any other way out of here. He slapped bees off his neck and cheeks, but they only stung him more fiercely than ever.

He looked around for a bucket of water to throw over himself when he spotted Ness cringing behind a barrel not far away.

"Shift, Ness!" Grant bellowed. "Shift now!"

"I cannae!" Ness shrieked. "The spell—it still holds me. I cannae shift!"

At that moment, the wall they were hiding behind detonated in Grant's face. A giant boulder smashed through it and brick and mortar peppered his leg. It almost crushed Elliot before Grant towed him out of the way.

"We cannae stay here!" Elliot yelled. "We must make a run for the chute."

Grant nodded, but he didn't see any way they could get there alive. He stole a peek over what was left of the wall. The wizards and guards advanced from all sides. If the brothers stayed where they were, they would be just as dead.

Grant measured the distance. A solid curtain of random stuff blocked the way. Glass shards, razor-sharp knives, fanged monsters slithering their furry bodies through the air—they filled the courtyard to bursting. The men couldn't make it to the chute without some protection.

Grant spotted an overturned wooden tub near the horse's stall and grabbed it. It wouldn't give him much cover against all the stuff flying around, but it was better than nothing.

Grant flipped it up, held it sideways in front of his head, and checked Ness. The prince gaped at him from his hiding place. Then he tightened his lips and nodded. They had to do this or die trying.

Grant took a deep breath. Elliot cringed under the tub against Grant's back and Grant burst out into the open. Random projectiles shattered off the tub and he bolted for the barrel where Ness dove behind him.

Knives sliced his legs and sides as Grant sprinted across the courtyard. Pinpricks stung him all over. He winced against the pain and kept on running until he spotted the chute a few paces ahead.

He skidded to a stop in front of it and bellowed over his shoulder. "Go! Get down there!"

He spun backward and braced himself to hold the tub in place, but he already felt it crumbling in his hands.

Ness leaped for the trapdoor and pried it back, but he didn't dive down it the way Grant hoped he would. The prince froze. Even Elliot stood stock still under the hail of missiles.

Grant looked over his shoulder and almost dropped the tub when he gazed down at Lily's face peering up at him. His lips formed her name, but he couldn't get the sound out.

At that moment, something stabbed him in the ribs. He flinched and cried out and the tub fell out of his hands.

It shattered on the paving stones and the full power of the wizards' attack hit him with all its fury.

Ness hopped into the chute and disappeared followed by Elliot, but Grant couldn't get away. Bees covered his nose and mouth. Stings hammered his forehead and cheeks and a dozen ravenous little monsters sank their teeth into his flesh.

Grant flew into a panic. He couldn't think. He slapped at his own face and tried to rip those things off him, but he only hurt himself instead. He couldn't decide what to do.

Powerful hands seized him out of the confusion and a female voice bellowed in his ear. "Come on!"

The next minute, those hands dragged him into the chute. There were too many hands to just be one person. Grant collapsed in blessed relief as the bees and monsters and knives and all the other weapons vanished and left him smarting in pain.

He tumbled down, down, down and slammed hard on the ground. Someone put their arms around him and that sweet voice murmured in his ear. "Come on. Get up. We're getting out of here."

He looked up at Lily gazing down at him. Every inch of his skin and body hurt, but he no longer cared. She was here. She had him. She would keep him safe and make sure he got away alive.

She helped him up and Elliot appeared on Grant's other side to support him. They staggered after Ness, Liam, and another figure fleeing through the city.

Chapter 23

Lily squatted down next to Grant. "Are you all right? Those look bad."

She raised her finger to touch one of the many stings on his face, but he batted her hand away. "Dinnae, lass. I cannae stand it."

"We have to do something about this. Your face is swelling up like a balloon."

"Don't worry about him," Liam added. "I can fix him up as soon as we get to safety."

"Why can't you do it now?" Lily asked. "He's bleeding all over the place and he's been stabbed in the ribs. He could have a punctured lung. He won't be able to walk pretty soon."

Liam started to answer when Edeena rushed him. "Ye said we'd go after the Lady Ilisa. Ye lied to me! I'm going back for her."

Liam caught her and held her. "You aren't going anywhere."

She tried one more time to fight her way around him, but he forced her off and slammed her against the wall.

He jabbed his finger in her face. "I'm ordering you to stand down. Do you hear me? Now be quiet. None of us is going back there right now."

Edeena glared at him and gritted her teeth, but she didn't argue.

Liam puffed out his cheeks and stood back to collect himself. "You saw yourself what it was like in there. You said we could sneak in through the laundry chute and find Lady Ilisa without anyone noticing us. There were wizards and soldiers all over the place. We would all be dead now if we went back."

No one said anything. Liam panted to catch his breath and hung his head. Sweat dripped from his forehead and his shoulders shook.

Lily got to her feet. Someone had to take charge of this disaster.

Before she could say anything, a troop of soldiers marched by outside the alley where Lily and the others were hiding. They tramped by without noticing the party.

"We can't stay here," Lily murmured, "and we have to find a place to take care of Grant."

"The slums...." Grant stammered. "Go back to Damerell."

Lily nodded and put out her hand to him. "Come on. You can lean on me."

He tried to straighten his legs and slumped. Elliot came to Lily's side. "I'll see to him, lassie. Ye go ahead and clear the way for me for I winnae be able to defend meself with him on board."

He took hold of Grant's wrist, heaved him up, and slung his brother over his shoulder.

Grant groaned in pain, but Elliot set his jaw and started off down the street. Liam and Edeena went first.

Lily kept near Elliot and checked each avenue and byway for soldiers before she waved him forward. Ness brought up the rear.

They covered miles of territory before they stopped to rest in the deserted alley behind a brothel. Elliot laid Grant's unconscious body in a corner and crouched down to catch his breath.

"Can we use one of your old safe houses to spend the night?" Lily asked him.

Elliot shook his head. "All the safe houses we used to hide the prince are known at Tyrekirk. Those will be the first places they'll look for us."

"What about you, Edeena?" Lily turned to the Buchanan captive. "Do you know any safe place where we can hole up until morning?"

Edeena shook her hair out of her eyes, but she refused to look at Lily. "If I did, they'd be full of Buchanans. They'd be the first to kill ye lot the moment they laid eyes on ye."

"She's right," Liam chimed in. "We can't use any Buchanan hiding place. We'll have to think of something else."

"What about the rebels?" Lily asked. "I heard at the inn there are elements in this city who oppose the Laird's rule. We could take shelter with them."

Elliot's head shot up. "Are ye out of yer mind? We're traveling with the Crown Prince. They'd have our heads."

Lily wanted to argue back, but Liam cut her off. "That's not an option, either. There must be somewhere else."

"Then we're out of luck," Lily returned. "We would have to find somewhere completely deserted where no one will see us. I'll bet nowhere like that exists in this city. There are too many people around and they're all hostile toward us."

No one said anything. Lily's heart sank when she scanned their faces. They were all thinking the same thing. They were doomed.

Elliot broke in on her thoughts. "I ken a place. Just give me a moment. He's heavier than he looks."

Liam kept stealing glances around the building, and when Lily took a look, she saw guards crowding around the brothel. They questioned the prostitutes and the customers.

She almost questioned Elliot about his hiding place, but when she looked at him, he was gazing down at his brother.

Grant lay unconscious in a heap. His eyes had swollen shut and he wheezed through puffy purple lips. The stings made his face completely unrecognizable.

Lily turned away feeling sick. She had seen much worse in Afghanistan, but she couldn't look at him. Somehow, caring about the injured person made it a hundred times worse.

The guards dispersed after a while and Elliot got to his feet. He threw Grant over his shoulder and nodded to the others. They took their positions around him while he made his way behind the building to another street.

Elliot took the lead this time. Liam and Lily flanked him in case of attack, but they didn't meet with any trouble.

Elliot wound deeper into Damerell through gutters and tenements. Lily didn't like the look of the neighborhood, but at least no one would bother their party here.

Elliot finally ducked into a forgotten doorway. The friends followed him into a burned-out hulk of a building with no glass in the windows and very little interior. Charred beams supported the roof and debris littered the floor.

Elliot carried Grant through the wreckage to a tiny room in the far rear. He eased his brother onto the floor and turned Grant onto his back under a broken window.

The others spread out to search the place and Lily drifted over to Elliot's side.

She wanted to be near Grant. As horrible as he looked, she didn't belong anywhere else. She couldn't explain it to herself, but Elliot showed no sign that her behavior was anything out of the ordinary.

Liam returned and scanned the room. "I guess this will have to do. Light a fire over there, Edeena. There's plenty of wood in this place."

Edeena slunk off somewhere and Liam squatted down next to Elliot. "All right. I can treat him now."

"What are you going to do?" Lily asked.

"Don't even ask."

Liam placed one hand on Grant's leg above a particularly nasty gash. He bowed his head over the fallen man, closed his eyes, and a stillness came over him. He kept quiet for a moment.

Little by little, a wave passed over Grant's body. It spread from the point of contact between Liam's hand and Grant's leg. It crept up Grant's knee and thigh, covered his midsection and his torn, bloody shirt, up his neck, and over his face.

The skin shrank in on itself. The swelling went down and Grant returned to his usual appearance, but he still didn't move. The wound in his side close and the skin sealed into a smooth, seamless whole.

Liam shook himself. "He's asleep. He'll stay asleep for a while, so don't try to wake him up."

He started to leave when Elliot grabbed Liam's elbow. "Thank ye, man. I mean it. Thank ye for me brother."

"Sure," Liam returned. "I was never going to let him die."

He walked away and left Elliot and Lily sitting side by side next to Grant.

Lily studied Grant now that he looked like himself again. Why did he fascinate her so much? He was just an ordinary guy. He wasn't a prince like Ness. Grant was just a man, a soldier.

That must be what drew her to him with such a powerful force. She saw herself in him. He was her in male form.

He offered her a way out of this endless misery of living in the past. He gave her hope that she could be a woman again instead of a relic of some military disaster that happened to catch her in the wrong place at the wrong time.

The fire crackled behind her back and everyone turned toward it in grateful relief. Lily and Elliot stayed where they were for a while, but pretty soon, they tore themselves away to sit near it, too.

Liam approached Ness. The prince crouched in a corner with his face turned away. He doubled over as if in pain, but Lily couldn't see any injuries on him.

"Come on, Ness," Liam told him. "I can break the spell that blocks you from shifting."

"Go on with ye!" Ness slapped Liam's hand away. "Leave me be."

Liam gaped down at him with his mouth open. "Don't you want me to break the spell? We'll need you if we meet any more wizards."

Ness kept his face turned to the wall and didn't answer. Lily thought about going over there and trying to comfort him, but she couldn't think what might be bothering him. He didn't almost die in that courtyard the way Grant did.

She watched Ness from her place by the fire until Liam drew her attention back to the group. "There must be another way to get into the castle."

"There isnae any other way into the castle," Elliot rumbled. "They'll execute this Lady Ilisa of yers in the morning and then ye winnae have any reason to get inside."

"They winnae ever execute her," Edeena snarled, "not so long as the Buchanans have ought to say about it."

"The Buchanans!" Elliot snorted. "A fat lot of good the Buchanans have ever done anybody or themselves. Ye cannae even save yerself, much less break into Tyrekirk to rescue a condemned prisoner."

"I still say it must be Lady Rhona using a different name," Liam remarked. "No one else matches the description."

"Does that mean you got a description of her from your source?" Lily asked. "Do you know what Lady Rhona is supposed to look like?"

"Well, no," Liam admitted, "but you have to agree it couldn't be anyone else."

"Her name's Ilisa," Edeena broke in. "She cannae be yer Lady Rhona. She's a Buchanan."

"That's impossible," Elliot countered.

"Maybe Ness can tell us who Lady Ilisa is." Lily swiveled around on her seat. "Come talk to us, Ness. Who was that woman you say you saw in the courtyard?"

Ness didn't respond. He stayed curled against the wall with his back to everyone.

"What's wrong with him?" Liam asked.

"He's in despair over losing his position as the Laird's heir," Elliot replied. "They groomed him all his life to become Laird. Now he's got naught. Leave him alone to nurse his injured pride. He's too wet to think straight."

Liam laughed. Lily bit back a grin, but she couldn't help casting a few more sidelong glances at Ness.

He didn't act like this when he went on the run last time. He didn't curl up in a ball and block out everything else. He kept arguing back. He kept throwing his false authority around.

Something else must be bothering him, but Lily couldn't put her finger on it. It must have something to do with that woman prisoner. Ness wanted to break off his own escape to rescue her. Who was she?

The conversation shifted. Liam and Elliot started talking about where the group ought to go in the morning. Lily tuned them out while she pondered the situation. A few minutes later, the two men got up and went off to scout the area around the building.

Lily brooded for a while, and when she shook herself back to the present, Ness was still cowering in the same place. He hadn't moved. Edeena sat a few feet away and stared into the fire.

Lily fought down the urge to return to her own thoughts. These two people had more information about her mission than she could understand. Why should she muddle around in confusion when she could just ask them?

She turned to Edeena. "What do you know about Lady Ilisa?"

"Hold yer tongue," Edeena snarled. "I may not be able to kill ye just yet, but he didnae order me to make a friend of ye. I can still hate ye and I'll go on hating ye as long as I live."

"That's okay," Lily replied. "You can go on hating me as long as you want, but it sure would help us get Lady Ilisa out of Tyrekirk if we could find out who she really is."

"I've already told ye who she really is," Edeena fired back. "She's wife to Neill Buchanan, our Clan Chief."

"And there's no chance she could also be Lady Rhona Armstrong?"

"No chance whatever."

Lily's shoulders slumped. "You know, Edeena, it would benefit you to help us as much as you can. We're your best chance of finding Lady Ilisa and getting her out of Tyrekirk. Once we do that, Liam will release you from the mate-bonding spell and you'll be free."

"Free!" Edeena rounded on Lily spitting through gritted teeth. "I'll never be free! Dinnae ye understand that, ye hag? The Highland tigers mate for life. He can break the spell all he likes. I'm stuck with him for life whether I like it or no. I can never go back to me own people now."

Lily stared at her in horror. Neither Liam nor Lily had ever considered asking Edeena if the bonding spell was a good idea. No wonder she protested so much.

Lily's stomach flipped. She hated Edeena for trying to kill her, but Lily couldn't help feeling sorry for her. If only Lily could take back that spell, she would do it to free Edeena from this trap.

It wasn't fair. That was the plain truth. If Liam knew, he would regret bonding Edeena to him for life. He never would have imprisoned someone like that if he knew. None of that helped Edeena now, though. The deed was done and it couldn't be undone.

Lily staggered to her feet and bolted for the door. She had to get away from Edeena. She had to go anywhere to put as much distance between herself and Edeena as possible.

That spell was a mistake. It wasn't Lily's mistake, but it still weighed on her mind. She would do anything to take it back. She would do anything to make this right for Edeena and now she couldn't.

Chapter 24

L ily drifted away from the fire until she came to the ruin's front door. Lamps lighted the streets. A few midnight prowlers wandered the neighborhood. They scurried here and there, put their heads together, and shuffled off somewhere else.

The stars showed up better here than they did in Detroit. The air smelled bracing and fresh even in this foul slum. She sat down on the step to observe the night. Maybe the breeze would clear her head.

She hugged her knees to her chest. What was wrong with her? She no longer felt any drive to continue this mission if she ever did. Why should she sacrifice herself for her country or even for some imaginary Lady Rhona? Why couldn't Lily just live her own life?

She understood how Edeena felt. Lily was just as trapped in a contract she never agreed to.

Liam lied to her about this mission. He lied about himself and now she couldn't get out of it.

If she knew when she left Ironforge what she knew now, she never would have gone along with this. That was why he lied—to trick her.

Someone startled her out of her thoughts when they came out of the building behind her. Grant sat down next to her and gave a deep sigh. He propped his elbows on his knees and let his chin fall on his chest. "There ye are, lassie. I wondered where ye'd gone off to."

Relief and joy burst her heart in half. He was okay! She threw her arms around him and laid her head on his shoulder. "Oh, thank goodness you're all right! I was so worried."

"Aye. I'm all right. I dinnae feel all too glamorous, but that's the price of war. That Buchanan lassie tells me yer brother fixed me up."

"Yeah, he did." Lily looked away. She blushed at her actions now that she didn't have to worry about him anymore.

She didn't really mean to hug him like that. Well, she did mean to, but she probably wouldn't have if she thought about it beforehand.

"Is Elliot...?"

"He's fine. He and Liam went to check out the neighborhood and see about where we're going to go tomorrow."

Grant nodded. "I meant to thank ye for.... I dinnae ken.... for getting me out of the castle."

"I didn't really do anything. It was...."

He shook his head. "I remember ye. I remember yer face. It's the last thing I saw before I.... Well, it was the last thing I saw and it was the first thing I hoped to see when I woke up. That's why I came to find ye."

His eyes burned in the darkness and she became aware of his presence so close and warm and sturdy. Her shoulder touched his shoulder. His body imprinted on her arms and chest and cheek where she hugged him.

He glanced down at her mouth and her world flipped on its axis. His lips woke hidden desires and yearnings in her innermost being. She fooled herself into thinking that need wasn't there anymore, but it had always nagged her in her most private moments.

Now here he sat, right in front of her. He offered her that faint hope that she could be more, that she could still feel something. She couldn't ignore it any longer. She couldn't ignore him.

He didn't shrink from the intensity of this moment. He stayed there, close to her. He must feel the tension between them, but it didn't seem to bother him. Why should it bother her?

She thought about it and realized it didn't bother her, either. Old loyalties and obligations told her that it should bother her, but it didn't. She accepted it.

It seemed natural and understood between them. Even her putting her arms around him fit the overall pattern leading up to this moment.

Before she could make up her mind, he kissed her. He kissed her the way he did in the forest—one little, innocent peck that grew and morphed into something so much more.

She couldn't argue with a little peck. Why should she?

Once his lips came to rest on hers, that kiss took on a significance beyond anything she imagined. It meant so much more. She couldn't break away.

His lips grappled at her mouth. He massaged her brain and spirit through his lips. He nudged her mouth open into deep, delicious ecstatic kisses that went on and on and on without end.

Electric heat scorched her being and she collapsed into it with all her heart. The structures that held her apart from all humanity until now dissolved in the dreamy wetness of his tongue and teeth and lips.

His hand touched her cheek. He cradled her head and she surrendered completely. Mind and soul liquefied in his grasp.

She let her head sink into his rough, broad palm. She wanted nothing but to kiss him, to put her arms around him, to hold him and protect him and be with him, as deeply as she could for as long as she could. Nothing else in the wide world mattered.

He slipped his other arm around her waist, tugged her closer to him, and lifted her partially off the step. Her body exploded in passionate tremors with all the possibilities struggling to become real at once.

She arched her back and crushed her body against his chest. His shoulders and arms tightened their grip around her. She fought to breathe against the overpowering flood of desire she kept buried all these years.

His breath quickened and he panted into her mouth. He nipped her lips and his strong hand slid up the back of her neck. She felt all control slipping away. She couldn't stop this in spite of all those ancient voices telling her she should.

Why should she stop it? Why shouldn't she satisfy this irresistible urge to throw all caution to the wind? This desire burned her insides in a molten core of fire that devoured everything in its path. It demanded more and more fuel to consume her entirely.

She couldn't bear the power of her own sensations. They drove her insane. They destroyed everything she was and wanted to be. She couldn't be this. She couldn't cope with it all.

She couldn't stand this. Her body forced her to pull away from him, to get to her feet and walk away. His arms and hands vanished. Her head swam and she had to concentrate to hold herself upright.

She paused to collect herself, teetered on her heels, and supported herself with one hand against a wall to catch her balance. She blinked. She was in one of the rooms in the building, but she couldn't remember how she got there.

Her cheeks flushed and her pulse pounded in her brain. Curious whispers translated through her body. What was happening to her?

Footsteps approached her from behind. She turned to see Liam and Elliot pass her on their way back to the fire, but they didn't notice her standing there. She existed in a different dimension from them and everything she knew. Even herself seemed to remain over there, in the normal world, while she watched from beyond the veil.

She couldn't form a thought to go forward or back. Nowhere in the universe offered her any haven from this whirlwind of thoughts and feelings.

Another set of feet crunched in the debris, and when she looked toward the sound, she wasn't surprised at all to see Grant enter the building following Liam and Elliot.

He saw her, though. He dwelt in that other realm, too.

He walked straight up to her, but he didn't touch her. One half of his forehead wrinkled when he cocked an eyebrow at her.

He studied her to the bottom of her soul. He could see everything passing in her and through her. She was transparent to him.

In his eyes and only in his eyes, she understood. She wanted. She wanted more of him. She craved him, more of what he did to her, more of the unimaginable intensity of his effect on her.

In that moment, she would have gone down on her knees and begged him for it if he told her to. She would have done anything.

She would have sobbed to get him to do it all over again, to wreck her with his touch, to dismantle the stifling armor that protected her from everything she needed.

He didn't have to ask. He didn't tease or hold it in front of her face. He wanted her to have it. He wanted her to be like that—pliant and fragile and responsive. He wanted her to respond. He wanted her to feel.

Nothing could hold them apart. Their mouths came together with that magnetic hold that no force under the sun could break.

She submerged in the intoxicating magic of his kiss, his tongue touching the back of her throat, his fingers laced into her hair, his arms guiding her where she needed to go.

She draped her arms over his shoulders. She didn't care what he did as long as they were together like this.

Her body hummed with all the desire he awoke in her. This painful, ravenous need screamed for him to satisfy her even as she knew nothing ever would.

Chapter 25

G rant gazed into the room where Liam, Elliot, and Edeena sat around the fire. Ness still lurked in the corner away from everyone.

Grant ducked back out of sight and drew Lily into a corner. "Listen to me, lass," he whispered. "I want ye to do something for me."

"What?"

"I want ye and Liam to go back to yer own world."

She jumped a foot in the air. "My own world! What do you mean?"

"Ye dinnae need to hide it from me anymore, lass. The Laird told me ye came from the future."

She stared at him wide-eyed. "The Laird told you? How could he know?"

"Will ye stop playing games? The Laird kens all kinds of things ye wouldnae expect. None of that matters. I ken the truth, so ye neednae pretend it isnae so. Ye came from the future. That's how ye were in the Army during the war. That's how ye were involved in that.... that Division of yers. It's in the future. I dinnae ken how ye came back here, but I want ye to go home. It isnae safe for ye here."

"I can't go back. We haven't found Lady Rhona yet. Besides, Liam has the time portal. He's the only one who can send us back."

"Then I'll talk to him."

Grant turned on his heel to reenter the room, but now she pulled him back. "Hold it, buddy. What the hell are you doing? We just did it and now you want to send me away. What's going on?"

Grant hung his head. He hoped it wouldn't come to this, but now he had no choice but to call a spade a spade. "Do ye think I dinnae ken how the land lies, lassie? Ye're from another time and another country. Ye winnae stay in this one. We had a nice time over there, but...."

"Is that all it was—a nice time? Is that all it meant to you?"

He lowered his voice to a hiss. "Ye ken ye mean a sight more to me than that, but ye must admit it to yerself the same way I do. For one thing, if Ness found out, it would be all over."

"What would be all over? How could he do anything about it?"

"Either way, it isnae safe for ye here. If we got caught, ye could be executed at a moment's notice."

"So could you," she returned. "I don't see you running and hiding."

"I've nowhere to run and hide. This is the only world I'll ever belong to. There's a way for ye to escape. Ye should take it."

She leaned back and crossed her arms over her chest. "You're trying to get rid of me. You had a nice time and now you want to go your merry way like nothing ever happened. Admit it."

He pursed his lips and took a deep breath. He had to stay calm if he wanted to convince her. "Dinnae ye see I'm trying to protect ye the only way I can? I nearly lost me life yesterday and tomorrow will likely be the same, but ye dinnae have to die. Go home. I would keep ye here with me if I thought there was any way to do it. I would keep ye with me for life, but that would only put ye in more danger. If I can save ye, I can sacrifice meself to do it."

"Well, how do you think I feel?" Her lip quivered. She seemed so much smaller, now that he saw her vulnerable and in danger. "Don't you think I would want to do the same thing for you?"

He hesitated to say the next words out loud, but if that's what it took to get her to safety, he would hazard even that. "Ye dinnae want that, lass. Ye said yerself ye've sworn off love for the rest of yer life."

She looked away and her face twisted in misery. He never expected her to react like this. He expected her to jump at the chance to get away with her life. "I don't want to go. We finally have a lead on this Lady Ilisa character. I don't want to walk away just yet."

He drew near her. Every minute he spent around her made him want to touch her all the more.

His fingers wrapped into hers. Her body spoke volumes to him. "Listen to me, lassie. If what happened over there wasnae just a nice time for ye, if ye care for me at all, do it for me. I must see ye safe if there's any way I can do it. I cannae protect ye from the Laird's men, much as I'd like to. This is the only way I can ken yer safe where the Laird cannae harm ye. What happened over there was....it was beautiful. I'll carry it with me for the rest of me days, but it's naught compared to this. If ye want to show me ye care for me at all, please.... please just do it. I'll carry on yer investigation. I'll try to find out anything I can about Lady Rhona in case ye ever manage to come back."

She peered up at him out of those bottomless eyes. He could look into those eyes forever and never find out all there was to know about her. "All right. If that's what it takes to show you, I'll do it, but I'll only leave if we're in real danger. I won't go now."

"Thank ye, lass." He indulged in one last kiss. "I'll talk to Liam so he understands." He turned away, but before he entered the room, he turned back. "One more thing, lass." She raised her eyes waiting for him to finish. "I think it might be wise to keep this from Ness."

She dropped her eyes and nodded down at the floor. He left her standing there in the dark. He had to muster all his strength to get away from her or he would stay with her always.

He sat down between Liam and Elliot. Elliot clapped him on the back. "There's me own man. How are ye, laddie? Still alive, I see."

"Thanks to ye lot," Grant replied. "Did ye find ought outside that could help us?"

"It isnae far to the edge of the city," Elliot replied. "We should be able to return to the forest tomorrow."

Grant turned to Liam. "And ye? Will ye return to the forest or stay in Kald?"

Liam shrugged. "I guess I'll talk to Lily about that in the morning. We may have tipped our hand trying to break into the castle. We might go to the forest for a while until we figure out another way to get inside."

Edeena broke in on their conversation. "What about Lady Ilisa? Do ye really mean to let the Laird execute her in the morning?"

"How can we save Lady Ilisa when we can't even save ourselves?" Liam asked.

"Ye promised me ye'd do everything in yer power to save her," Edeena growled back. "Ye trapped me in this wretched spell of yers on yer word that ye would get into the castle and save her."

Liam bowed his head. "You're right. I did."

"Ye're naught but a liar," she spat. "Ye arenae a man. I ken a man when I see one. The Buchanans are men who ken the value of their word. When they pledge to do something, there isnae any force in Heaven or on Earth to stop them. If any man of me Clan gave his word to free the lady, he would do it. He wouldnae slope off to the forest to save his own sk in."

Liam stared into the fire. Grant and Elliot exchanged glances. She was right, of course. The decision to turn their backs on a lady in difficulties didn't sit right with Grant, either.

Ness watched and listened from the corner. The prince's mouth turned down at the corners in a miserable grimace that Grant had never seen before.

Liam raised his head and confronted Edeena. "I'll tell you what. If there is any possible way we can get back to the castle tomorrow morning, we'll do it. Does that satisfy you?"

She relaxed. She didn't smile or nod, but she softened her hostile attitude—for now, at least. A few minutes later, Elliot stretched himself out on the floor, closed his eyes, and went to sleep.

Grant stayed awake and waited until Edeena curled over on her side, too. Her eyes drifted closed and her breathing lengthened. Ness rested his head on his arms. The room fell quiet except for the fire popping.

Grant chose his moment. He had to do this before Liam went to sleep, too. At last, he summoned the courage to speak. "Ye did right giving her assurance that ye'd keep yer promise. It was well done."

"Yeah, well, I'm not here to see anybody get killed, least of all myself. I have a mission to fulfill and I can't do that if I'm dead."

Grant took a deep breath and plunged in. "About that, I want to ask ye a favor for meself."

Liam gasped and threw up both hands. "Jesus Christ, not another one!"

"Just hear me out, man. Ye say ye arenae here to see anybody get killed. I'm certain ye arenae here to see yer sister get killed, either."

Liam's head whipped around. "What about her?"

"If things go against us, tomorrow or any other time, ye have the power to take her and yerself to safety. Ye can take her back where ye came from."

Liam cocked his head and his expression changed. "What exactly are you saying?"

"I'm not saying," Grant murmured. "I'm asking, as a favor to me, that ye take Lily to safety if things go against us. I've given her me own word as a man that I'll continue yer investigation into Lady Rhona in case ye ever come back."

Liam cast a glance toward the doorway. Grant couldn't see anything in the dark beyond. Was Lily over there listening to this conversation right now?

Liam pierced Grant to the core and his voice took on a hard edge. "I have no desire to see Lily get hurt—by the Laird or anyone else. She's been through enough in her life. She doesn't need that, too."

Grant heard what Liam didn't say and he held Liam's gaze. "I winnae ever hurt Lily—never. Now I want yer word as her brother that ye'll do the same. If it comes to a battle we cannae win, take her home where she belongs."

Liam looked deep into Grant's eyes. Grant met him in that place where both men understood exactly what Lily meant to both of them. "You have my word, Grant. If it comes to that, I'll take her home."

Chapter 26

Grant shoved Edeena into an open space where four tall buildings formed an enclosure. "Go! Go now!"

Edeena bolted across the gap, skidded for cover, and dove into a hollow under a crumbling cellar. One wall had collapsed to reveal the partially hidden room underneath.

Elliot came to Grant's side, but Grant held him back. "Hold hard, lad. Not yet."

The friends held their breath and hid from another battalion of soldiers trooping into view. The Laird's forces halted there while five wizards held a hasty conversation. They pointed in different directions before they spread out to search the enclosure.

Lily shrank back, but the group couldn't exactly hide in plain sight. The soldiers drew closer and closer. They searched every alley. They would discover the party any second now.

A high-pitched whine hummed in Lily's ear. She turned to see Liam splay his fingers toward the corner between the guards and the friends hiding behind the wall.

A net of fibers threaded from his fingertips and stuck to the buildings on either side. They laced into a web gleaming white.

The guards tramped closer and two of them poked their heads around the corner. They scanned the street where Grant, Elliot, Liam, and Lily stood stock still and breathless with tension.

The two soldiers looked right at the party and then walked away to check the rest of the street. In a few minutes, the troop marched away to another part of the city.

Lily whispered to Liam, "What did you do?"

"They'll be back in a few minutes," Liam murmured. "They're tracking us. We have to get out of here now."

"How can they be tracking us? How do they keep finding us no matter where we go?"

"They're using locator spells," Grant replied.

"I can mask us for a little while," Liam told him, "but they're bound to find us sooner or later with so many wizards working together. Once they realize what I'm doing, they'll use counter-magic to unmask me."

Grant gave Elliot a push. "Go, lad."

Elliot dashed across the enclosure and slipped into the cellar alongside Edeena. Liam followed next. Grant laid his hand on Lily's shoulder. "Go, lassie."

Lily cast a glance over her shoulder. "What about Ness?"

The prince lagged several paces behind the rest of the group. Every time Lily checked on him, Ness was looking over his own shoulder. He kept peering backward and lingering.

"Ye go on, lass," Grant told her. "I'll fetch him."

"No. I'll go."

Lily didn't wait for Grant to argue and she strode back to where Ness stood. He shuffled his feet in the middle of an intersection where anyone could see him. He didn't even try to hide.

"Are you all right, Ness? Is anything the matter?"

He didn't turn around. "We must go back. We must go back to Tyrekirk."

"We can't go back to Tyrekirk. The Laird is already trying to kill us. We can't walk right into his castle."

He shook his head. "We shouldnae have left her behind. We should have at least tried to get her free."

Lily's heart sank. "Do you mean Lady Ilisa? She's probably dead by now."

He spun around and his eyes flashed with more fire than she'd seen from him since they first met. "She isnae dead. I ken that. She's still alive. We can still save her."

"What makes you think that? The guards told you she was due to be hung this morning."

"She isnae dead," he insisted. "I ken it."

Lily let out a heavy breath. "All right. If she's still alive, we'll work out a way to rescue her, but right now we have to get out of here. The Laird's troops are right on our tail. Come on."

Without warning, he grabbed her by both shoulders and kissed her. Lily jumped back in surprise. "What are you doing?"

"It's Grant, am I right?" he demanded. "Is that the reason ye dinnae care for me?"

Lily's cheeks flushed remembering her encounter with Grant. She couldn't destroy Ness's only hope by telling him that she'd already given herself to someone else.

She thought fast to come up with some excuse to put Ness off. "It's not that. Some bad stuff happened to me back in my own country. I swore never to love anyone again and to dedicate my life to serving humanity. That's the only reason I can't be what ye want me to be."

He studied her so closely that he made her fidget. Then he shook his head. "It's Grant. I ken it is. I felt it when I kissed ye just now."

"Listen, Ness...."

Before she could get the words out, he dove in and kissed her again. This time, she stiffened and didn't pull away. His lips remained there glued to her mouth for a long minute. His eyes searched her soul before he broke away. "Ye see? Ye dinnae have to soothe me feelings. Just tell the truth."

She started to answer when Grant came striding down the street. He came up behind her. "What's going on?"

A cloud crossed Ness's face and he pulled his head down between his shoulders. "I ken about ye two. Ye dinnae have to hide it any longer."

Grant kept his expression totally blank. "Ye ken what about us?"

"Don't bother," Lily told him. "He already knows."

Ness leapt at him and jabbed his finger in Grant's face. "I told ye to back off, but ye didnae listen. Ye're so full of what a fop I am that ye think ye can tread all over me. Ye think a common soldier like ye can take what's mine and walk away."

"I'm not yours, Ness," Lily cut in. "I told you that. When are you going to....?"

Ness completely ignored her. He focused all his fury on Grant. "I can destroy ye. Ye ken that. Ye think ye're bigger and stronger and braver because ye're a soldier. Ye dinnae ken what I can do."

Grant didn't lose his temper. He murmured low under his breath. "I ken what ye can do, laddie. I've seen it meself."

"Dinnae ye call me a laddie!" Ness spat. "I'm not a laddie any more than ye. Would ye prefer to find out for yerself? Is that what ye're asking for, that ye think ye can walk all over me life and take the one thing that's....?"

Lily saw the darker color of his scales showing through his skin. The more irate he got, the more signs he showed of getting ready to shift into his dragon form. Even his facial bones changed until she thought she saw the monstrous figure forming under his skin.

Grant must have seen the same thing, but he didn't show it. He confronted Ness with the same blank expression. He made no move to touch his weapons.

Ness bellowed in his face. He talked so fast that Lily couldn't quite make out what he was saying. She got so engrossed in watching the dragon seething under his skin that she lost the thread of his meaning.

She tensed to spring away or fight, one or the other. She couldn't know for sure if Ness wouldn't attack her, too, now that he realized he'd lost her to someone else.

Ness didn't see Grant straighten his arms. Grant let them fall to his sides and relaxed them, but that was only a prelude to stiffening them. He was preparing himself to fight, too.

A shriek out of nowhere startled Lily into spinning around. She searched the surroundings to find the cellar where Edeena, Liam, and Elliot were hiding when she spotted a dozen large cats bounding over a nearby wall.

They rushed into the enclosure and half streaked for the cellar while the others went for Lily, Ness, and Grant.

Grant side-stepped away and slid out his saber. A muffled explosion poofed from the cellar before the cats closed in on Lily's position.

She thrust out her hand to Grant. "Quick! Give me your dirk."

He pulled it from his belt, but he didn't have time to hand it to her before the cats closed in. One of them soared at Grant while another two cut the pair away from each other.

He surveyed the scene for a fraction of an instant and then tossed the weapon into the air. It made a majestic arch and fell handle downward so she caught it easily. She grasped it and rounded on the advancing enemy.

The cats' piercing stares struck terror into Lily's heart. Fighting one of them was bad enough. She couldn't face this many.

Another blood-curdling screech ripped across the street and two cats tumbled in the dust. They kicked and scratched and bit each other in deadly fury and Lily recognized Edeena fighting one of the strangers.

Lily's mind switched into overdrive. Why would the Buchanans attack one of their own? It made no sense, but she didn't have time to think about it before the first creature coiled its legs and launched at her.

It rocketed through the air and she dropped back on one foot with her dirk ready. The creature extended its claws to catch hold of her.

At the last second, she punched her blade at its chest and rotated away. The cat howled to wake the dead and Lily tossed it aside.

Battle frenzy took hold of her, but she didn't get a chance to face the next attack before another cat landed on her back. Its claws hooked her clothes and its teeth sank into her neck.

The stabbing pain sent her into a rage. She slapped her free hand over her shoulder and grabbed a fistful of flesh.

She didn't see what she was holding, but she felt something wet and her finger touched the thing's eye. She clenched her teeth in demonic fury and gouged with all her might.

The cat's teeth broke loose and Lily lashed out harder than ever. She ripped her hand away and the flesh separated. Her fist came away holding a bloody lump of sodden tissue with a few scraps of fur sticking out of it.

She seized one of the paws on her shoulder and wrenched it sideways. She jerked the cat off, flipped it onto the ground, and slammed her foot down on its head. The skull split under her heel and the cat lay still.

Lily stared around her searching for her next victim. Blood rage clouded her mind when she saw her friends locked in mortal combat with more cats. Her friends wrestled and fought all over the enclosure.

Four tigers surrounded Grant. He cut and stabbed at them on both sides just barely keeping them at bay.

Elliot pressed his back to a wall with seven of the creatures blocking him in. He brandished his saber in one hand and his dirk in the other, but when he slashed at one cat, the others raked his legs and shoulders with their claws.

Liam lay flat on his back across the street with a cat perched on his chest. The animal dove for his throat again and again while Liam struggled to hold the thing off. He thrust his forearm into the cat's mouth and its fangs mangled his arm to bloody ribbons.

At that moment, the two cats fighting each other burst apart. One of them bowled away and crashed into a lamppost. The other rolled to its feet and changed into Edeena. "They arenae Buchanans. Look at their eyes!"

Liam paused just fight long enough to glance over at her. "Are you sure?"

She barely got the words out before another three cats broke off their attack on Elliot to come at her. "They arenae Buchanans! I'm telling ye."

Liam let go of his attacker long enough to sweep his hand over the area. In a blink of an eye, all the cats changed into people.

The Laird's wizards shrank back from the Ritchie brother's weapons and Liam found himself wrangling a man instead of a cat.

Just then, a frightened squeal rang out from the other side of the enclosure. "Liam! Liam, help me!"

Lily turned to see Ness pinned to the ground. A man sat on Ness's chest with his beefy fists locked around the prince's neck. The man's cheeks swelled and his arm and shoulder muscles flexed from choking out the prince's life.

A soldier towered over Ness raising his sword on high. The soldier aimed the blade downward to stab the prince through the body.

The whole scene slowed to a standstill in front of Lily's eyes. Ness couldn't shift. The spell the Laird cast on him trapped him in his human form so he couldn't defend himself.

Liam still lay trapped under his attacker, but he managed to yank one hand free. He traced a mysterious squiggle in the air and a twisted line of yellow light shot from his finger. It snaked past Lily and enveloped Ness.

The soldiers didn't notice. Neither of the men attacking Ness realized what was happening until the prince lifted off the ground taking them with him. The two men went flying as the golden dragon exploded into the air.

Lily stumbled back to make room for him. A low rumble shook the ground and the air crackled with electricity. All the wizards and soldiers rounded on the dragon at once. They left Elliot and Liam and Grant alone and the soldiers converged to defend themselves against the prince.

Ness drew himself to a towering height. He blocked out the sun and growled at the wizards. He stomped into the enclosure and left no room for anything else.

The Laird's men retreated before him and Lily scrambled to get behind him. Grant and Elliot slipped along the walls under Ness's protection.

Ness distracted Liam's assailant. Liam pushed the man off and leaped to his feet. He took two steps toward Ness when a high-pitched scream made him look back.

Ness spun around and Lily's jaw dropped when ten more dragons whizzed overhead. They appeared from behind one of the buildings and rocketed into the enclosure where Lily and her comrades cowered in shock.

Ness reared on his hind legs. He spread his great wings to occupy all the space over Lily's head and he let out a deafening roar of challenge. His long neck whipped from side to side and he sprayed a vicious plume of fire at his enemies.

He caught four dragons on the wing. He blasted them out of the sky and they tumbled over themselves to get their wings working. The flames licked their bodies and torched them to ash, but the other six dragons dive-bombed the party.

They swooped past Ness and pelted him with their fire. He broke off killing the other four to confront them, but they buzzed around his head so fast that he couldn't fight them all.

Lily stretched out her hand to her brother. "Come on, Liam! Get over here."

At the same moment, a dragon whooshed around Edeena and stopped her from running for cover under Ness's wings. Lily, Grant, and Elliot had to keep dodging back and forth to avoid getting trampled by Ness's huge feet.

Liam darted for Lily's outstretched hand and dove under Ness's wing. Grant roared in his ear over the noise. "Open the portal! Ye promised. Get Lily out of here."

Lily looked up at him and the expression on his face told her that arguing would get her nowhere. They couldn't win this fight.

The Laird and his forces would keep escalating until they killed her and her companions. Everyone would end up dead or captured in the end.

Liam stole a peek out at the battle and shrank back when two dragons zoomed past. Their fiery breath pelted Ness's enormous sides.

Ness stumbled under the impact and everyone scrambled to keep clear while still sheltering under his massive body.

Liam put his hand in his pocket and pulled out the box. Lily lost awareness of everything else and time slowed to a standstill when he put the box on the ground and pushed the symbols on its side.

A scream split the halo of silence. The whole party looked up to see a brilliant blue dragon attacking Edeena.

It snatched at her hair, tore at her clothes, and darted out of reach. She lunged forward to counterattack, but it fluttered away only to come back at her again from the other side.

She shifted into her cat form and crouched on the ground to spring, but the dragon descended, caught her in its claws, and lifted her off the ground.

The cat contorted and screeched in rage and agony, but she couldn't get her teeth or claws anywhere near her attacker.

The dragon carried her twenty feet off the ground before it released its claws. The cat slammed onto her back and shifted back into a woman.

Edeena barely got her arms up before the dragon pounced on her. It shredded her with its claws while it flapped its wings to hold itself out of her reach.

Liam charged for her. Lily grabbed him and tried to hold him back. "No, Liam! Don't!"

"I can't leave her out there." He shrugged her off and ran.

Ness flailed the air again, rose on his hind legs, and beat his wings. The wind caught the other dragons and swept them away, but two of the enemy still hovered around. One landed on his neck and sank its fangs into him.

Ness arched his spine thundering in pain and one of his wings flicked the box on the ground. The device pitched over and rolled several paces away. It clicked and a vortex erupted out of it.

A gale-force wind ripped Lily off the ground and yanked her toward the box. She grappled to hold onto something and found herself clutching a hand. She opened her eyes to find Grant standing in front of her.

He clapped his other hand over her fingers. "Go, Lily. Go."

Her instincts told her to fight the undertow and hold onto him. She didn't want to go no matter what she said last night. She couldn't leave him behind.

The glacial calm of his face told her she had to go. She couldn't survive here. No one could. Going back to modern times was her only hope.

A cry made her turn around again. Liam supported Edeena by the shoulders and the pair staggered across the enclosure toward the portal when, out of nowhere, the same blue dragon and another red one rushed them from behind. They collided with Liam and sent him pitching onto his face.

Edeena tried to help him up, but the dragons distracted her with constant attacks.

Ness lashed his tail around and smacked off the creature annoying him. The dragon somersaulted through the air and smashed into a building.

The blow knocked a spurt of fire from its mouth that hit Ness in the leg two inches from Lily's head.

She ducked under her arms for cover. Grant yanked her out of the way by pulling her toward him and she fell into his arms.

Ness shot out his head to snap his teeth on one of his enemies. He bit the dragon in half and hurled it away.

He cracked his neck the other way in his rage to get rid of these pests. The sudden movement made him take a step and he accidentally bumped Grant and Lily. He bowled them a few more paces away from the portal.

The suction coming out of the box built with every passing second. It stripped Lily's hair away from her head.

She stole a glance over her shoulder and saw not only Ness's massive body blocking her path to the portal, but three more dragons perched on the ground. They surrounded Ness and bombarded him with fire.

He rounded on one, only to suffer a brutal assault from the other two no matter which way he turned. He couldn't fight them all.

The wizards formed ranks on the other side of the street. They gathered into a tight formation under the dragons' cover and the wizards joined hands.

Liam pushed Edeena toward the portal, but she fought him every step of the way. Lily didn't dare go near it with all those dragons around.

At that moment, the wizards unleashed what looked like a spiral torrent. It erupted from their joined hands and gathered into a hazy bubble in the air. As soon as it formed, it imploded into a giant spearheaded projectile that shot straight for Ness.

One of the other dragons rose off the ground and blasted its fire in his face. The blow distracted him so he didn't see the spear until it plunged into his shoulder where his neck joined his body. He spun around to confront the wizards and all the dragons ambushed him at once.

The vortex howled louder than ever. Liam snatched Edeena by the dress and tried to manhandle her toward it. She gave a forceful twist and slammed her hands against his back. She broke his grip and darted away. Liam stumbled backward and the vortex caught h im.

The whirlwind picked him up and yanked him toward the portal. Lily saw him flying away from her and Grant pushed her forward. "Now!"

She dove for the portal when, out of nowhere, Ness's massive tail came crashing down in front of her. The impact bounced her off her feet and she fell on the cobblestones.

Her ears popped with the portal collapsing. Grant barely dragged her out of harm's way in time before the vortex sucked in on itself and vanished.

Chapter 27

Grant didn't have time to react to the portal disappearing before Ness gave one last ground-shaking bellow of pain and confusion. Grant looked up at the golden dragon heaving and convulsing above his head. The spear stuck out of the prince's neck and black blood poured down his scales.

The wizards collected themselves into a circle again. Grant knew that movement only too well. They would form another magical weapon to shoot the prince down and then nothing and no one would stop them from annihilating Grant, Elliot, and Lily.

Grant rushed into the enclosure without stopping to think. He raised his saber on high to kill as many of those wizards as he could. He took a flying leap to hack them to pieces.

They either didn't see him coming or maybe they were so focused on their spell that they ignored him. He launched himself off the ground roaring at them to draw their attention away from Ness.

At that moment, another one of those mysterious clouds broke out of their hands and congealed in the air in front of him. He couldn't stop himself before another spear formed and shot straight at him.

It punctured his chest and smashed him backward so hard he didn't feel any pain. He watched himself hurtling back until the spear buried its point in the brick surface of a building behind him. For one terrible instant, he hung there with the shaft sticking out of his chest.

Then the spearhead flopped out of the hole it had made. Grant's weight dragged it loose and he hit the ground. Pain exploded through him and his mind swam. The next thing he knew, something awful happened deep inside him.

He couldn't pinpoint the moment it happened. It seemed to creep up on him from years ago. Even then, it overtook him so fast he couldn't stop it. It poured out of him through the hole in his body to become something ugly, something disgusting, something devilish.

He looked down on the battle from a great height and his brother Elliot scrambled to get away from him. Elliot's eyes bulged and his mouth hung open. The wizards all gaped at Grant in shock. They broke their magical circle and backpedaled to get away from him.

Lily cringed against a wall across the street with four dragons beating their wings around her head. They didn't see Grant. They didn't see Ness fighting his enemies with the last of his strength. They didn't see anything until it was all too late.

Grant stalked them fuming with rage. Murderous fury boiled out of his soul at the sight of these creatures threatening the people he loved. Yes, he loved Lily as much as he loved Elliot if not more so.

Ness broke Grant's line of sight before he got anywhere near her. Ness turned his back on his enemies and lunged for the dragons threatening Lily.

He nipped one of them out of the air and snapped it in half. He dropped it to the ground and pulverized it under one giant foot. He whipped his tail around and sent another spinning far away.

The other two dragons wheeled to face him. They joined their comrades surrounding Ness from all sides. Grant couldn't stand that. Seven against one was no fight at all.

He advanced on them to annihilate them all. He didn't think how he would do it. He only knew he had to get rid of them by any means necessary. He bellowed at them and they all turned to face him. Even Ness turned around.

In that moment, Grant saw himself reflected in the prince's shimmering eye, but Ness didn't see a soldier. He didn't even see a man. He saw a huge seething black dragon more ferocious and horrible than any he'd ever seen before.

Even that made sense to Grant's dragon brain. He already knew what he was. He kidded himself all these years when the real truth lay buried in his being. He was a dragon underneath it all.

The next minute, his enemies rushed him en masse. They left Ness standing stricken and dying in front of Lily and they all collided with Grant.

Their claws slashed his scales. They ripped at him with their teeth. They bombarded him with their flame, but it did no good. His skin was ten times thicker than theirs. Nothing they did penetrated his tough scales.

He unleashed his fury on them one pathetic body at a time. He narrowed his eyes at one dragon after another, chose his weapon, and killed without mercy. He broke a neck here. He flicked his tail and cracked a spine there. He incinerated another with a quick puff of his fire.

He stalked them down one after the other and sent them plummeting to Earth, never to rise again.

The last three dragons took wing and soared high over the city. They formed ranks wingtip to wingtip over Kald and plunged for him.

They bombed out of the sky going a hundred miles an hour. Grant gathered his resolve and crouched where he was waiting for them.

Menacing hatred seethed inside him. The dragons unloaded their fire on him all at once, but he didn't move. He let their fire bounce off his face and chest. He closed his eyes and reveled in his own strength.

He didn't even bother to open his eyes to return their fire. He blew out a gentle puff of breath and they exploded in screaming balls of flame. They tumbled far away until nothing but a plume of ash floated on the breeze.

A concussion drew his attention back to see Ness arched on his hind legs. He spread his great golden wings to cover the street. Lily crouched behind him huddling under her arms. The wizards stood in a row facing Ness and pounded him with one volley after another.

Twenty wizards held hands in a semi-circle around the stricken prince. They aimed their joined hands at him and an eruption swirled from them.

It rotated in a twisted tube spinning rapidly at the tip. The point struck the prince, drilled into his skin, and ate at his scales until it shredded them out of the way to reveal the bloody flesh underneath.

The wizards shot a fork of lightning at the prince. It surrounded Ness's head in a cage that sent him into confusion.

The golden dragon screeched and thrashed in agony, but through it all, he stood tall and unmoving with his wings outstretched to protect Lily.

The wizards lifted their hands at the same time and chopped them down to unleash their last, most terrible weapon yet.

Mist collected in the air over Ness's head, and when they brought down their arms, the mist formed into a massive axe that cleaved Ness's body in half.

He crashed to Earth and his wings crumpled to the ground. The cage around his head spluttered out and vanished.

The sight snapped Grant out of his stupor. He didn't stop to think about what he was doing. He roared at the wizards and thundered all his fury at these men, but instead of sound, fire came out of his mouth and he torched the wizards to ash the same way he torched the other dragons.

In a split second, he was looking at Lily from ground level. He was a man again. He had changed back without realizing it. Ness's dragon body had disappeared, too, and the prince lay broken and blood-spattered on the ground.

Lily blinked up at Grant with a mixture of horror and amazement. He panted to catch his breath. He still couldn't fully comprehend what just happened.

A gurgle drew Lily's attention to Ness. She scrambled over the cobblestones to where he lay barely breathing. She rolled him over and a trail of bloody saliva dribbled from his mouth.

She stroked his cheek and did her best to pick him up. "Ness! Are you...what are you....?" She couldn't finish.

"Dinnae, lass," he choked. "Ye're hurting me."

She wouldn't stop tugging at him. "You have to get up, Ness. We have to get out of here before they come back."

"I winnae be going anywhere, lassie." He coughed and another bubble of red popped between his lips. "Ye go on with ye. Ye go with Grant. He'll look after ye."

"Ness, I...." she stammered.

"Promise me, lass," he rasped. "Promise me ye'll find Lady Ilisa and get her out of Tyrekirk."

"I promise, Ness, but...."

"She's me mother, lassie. She's me mother and she's still alive in there. I ken she is. She's Lady Ilisa Creighton, the Laird's own daughter. He wouldnae kill her—not ever. He wouldnae. I ken it. He might threaten and put her on the schedule for the gallows, but he'd never go through with it. Ye must believe me, lass. I never should have left her behind. I kenned it was wrong at the time, but I was too cowardly to go back. I was too concerned with escaping meself. Do ye understand?"

"I understand." Lily cradled his face in both hands and caressed his cheeks while she fought back tears. "I promise, Ness. I promise I'll find her."

Ness swallowed hard. His eyes took on a glazed appearance, but he kept staring up at her face. "I loved ye, lass. I've never loved any other woman. Ye must ken that."

The words hadn't escaped his lips before he froze. He didn't move and he didn't look away. He just stopped. Everything about him stopped and went dead.

Lily's shoulders shook, but she didn't make a sound. She held him and bowed her head in silent agony.

Grant stared down at the prince. Through the whole fight, Grant never really let himself believe it could end like this.

Ness looked so small and fragile compared to the dragon that did so much damage to the Laird's forces. A frail man like that didn't seem capable of demanding the efforts of so many wizards and soldiers and dragons.

Even now, Grant couldn't bring himself to believe that Ness was really dead. Grant dedicated weeks of his life to protecting this man.

The golden dragon seemed too big and powerful to be killed by anyone. Yet here he lay, bloody, unblinking, a wreck of what used to be a prince.

Lily got to her feet, ran her wrist across her nose, and sniffed. She faced Grant and her face wrenched all the wrong ways in a mess of emotions.

She glanced sideways and her voice cracked. "I guess we.... uh.... I guess we should get out of here."

Grant surveyed the enclosure. Bodies lay strewn everywhere, but they were all men. No sign remained of the dragons that wreaked so much havoc on the party. Grant didn't see Edeena anywhere.

Grant's stomach flipped and he cringed in shame when he saw Elliot. His brother stood still across the street and fixed his gaze on Grant. Elliot had seen everything.

He saw Grant change into a dragon. He saw Grant slaughter his enemies with his fire and his teeth. How could Grant face his brother after this?

Elliot turned away, picked up his saber, and slid it into its scabbard. Then he set off to cross the street.

Grant jumped into his path and caught his brother's arm. "Elliot, wait...."

Elliot knocked his hand away. "Get off me! Dinnae ye touch me!"

Grant let his hands fall. He didn't know what to do. "Wait, Elliot, please...."

Elliot spun around to confront Grant and Elliot's mouth twisted in the same hideous screwed-up grimace as Lily's. "Ye're one of them. Dinnae ye see that? Ye're Creighton."

"No, lad," Grant groaned. "Dinnae say that."

"Ye're a dragon," Elliot croaked. "How can I even ken if ye're me own brother or no?"

"Elliot," Grant whimpered, "Elliot, please...."

Elliot waved him away. "I cannae stand to look at ye. I cannae look at ye without seeing.... *that*. Just leave me alone."

He walked off. Grant tried to touch him again, but Elliot chopped the air and stormed away. In an instant, Elliot turned a corner and vanished out of Grant's life forever.

Grant gaped at the spot for what seemed like an eternity. That did not just happen. Elliot, his brother, his other half, his best and closest friend, his only living relative, did not just walk away from him. Elliot did not just say he couldn't stand to look at him.

Grant's heart plunged into his shoes. He didn't want to live with those words ringing in his ears.

Only now did the realization hit him. The rush of the fight faded and left the horrible truth staring him in the face. He couldn't ignore it anymore.

He was a dragon and that meant one thing. He was a member of the Royal House of Creighton.

How was that possible? He and Elliot grew up the sons of a poor, unwed mother who worked as a servant in Tyrekirk. That was the only way the brothers got a chance to become members of the guard. They would have become criminals in Damerell if they had been born to anyone else.

He couldn't be a Creighton. He and Elliot hated all Creightons. The brothers served them as masters, but Grant never liked or respected them. He never wanted to be one of those disgusting lizard people.

Lily touched his arm. "Come on. We have to get out of here."

He surveyed the street one more time. He didn't want to get out of here. He wanted the Laird's troops to come back and kill him to put him out of his misery. He would rather be dead than face the world after today.

Lily took his hand and gave him a tug, but he didn't move. She said again, "Come on," but the words deflected off him. A thick layer of numbness enclosed him and blocked him off from the rest of the world.

She rotated around to stand in front of him. Her face occupied his vision and she raised her voice. The words cut razor sharp. "Let's go, Grant."

Some buried part of his mind recognized a command when he heard it. The soldier in him took over and he followed her.

She set off at a walk and eventually broke into a run. He ran behind her. He didn't care where she took him. Nothing mattered anymore.

Chapter 28

Lily gasped for breath climbing the stairs to the roof of one of Damerell's countless buildings. The sun sank behind the city by the time she got to the top and the stars started coming out overhead.

Grant propped his hands on his knees and panted for air, too. He bowed his head and his loose hair covered his face.

Lily scanned the horizon. They hadn't seen a single soldier or wizard or guard since they left the battle. "I guess this is as good a place as any."

Grant crossed the roof, turned his back to the parapet, and slid down it. He rested his elbows on his knees and his chin fell on his chest.

Lily regarded him from a distance. He hadn't been the same since Ness died, but she already knew that wasn't what was really bothering him. Elliot was the one who really drove the dagger home.

She hesitated to approach Grant now. What could she say to make up for losing his brother? Grant was a dragon, so Grant was a Creighton. How it happened didn't matter. Nothing could go back to the way it was before.

She gazed up into the growing darkness and read her own predicament in all its stark horror. She had lost her brother, too, but under different circumstances. She also lost the only way she could ever get back to her own time. She was stuck here forever.

She never really had a relationship with Liam—not as an adult, anyway. She spent a handful of days with him since they both left home. Now he was gone and she would probably never see him again.

She also lost Ironforge. She lost the Last Division, but she couldn't bring herself to be wholly unhappy about that.

Maybe this was for the best. Now she had no choice but to fully embrace a completely different life.

She was here, alone with Grant. They had no one else in the world to rely on besides each other.

She took a long time to decide to go sit down next to him. As awful as this situation must be for him, he had no one else. No one else could comfort him.

She crossed her legs on the rough shingle roof. A bitter wind swept over the city and robbed the air of all warmth. She and Grant could look forward to a cold night up here with no blankets and no shelter.

"Your shoulder's bleeding," she murmured. "Let me take a look at it and bandage it up."

He made a choking noise in his throat. He kept his head bowed so she couldn't see his face, but she didn't have to see. She could picture the anguished convulsions struggling to break out against his best efforts to control them.

She peeled back the bloody shreds of his shirt while she fumbled for something to say, but nothing made sense right now. Only silence explained the depth of pain and hopeless despair tearing him apart.

"I hated him," he blurted out. "I hated that stuffed-shirted coxcomb. That's the worst of it."

"Ness?"

"I could have killed him meself a hundred times, he made me so foaming mad." His voice shook more and more the longer he talked. "I wished him dead so I didnae have to drag me carcass through the streets protecting him from some phantom out to kill him. Elliot! Christ, Elliot hated that overblown fool!"

He shook his head and his eyes darted around the roof. Lily couldn't hold herself back from him anymore. She squeezed his shoulder, but he didn't respond.

"I never kenned. That's what I cannae live with. I never kenned what he really was. I thought he was a bleeding-heart spoiled bairn who would throw any tantrum to get what he wanted. I never kenned he could do that. I never kenned."

She understood because she felt the same way. Ness gave his life protecting her. He took that spear on the chance that she and Liam could get through the portal. He made the ultimate sacrifice for her sake.

"I cannae love ye, lass," Grant croaked. "I cannae love ye kenning what he did out of love for ye. It isnae fair that I should be here with ye and he is not. Och, Christ, Elliot! What am I to do?" He rocked back and forth and turned his head from side to side.

Lily didn't know what she wanted to say, but she had to say something. She couldn't let him spin in misery while she sat here doing nothing. "It's all right. You heard what Ness said. He told me to go with you. He would want you to....to love me."

Getting those words out took all her effort. Love him? Let him love her? Could she really do that?

Could she bring herself to cross that bridge? She could do it. She had to do it. She wanted to and Ness gave her his blessing with his dying breath.

Grant shook his head. "How can I be? How can I live like this? I cannae stand the Creightons."

She bit back a smile. He hated the Creightons and now he found out he was one. She couldn't let him dwell in that dark place any longer. She was the only one who could pull him out of it.

His shoulder looked bad, but for some reason, it wasn't bleeding anymore. Maybe the act of shifting made it heal. How should she know?

She slipped her hand around his jaw, steered him to face her, and kissed him before he could protest. She took hold of his lips and drew him into the warm ripple of their kiss. She caressed his fevered cheeks until she felt him soften.

His strong hands rested on her shoulders, and after a moment, he brushed her hair back. He responded to her touches and matched them with his own. He let her enfold him in her healing presence.

His burly body drove off the cold and she snuggled into his protective embrace. He sheltered her the same way she sheltered him. He healed her loss the way she healed him. They were alone against the world and she could finally accept that.

The whole sequence of events brought her to this moment. It thrust her into this situation. Now she had no choice but to turn her back on Ironforge and the Last Division. They were all wrong for her and she would never have admitted it to herself otherwise.

She would never have walked away from her friends to get with a man no matter how much she loved him. She needed Fate or circumstance or something to force her hand.

As soon as that thought formed in her mind, Grant broke the seal of their kiss. He burrowed into her neck and the passion of last night erupted all over her. She hugged his head into her and pressed her ear against his head.

She wanted everything that would happen between them. She no longer held herself apart for some lofty idea of serving mankind. She served herself and the primal desire to love him and hold him and experience him.

She no longer worried about what this meant. She didn't bother thinking this moment might be a meaningless encounter in the darkened corners of a burned-out building.

This was all her and him and it meant everything. They didn't have to hide it from anyone, least of all themselves.

He crawled up her neck to kiss her again. She opened her eyes and couldn't see his face against the darkness behind him, but she didn't need to. She heard the pulse of his blood in his veins, and this time, she heard the dragon in there, too.

It was part of him. She loved that monstrous black beast as part of him. It *was* him. It was him as much as his hair and his shoulders and his knees. She wanted him. She wanted all of him in all of her. She wanted the dragon to take her and love her and make her love him.

They sank down together on the roof and his head came to rest in the crook of her neck. She held him there in the silent radiance of loving him.

She gazed past his head at the sky. The stones dug into her back and hips, but nothing could disturb the rapture of finally finding where she belonged. She thought she belonged at Ironforge, but that was just another delusion to hide her from this.

She shrank to a speck until her whole being existed in that microcosmic nexus where he became her and she became him.

Chapter 29

Grant's eyes snapped open and he stared straight up into a flawless blue sky. He blinked once and felt a weight crushing his chest.

Just then, it shifted and breathed. A head of brown hair scattered across his neck and he remembered everything.

Lily murmured and shifted in her sleep. Her body lay draped across him and pressed him down into the sharp shingle roof. If he hadn't been completely exhausted after yesterday's fight, he never would have been able to sleep like this.

He did his best to lie still and she settled down again. He wasn't ready to get up and face reality yet.

He relived all the horror of the day before. He had changed into a dragon and then he stood by and watched Ness die of his injuries. Then, to cap it all, Elliot had abandoned him.

That terrible moment, the look of horror and disgust on his brother's face—Grant would gladly gouge that memory out of his brain, but that would never happen. Elliot was gone and under the worst possible circumstances.

This would be the first day Grant had ever faced in his life without Elliot by his side. Instead, he had Lily.

Grant hated himself for being happy about that, but he couldn't trade one for the other. If he had to choose, he would have kept them both.

He couldn't choose between them. His heart broke at the very thought of choosing. Fate did the choosing for him. It left him with no choice and no brother.

Lily stirred again, and this time, she didn't go back to sleep. She groaned and rolled off him. She sat down hard on the shingle and rubbed her forehead.

She looked up and scowled. Grant watched thoughts and emotions race across her features while she remembered. Liam was gone. The portal was gone. Ness was gone.

She slouched and stared around the roof while the devastating reality sank in. It rested heavily on her the same way it rested on Grant. Neither of them had any choice but to face a situation they would rather not.

She finally ran her fingers through her hair and straightened up. "Well, I guess that's it, then."

"Aye." Grant went back to staring at the sky. It didn't give him any answers, but it didn't change anything, either.

That sky might be the one thing in the known universe that didn't attack him or threaten him or make his life more difficult than it already was. He could live with that.

"What do you want to do today?" she asked. "Where should we go?"

"There's only one place left to go and that's Tyrekirk."

She whipped around and her eyes fell out of their sockets. "Tyrekirk! Are in out of your mind?"

"If we run, the Laird will track us down. We're both alive, but we may not be after the next battle. Running isnae any use. We must go straight into the eye of the storm. Besides, all the answers to all our questions are at Tyrekirk."

"What makes you think the Laird won't kill us on sight? What makes you think we'll get anywhere near the place before his soldiers cut us down?"

"I wouldnae be surprised if they did. In fact, I fully expect them to, but at least I winnae die running like a scared rabbit in search of a hole to hide in. I'm going to the castle, lass. If ye dinnae want to come, I winnae make ye."

She narrowed her eyes at him. "Do you honestly think I would let you go within a hundred miles of that place alone? What do you take me for?"

He shot her a grin. "I didnae think ye would."

She shrugged it off. "I guess you're right. What do we have to lose, right?"

"Ye promised Ness ye'd go find Lady Ilisa. She'll be there if she's alive at all. The Buchanans put a heap of stock in her and I want to ken how I came to be a Creighton when I didnae ken it all these years. No one can tell me that but the Laird himself."

"You're right." She burst into action. She tore the tie out of her hair and started raking it into shape with her usual businesslike energy.

She hopped to her feet. "All right. Let's go. I'm hungry. Maybe the Laird will give us breakfast when we get there."

Her attitude infected Grant. He got up and they marched down to the street. They became soldiers again walking arm's length apart and taking turns checking behind them and to either side.

They walked for a mile before Lily murmured in his ear. "Where are all the guards?"

"I dinnae like this," he muttered back.

"What do you think it means?"

"It can only mean one thing. It means the Laird isnae hunting us any longer."

"How is that possible? Why would he suddenly stop hunting us after trying so hard to kill us?"

He shook his head. "I dinnae like to think about it."

She pulled up short and grabbed his arm to stop him. "Hold it. If you want to go back to Tyrekirk, we have to think about it. We have to anticipate the Laird's every move if we want to stay alive in there. Now what are you thinking? Why do you think he's not hunting us anymore? He's been trying to kill us for days."

He lowered his voice to a hoarse whisper. "Think on it, lassie. He's been hunting us for days, but all of a sudden, Ness dies and the pursuit stops. It can mean only one thing."

Her eyes fell out of her head staring at him. "Are you seriously telling me he was hunting Ness and not the rest of us?"

"Why would he let us go, now that Ness is dead? Think on it. No other explanation fits everything that's happened. First, someone tries to kill Ness. We go on the run and the Laird pursues us. The Laird's wizards attacked us in the form of Highland tigers to frame the Buchanans. The wizards killed Ness and now they arenae after us any longer."

"That would mean the Laird had Ness killed on purpose."

He nodded. "That's how it looks from where I stand. Can ye explain it any other way?"

She fixed her eyes on the street ahead, set her jaw, and snarled through gritted teeth. "I certainly hope you're wrong. If he did kill Ness..." She didn't finish her sentence.

Grant flanked her and they walked the rest of the way in silence. He turned the last corner and Tyrekirk came in sight. He ducked behind a wall to steady his nerves for the coming confrontation.

Lily eased in next to him. "Are you sure you want to do this?"

Grant eyed the castle and nodded more to himself than to her. "It's the only way. We winnae get our questions answered anywhere else. If I'm to be this, I bloody better ken the reason why."

He didn't give himself time to change his mind. He stepped into the open, marched up to the gate, and barged right up to the guard ready to fight. "I'm going in."

To his astonishment, the guard stepped aside. "Proceed."

Grant narrowed his eyes, first at the man and then at the gate. He wasn't expecting this at all. He braced himself ever since last night to fight his way into the castle.

The guard pulled his lever, the gate swung open before Grant's eyes, and he frowned. He didn't dare go in there. "What's the meaning of this?"

"He's expecting ye," the guard replied. "He's waiting on ye. He told us ye'd be coming in this morning. Ye're expected."

Grant cast a glance at Lily, but she only shrugged. They wanted to get inside. Now they found the way open for them.

Grant took a deep breath. Here went nothing. He crossed the threshold and entered the courtyard.

A few other guards stood on duty, but none of them offered any resistance. Grant stopped and eyed them before he could bring himself to go on.

He made his way to the audience hall and found Maxwell in his usual place. The Chamberlain smiled. "Och, Mr. Ritchie. So good of ye to join us."

"I'm told I'm expected, Maxwell."

"Aye. Ye can go right in."

Grant paused again. Go right in? That never happened to him before. He always had to wait for the Laird to be ready for him. Now the Laird was waiting for him instead.

Maxwell swung open the doors and Grant and Lily walked into the hall. To Grant's further surprise, he met the Laird coming toward him with his arms out. "Me dear Grant! How wonderful to see ye back again."

He clapped Grant on both shoulders before he pulled him into an embrace. He slapped Grant on the back and turned to Lily. "Och, and this is the delightful Miss Barnett, is it no?"

Lily colored and tried to look away. "Not really."

"Of course ye are. I've been waiting for ye two to show up. What took ye so long? Never mind. We've so much to discuss."

"Such as?" Grant cut in. "What's this all about?"

"Why, yer ascension, of course," the Laird exclaimed.

"Me ascension!" Grant blurted out. "Ascension to what?"

"To me right hand. What else? Now that Ness is dead, ye're me heir to the Lairdship. Ye'll be Laird of Kald after me and yer lovely intended here will be Lady Lily Armstrong."

Lily gasped out loud. "Intended! Now just hold on there a second...."

The Laird waved her objections away. "Never mind about that. We've a great deal to arrange now that ye're both here, but before we do that, I see ye're both tired. Ye'll want a hot meal and perhaps a bath and a change of clothes. Maxwell has assigned ye a suite of rooms in the Fourth Tower."

"The Fourth Tower!" Grant snorted. "Ye must be joking."

"I would never joke about that. I ken ye're used to a different class of accommodation, me dear lad, but ye must get used to yer change in circumstances. Ye'll soon find it more comfortable than yer old quarters downstairs."

Grant cast his eyes to the floor. "I dinnae think I could live down there anyway, not without Elliot."

The Laird started to turn away, but Lily called after him. "If you don't mind...."

"What is it, me dear?"

"We have some questions about Lady Ilisa Creighton. We heard you were keeping her a prisoner here. We even heard you planned to execute her."

The Laird cocked his head. "There isnae any Lady Ilisa Creighton."

"She's your daughter," Lily insisted. "Ness claimed she was his mother and we heard a report that you were holding her in the Black Turret. Does that ring a bell?"

A faint smile played on the Laird's lips. As well as Grant knew the man, he could never tell when the Laird was lying or when he was telling the truth.

"I only had one daughter, me dear, and that was Lady Saundra. She was Ness's mother and wife to his father Camdyn Carmichael. She died years ago giving birth to Ness. Ask Grant if ye dinnae believe me. I think I would ken if I had a daughter by the name of Ilisa and there isnae any Black Turret in this castle, either. I'm afraid ye've been misinformed."

He turned away one more time and Lily called after him. "If Lady Saundra was Ness's mother, who is Grant's mother? You must know. He can shift into a dragon which means he's of Royal Blood. He must be a direct relative of yours, so who is he?"

Grant watched the Laird's back for any sign of a reaction, but the old man didn't move. He stood there with his back to them. Then he swept up the steps and settled himself on his throne.

His withered face showed the same impenetrable calm that Grant recognized from years of serving in this castle. The Laird never answered any question unless it served his purpose to do so. He didn't want Grant and Lily to know who Grant's mother was so he simply ignored the question.

Lily drew in a breath for another volley of questions, but Grant laid his hand on her arm to stop her. He shook his head. She closed her mouth, but a defiant sparkle still flashed in her eyes. He knew her better than to expect her to give up on this.

He led her out of the hall before any trouble could break out between her and the Laird. Grant was too relieved that he wasn't on his way to the gallows again. He and Lily would have to get their questions answered some other way.

Maxwell met them in the corridor. "I have yer rooms assigned."

"Just please tell me ye didnae assign either of us to Ness's old rooms," Grant muttered.

"Quite." Maxwell snapped his fingers and a maidservant escorted Grant and Lily upstairs. She showed Grant into a spacious bedroom the like of which he'd only seen at a distance. She placed Lily in another room across the hall.

Chapter 30

The door shut on the outside world and Grant surveyed his new domain. So this was how Ness had been living all these years while Grant and Elliot shared a bunk in the guard room under the kitchen.

A giant window looked out over Kald. People, carts, and animals looked so small and insignificant from up here. No wonder the Creightons found it so easy to dominate their subjects.

Just then, his door flew open and Lily charged in. She shut it behind her and shot the bolt before she rushed over to him. "Did you hear that ridiculous tale of his about how Lady Ilisa doesn't exist? Does he really expect us to believe that?"

"It's true," Grant replied. "Lady Saundra was Ness's mother."

Lily's head whipped around. "You can't mean that. You heard Ness."

"I heard him, but everybody kens Saundra was his mother. It's common knowledge."

"How do you explain him telling us about Ilisa? Are you saying Ness was lying? How do you explain you being a dragon? Obviously someone had a child that no one knows about and sent you to live somewhere else. Things aren't exactly as the Laird would have us believe. He didn't bother to tell us anything about your origins and now he wants to elevate you to being his heir. How do you explain that?"

"I cannae explain it. I only ken what I ken. I've worked in this castle for nearly ten years and never heard mention of any Lady Ilisa before. I think I would ken about it if I had and the Laird kens his own flesh and blood."

"What if he's lying?" she asked. "What if he made it up to hide the fact that he's keeping Ilisa locked up in the Black Turret?"

"There isnae any Black Turret. He's right about that, too. I've been all over this castle and never even heard of it before."

Lily's eyes snapped. "Are you seriously going to stand there and defend him? We have to investigate this."

"There's naught to investigate, lass. Everybody kens Saundra was Ness's mother, and if there is a Black Turret, it doesnae exist on any map of this castle I've ever seen."

She threw up her hands and stormed for the door. Grant jumped after her to catch her. "Hold it, lassie."

She rounded on him with her teeth locked. "You heard me promise Ness right before he died that I would find Lady Ilisa and free her from the Laird. You also promised me that you would keep investigating Lady Rhona and find out everything you could about her. Don't you see this is the same thing? We can't just leave this alone."

He eased her into his arms. "Easy, lass. I dinnae say to leave it alone. I'm saying we play the Laird's game while we can. Ye cannae deny this is a better way to pass the time than what we were doing out in Damerell."

She held herself stiff and didn't soften. "Do you agree to investigate this because if you don't, I'll do it myself."

His shoulders drooped. "Please, lass, just let a man get a bite to eat and a night's sleep in a decent bed before ye consign us to the gallows all over again."

Lily glared at him for a minute more before she relaxed. "All right. I'll go along with it, but I won't give up on this."

"I never expected ye to." He kissed her and eased closer.

She relaxed in his arms, but at that moment, the bedroom door burst open. Two maids and two manservants bustled in carrying piles of clothes. The older manservant marched right up to Grant.

"Chamberlain Maxwell sent us to measure ye up for a new kilt and tartan. The housekeeper will send up all the peripherals ye need as soon as we're done and me Lady will find the maids over in yer own chamber waiting to fit ye for new gowns and linens. If you please, me Lady...."

The manservant bowed in a significant way, but Lily only stared at him. "I think," Grant told her, "he's trying to tell ye to piss off to yer own room so they can get to work."

Lily blinked up at him. Then she snorted with laughter. "Is that what he's trying to tell me?"

Grant turned to the man. "Ye can measure us up later. Leave us alone for a bit, if ye please."

The man wrinkled his nose, but he couldn't exactly argue. Maybe being the Laird's heir had some advantages. The whole gaggle trooped out of the room and shut the door a little too loudly when they left.

Grant glanced at Lily, who stifled a snigger. "Is this what we have to look forward to around here?"

"I'm afraid so, lass. We winnae have any end of everyone telling us what to do. Even the servants will have us at their beck and call." She started to say something, but before she could get the words out, he pulled her in tight. "Now where were we?"

She relaxed into his arms and lips without a moment's hesitation. In an instant, they were kissing in that delirious passion that drew Grant to her in the first place.

Her arms slipped around his neck. She excited him as much now as the first day he met her in the avenue.

He broke off kissing her to peer down into her eyes and heavenly light shone out of her features.

Her pupils dilated drinking in the sight of him. Would any woman ever look at him the way she did? Would any woman ever surrender to his touch and his presence with such utter abandon?

He didn't want to find out. He never wanted to see another woman looking into his eyes or feel another woman's body against him.

She filled every need and he couldn't imagine anyone else. She erased the rest of the world until she existed alone and unchallenged in his heart.

He trailed his fingers through her hair, down to her neck. Her lips trembled and she shuddered when he grazed her throat. Her whole being hung on a tremulous thread waiting for him to touch her and take her to Heaven.

Chapter 31

Lily pointed down at the map on Grant's dressing table. "It can't be there. We've searched that entire wing room by room."

"If it isnae there, it must be somewhere else."

She traced the halls and winding passages of Tyrekirk on the map. "We've searched this section and these towers and we can rule out the whole West Wing."

"That leaves the South Wing, the North Wing, and the other four spires."

"There has to be a way to narrow it down. Don't you think it would be in one of the spires? Why else would they call it the Black Turret?"

Grant chuckled. "I can think of a dozen reasons they would call it that when it isnae a turret at all. They might have changed the name to throw off curious intruders like ye, lassie."

She flashed him a wicked grin. "You're right. So that leaves us with four spires and two wings."

"We can cover more ground if we search separately. Ye do the South Wing and I'll take the North. Ye do these two spires and I'll do these two. We'll meet back here for lunch and compare notes."

She rose on her tiptoes to kiss him before she hurried off. She lifted the skirts of her long gown so she wouldn't trip on them. After a week in Tyrekirk, she was only just starting to get used to the fancy clothes and corsets everyone expected her to wear.

She had to look the part of the future Lady of Kald and Grant never wore his old clothes anymore. He always wore a freshly laundered Creighton tartan kilt and his manservant spent hours a day polishing the silver buttons on his immaculate forest-green jacket.

Grant's ascension still hadn't sunk into Lily's brain yet. Something would go wrong. The Laird would change his mind and she and Grant would go back to being nobodies.

If they succeeded in this investigation and found out whatever secret the Laird was keeping hidden, he would retaliate by doing a lot more than that. If she and Grant got really lucky, the Laird would throw them into the gutter to fend for themselves. More likely, he would destroy them both to keep his secret.

Lily still couldn't reconcile all the conflicting information she had discovered since coming to Scotland.

Grant was a dragon. That made him a member of the Royal House. It meant someone connected with the Laird's own family had at least one child they shouldn't have had. Elliot was almost certainly a dragon, too. He didn't want to admit it, but he couldn't deny what he was.

Lily believed Ness no matter what the Laird said or wanted everyone to believe.

The Laird went to a lot of trouble to make it look like Lady Saundra was Ness's mother, but Lily could never believe that.

Ness's eyes hovered before her whenever she thought this mystery over. She found herself gazing down into his dying face while he made her promise not to give up until she found Lady Ilisa.

She thought about it now as she rushed up the stairs into the spires. She worked her way to the very topmost pinnacle and worked her way down, down, down. She opened every door and searched every passage. There was no Black Turret.

She made her way back to the South Wing and met Grant coming the other way. "Any luck?"

She shook her head. "Nothing. You?"

"It isnae a turret. I'm certain of that."

"So what's next? What else is there to investigate?"

"I'll go with ye to search the South Wing. It must be there. We've covered everywhere else."

They entered the South Wing. Grant flung the doors wide and entered one room after another while Lily searched the other side of the corridor. They worked all the way to the far end where they came to the stop.

"This is it," Lily told him. "There's nothing more to search."

Grant didn't answer. He stared at the blank stone wall.

"What's the matter?"

"This." He waved to the wall. "Something's amiss here."

"What's amiss? It looks normal to me."

"Do ye remember the other four wings, lassie? They all end in those high bay windows looking out over the city. They all have those dark curtains surrounding them, but this one doesnae."

"What are you saying? Are you saying there's something on the other side of this wall? How could there be without someone noticing it?"

He marched to the nearest door and strode into one of the many state bedrooms in this part of the castle. He surveyed the room with a calculating eye and pointed to the wall adjoining the end of the building.

"There. Right there. There ought to be another window there. See? Look." He threw aside the curtains blocking the next window along. "It gives a perfect view across the Boundless. There isnae any reason under Heaven there shouldnae be any window there. They're hiding something in plain sight."

"But we can't see the end of the building. We can't see if there's anything there."

He grabbed her hand. "Come on!"

He raced outside with Lily right behind him. They charged around the castle to the Boundless side. The castle walls came nearly down to the water's edge. A narrow gravel beach separated the high walls from the estuary itself.

Grant sprinted around the castle and pulled to a sudden stop. "There! Right there!"

He pointed up at Tyrekirk's majestic spires rising to the sky. Only from here, with her back to the Boundless and the open sea beyond, could Lily see a tower attached to the end of the South Wing. The whole castle had been constructed to conceal it. No one could see it who wasn't looking for it.

Grant cackled with glee and spun the other way. "Come on, lassie. We're going into the Black Turret.

They ran back to the South Wing, back to the solid wall where the window should have been. Grant traced his fingertips through the mortar between the stones.

"Now what?" Lily asked. "How do we get in?"

"I dinnae ken. There must be an entrance."

"What I wouldn't give to have Liam here right now," she remarked. "He would get us inside."

A curious grin spread over his face. "I may not be a wizard, lass, but I'm something. Stand back. I'll get us through."

"What are you going to do?"

He straightened his arm to push her a dozen yards away while he eyed the wall.

He shifted so fast that Lily jumped back with a squeal. The black dragon filled the corridor so tightly that he had to crouch under the ceiling.

Lily plastered herself against the wall to get out of his way. Anything could happen when he took that form.

He coiled himself tighter and, with one powerful lunge, he smashed his giant head into the stone wall blocking their path.

The wall disintegrated and Grant nosed the rubble out of the way with his pointed snout. He shifted just as fast and returned to his normal form to find Lily gaping at him with huge eyes.

She swallowed hard. "I don't think I'll ever get used to that."

"I didnae mean to scare ye, lass" he murmured. "Is it as bad as all that?"

She pulled herself together and touched his hand. "It's okay. I like you like that."

"Ye do?"

She rose on her tiptoes to kiss his cheek. "Yes. I do. Now come on. We need to find her before the Laird figures out what we're doing."

She clambered toward the hole and picked her way through the debris. She and Grant climbed over stone blocks and entered a dim chamber where a spiral staircase wound up into the tower.

Lily climbed one foot after another up the steps. The urgency of possibly getting caught kept her moving forward and her pulse quickened. If Lady Ilisa was in this tower, they had to find her and get her out. The Laird might have set up alarms and booby traps to stop anyone from rescuing her.

Grant followed, but they didn't find any doors or rooms that Lily could see. The stairway seemed to fill the structure's whole circumference.

She realized her mistake when the stairs ended at a plain wooden door. From here, she could make out part of the tower's top section divided into a large apartment.

Lily put out her hand for the door latch, but Grant stopped her. "Hold hard a moment, lass. It could be rigged."

"There's no way we can get in if it is. We can only try."

She held her breath and push down the latch. She jumped out of her skin when the latch clicked, but the door swung open easily. If the Laird put the lock under a spell, it must have been enchanted from the inside.

Lily stepped into an ordinary bedroom like her own downstairs. A tiny window gave a magnificent view across the Boundless to the mountains beyond where the Buchanans lived.

A petite lady with brown hair and deep blue eyes turned from the window to look at Lily.

Grant's footsteps stopped behind Lily and the lady's eyes drifted away from Lily's face to a point beyond Lily's shoulder.

No one breathed for one tense moment. Then the strange woman's eyes popped and she gasped, "Grant!"

Chapter 32

Grant stared at the woman in astonishment. He'd only seen Lady Ilisa once in his life and that was in the courtyard when he and Elliot and Ness had escaped from Tyrekirk. Grant didn't recognize her then.

He didn't exactly recognize her now, either, but some part of him realized the terrible truth. His destiny would always and forever remain tangled up with her. He was bound to meet her sooner or later and he couldn't even explain to himself why.

She looked strangely familiar from a forgotten nightmare he'd worked all his life to forget. He couldn't place her, but he knew her.

She smiled at him and tears sprang to her eyes. "Grant! Me own Grant!" She rushed toward him with her hands out.

He couldn't understand why she would act that way, but something inside him made him feel the same way. He would have rushed into her arms if the shock of finding her here hadn't startled him into a shocked daze.

He saw her in the courtyard. He pictured her a hundred times since then while he and Lily had been searching for her, but he had never expected to react to her like this.

His heart exploded for this woman he'd never met. He raised his arms to catch her, and at that moment, the tower exploded behind his back.

Bricks and beams smashed into his back and head. They flattened him onto his hands and knees and a cloud of dust enveloped everything.

The blow stunned him and he shook his head to clear his mind. He tasted blood and searing pain stung him between the shoulder blades.

"Grant!" A female voice reached him through the confusion. "Grant, where are you?"

He roused himself when he recognized Lily's voice. "I'm here, lass. Where are ye?"

A hand touched his back, but it was a different voice speaking to him now. "The Laird! He's coming for us."

Grant pried his eyes open to peer through the haze. Bodies raced into the room through the mangled hole where the door used to be.

Lily knelt on her hands and knees not far away. Lady Ilisa crouched at Grant's side trying to pick him up.

He braced himself to get to his feet when a breath of wind blew through the window. It cleared enough of the dust for him to see the Laird's men surrounding him.

Alarm bells went off in his head. The blood in his mouth sent him into a frenzy and the dragon took over. He never would have believed he could give himself to it with such ferocity.

It ripped him in half as never before. It split his skin and the black monster boomed out of him to unleash his fury on his enemies.

He didn't stop to think he might be too big to fit in Lady Ilisa's apartment. His dragon soul didn't care about anything but tearing these bastards to pieces.

His body shattered what was left of the room. He caved in the walls and stone and plaster chips erupted outward over the Boundless. The roof popped off over his head and sailed clear into the sky.

The wizards and soldiers checked their advance, but only for a second. The guards dropped back to let the wizards move in on Grant. So much the better. He eyed them with venomous glee and salivated for their blood.

He roared his fiery breath at them and let loose such a tidal wave of flame that he lost sight of them. He didn't see until he stopped that they had taken refuge behind a magical shield that deflected his attack.

The walls and roof no longer held him back. He spread his wings in the fresh air, arched his spine, and craned back his head. These pests could trot out all their tricks. He wouldn't let them live.

He thundered to the skies and flicked his tail around. He caught the shield with the whip end and cracked ten wizards skyward. They catapulted off the tower on a soaring arc toward the estuary.

He spotted Lady Ilisa out of the corner of his eye. She helped Lily out of the way and the two women retreated behind Grant's wings. Even then, the wizards focused more attention on the women than they did on Grant.

The wizards put their heads together under their gleaming shield, but Grant couldn't hear them over his own deafening bellows. They faced him and another dragon materialized out of thin air. It grew out of the space between the wizards.

Grant's lizard brain couldn't understand it. He only knew he had to defend himself against that dragon.

The glowing blue creature swelled bigger and bigger and it flexed its wings to beat the air. It opened its mouth and a luminous blue-white light erupted out of the nothing.

Grant reared back to fight the thing. He rose off the floor and shot his head forward to bite it, but it didn't launch at him. It stayed seated in that hollow between the wizards' clustered bodies. What were they doing? He understood the trick too late.

Lady Ilisa screamed, "Grant! Watch out!"

One of the wizards ducked, dropped to one knee, and fired a whistling projectile at Grant. It rocketed him in slow motion, but it was coming too fast for him to get away from it.

Another dragon pounced in front of him out of nowhere and rounded on the wizards to protect him from their attack.

Grant didn't have time to figure out where the creature came from before the missile aimed at him buried its point in the stranger's chest. The dragon changed in an instant and Grant stared down in a daze at Lady Ilisa.

The next instant, a catastrophic barrage pommeled him backward. He never got a chance to look up. His eyes refused to leave her face, not even when the wizards bombarded him with spells that collapsed his dragon body to the pathetic form of a man.

His knees buckled and he hit the floor next to her, but he still couldn't force his mind to put together what just happened. The long shaft of a spear stuck out of her chest at a strange angle. Blood stained her chest and her hair scattered across her neck and cheeks.

A sphere of power held him immobile, but he was too stunned to shift again even if he could find a way to do it. He only just found her and now she lay destroyed at his feet. He put out his hands, but he didn't dare to pick her up.

She turned her bottomless eyes up to his face. "Grant! I can die now that I've seen ye again."

His fingertips grazed her cheek. "I never kenned ye. I never kenned or I'd have come sooner."

She smiled and shook her head. "Ye're here now. That's all that matters. I love ye, Grant. Ye must ken I love ye."

He didn't understand how she could love him, but he knew it was true. He saw that in her eyes.

"I'm yer mother, Grant—yer real mother," she whispered. "The Laird threatened to kill ye and Elliot, so I sent ye to live with a servant. I got a wizard to hide yer identities so the Laird wouldnae find ye. I had to leave, Grant. I couldnae take ye with me. I never would have left ye and yer brother alone otherwise."

So it was all true. Elliot was his brother after all. That meant Elliot was a dragon shifter, too, and he didn't even know it.

Where was Elliot now? Grant would give anything to see him again.

"When I came back, I had Ness and the Laird took Ness for his heir. I caused the Laird too much trouble and embarrassment, so he arranged to get rid of me by locking me in here. He gave Ness to Saundra to raise and he made it out that Saundra was Ness's mother all along, but he couldnae stop me loving ye lads. Ye must ken that. I never stopped loving ye all these years."

She touched his cheek once before her arm flopped to the floor. Her head sagged, her body went limp, and Grant blinked down at the still form.

Lily's hand came to rest on his shoulder, but he couldn't feel a thing. He'd seen his mother for a matter of minutes and now she was dead, just like that. He spoke to her once in his life. Now she was gone and he would never get her back.

He lost awareness of everything else. He didn't even try to fight back when the Laird's men bundled him and Lily downstairs and dumped them in the corridor at Maxwell's feet.

The Chamberlain scrutinized the pair over his spectacles and he said nothing. Lily rotated onto her knees and yelled at him. "You can't do this to us! You can't keep a woman locked up in a tower for years and get away with it."

Grant came out of his trance enough to look around for the first time. Invisible chains bound Lily's arms behind her back. She could move her legs, but she couldn't stand up. A dozen guards surrounded the pair with a bunch of wizards on hand in case anybody tried anything.

Grant sat down on the floor, defeated. Nothing mattered anymore after this disaster. "Never mind, lass. It's all up."

"How can you say that?" she roared. "How can you just give up? They killed her and now they're going to kill us."

Grant kept his eyes fixed on the floor. He never doubted the Laird would execute them both now to hide his secret. They did his dirty work for him by getting Lady Ilisa killed. Grant would never forgive himself for that.

He tried to move and found his own arms bound the same way. When the time came for him and Lily to enter the Laird's audience hall, the guards laid hold of them, dragged them across the floor, and deposited the pair at the foot of the Laird's throne.

The Laird stood up, descended the steps, and lifted both hands. "There, there. There isnae call for that sort of thing."

Lily drew herself into a compact ball, crouched on her knees, and glared at him. "You can't do this to us. You'll pay for this."

The Laird waved his hand. "Release them immediately."

"But me Laird, they....," one of the guards stammered.

"I said release them."

A wizard came forward and did something behind Lily's back. In a few seconds, Grant found himself free to move, too.

"Come," the Laird exclaimed. "Get up. This will never do."

He helped them both to their feet, but Grant couldn't relax. He braced himself for another attack, but it never came.

"You can't get away with this," Lily snarled. "You can't execute us without suffering some consequences. I hope you know that."

He bestowed a patronizing smile on her. "Me dear Miss Barnett, I wouldnae dream of executing ye. Grant is my heir now, and ye, me dear, are to be his wife."

Her jaw dropped. "His wife!"

He laid his hand on her shoulder. "We have many plans and arrangements to prepare for such a large state wedding. I wouldnae trouble ye with any unpleasantness such as executions or the like." He chuckled to himself.

Lily glanced over at Grant, but he couldn't help her out here. If he had to choose between being the Laird's heir and marrying Lily or facing the gallows, he had no problem choosing the former.

The Laird steered them both toward the door. "I think we can all go on the way we were before. We can forget all this bother ever happened."

"We won't forget it," Lily snapped. "We won't forget about Lady Ilisa and we'll never stop trying to find a way out of here. You can't keep us here. We won't forget what you've done."

The Laird stopped in his tracks and leveled her with a chilling glare. "Ye will never leave here. Grant will become me heir and ye, me dear Miss Barnett, will take yer place as Lady of Kald. If ye dinnae or if ye undermine me plans in any way, I'll track down that brother of yers. I'll make sure yer own time and yer own world pays the price."

She gaped at him in shock and then glanced over at Grant, but Grant only hung his head.

He should have known it would come to this. The Laird would stop at nothing to get what he wanted. He didn't care who he hurt or killed.

The Laird turned away and murmured to himself as he walked back to his throne. "We'll launch another campaign against the Buchanans. We must punish them for their incursion into our city and for murdering Prince Ness in cold blood."

Grant's head shot up and he stared at the back of the Laird's head. Did he just hear that right?

The old man swept around and lowered himself into his seat. "Ye, Grant, will help me with the preparations. When the time comes, ye'll lead the campaign to wipe out those troublesome cats once and for all. Maxwell will see ye're adequately informed on all our positions."

He waved his hand by way to dismiss Grant and Lily. When they still stayed there gawking at him in disbelief, the guards seized them and hauled them out of the audience hall.

Chapter 33

Lily blinked at the closed door to the audience hall. She still saw the Laird's ghastly figure passing judgment on her and Grant....and on Liam and the rest of her world.

Grant sighed. "Well, that's that. We're boxed in, lass. We dinnae have any choice but to go along with this."

She rounded on him bristling. "How can you even think that? He killed your mother. She died saving your life. How can you turn your back on that?"

"What would ye have me do—turn me back on Liam and the future, too? Ye heard him. We'll do as he says. I'll have to become his heir and ye'll have to become me lady. Perhaps we can do some good from the inside, and once he's gone, there'll be naught to stop us from doing things our own way. We must simply stay in his good books until then."

Lily shot another hateful glare at the door. "This is bullshit. I won't go along with it."

He slipped his hand into hers. "Is the idea of marrying me so repulsive to ye?"

She whipped around and gasped in surprise. Then she wilted. "Of course not. You know I didn't mean that."

He put his arm around her shoulders and hugged her against his chest. "At least one good thing has come out of this."

She let him guide her back to the Fourth Tower. He took her to his room and shut the door behind them.

She sank down on the bed and rested her throbbing head in her hand. "I can't believe he's going to frame the Buchanans for Ness's death when he was the one who did it."

"Aye. No doubt that's what he had in mind all along. He fabricated the story about the Buchanans making attempts on Ness's life. Then he disguised his wizards as cats to attack us. He planned to make it appear the Buchanans were responsible so he could mount another war against them."

"Here's what I don't understand. How could Lady Ilisa be your mother? Edeena says she was a Buchanan, but how could she be? She was obviously a Creighton dragon.

Edeena and the other Buchanans came into Kald to find her and rescue her because she was the wife of their Chief, Neill Buchanan."

"Are ye sure Edeena was telling the truth when she said that?"

"She was under a truth spell when she said it. Liam bewitched her to get information out of her. She wasn't going to tell us anything otherwise."

He frowned and rubbed his chin. "It's a curious question."

"The whole timeline makes no sense. She had you and Elliot. Then she hid you, but you said yourself the Laird can see anything he wants and find anyone he wants. What was there to stop him from finding you? You said he's the most powerful wizard in the country. Then she had Ness before the Laird took him and locked her up. None of it fits together."

"Ye're right about that, but I'll tell ye one thing, lass. If we're ever to find the answers, we'll find them here. There's bound to be some trace of the secret hidden here. Our best hope of finding it is to play along with his game. We can do the most good here and we're most likely to uncover the truth if we stay. Do ye understand?"

Her eyes drifted toward the window, but she didn't see the stunning view outside. She surveyed the whole interwoven mystery from one end of the cosmos to the other.

She saw her friends back at Ironforge. She saw Elliot somewhere far on the fringes of her awareness. She saw Edeena and the other Buchanans up in their mountain home.

She understood. She understood a lot better than she cared to admit. She wouldn't be going back to Ironforge—not now, not ever.

That part of her life had closed behind her forever. She was here and she would stay here. She was up to her neck in this mystery and this was where she would stay.

If anyone could solve this puzzle, she and Grant would do it. They had to. She still hadn't found Lady Rhona, but that didn't bother her.

Lady Rhona was still alive. She sensed that with some of Ness's deep certainty.

Lady Ilisa was not Lady Rhona. Lily couldn't explain how she knew this, but Lady Ilisa's death didn't end the mystery.

Lady Ilisa's death didn't solve anything, nor did it accomplish whatever Lady Rhona's unknown enemy had set out to accomplish. Lady Rhona was still out there and Lily still carried the responsibility of protecting her.

Either way, if Lady Ilisa and Lady Rhona were one and the same, that left Lily in the same predicament.

She couldn't leave. She was stuck here with Grant—not that she minded. She wanted to stay with him. She even wanted to marry him. She just didn't want to play into the Laird's hands by doing it.

Grant appeared in front of her. He stood before her and cupped her chin in one hand. He raised her face to meet his gaze and profound rapture overflowed her heart when she looked up at him. She sank into that immense vacuum where nothing existed but him and her, alone together.

"Do ye understand, lass?" he murmured.

"I understand."

She understood. She understood that she wanted him and she would do a lot more than stay here and be his lady to get him.

He brought her lips to his mouth and she closed her eyes and kissed the dragon in his soul. It loomed above her in all its gargantuan horror, but it only sparked a deeper desire to give herself to him. He was no ordinary man. He was something magical, something fantastic, something mythic.

She peered up into his smoldering blue eyes and saw the dragon. The dragon pulled her into his arms and demanded her very soul as his own. The dragon's burning slit eyes glared down at her and read her deepest being.

Whatever she might have been, she would never be again. He made her into something different, something whole, something more uniquely alive.

He broke the link binding her to the past. He stole her from the Last Division so she could never go back. She didn't want to go back. She wanted to dwell in this place, in the hollow next to his heart, for the rest of her natural life.

Chapter 34

Grant raised a spyglass to his eye and scanned the mountains beyond the Boundless. The Buchanans were hiding up there somewhere. Was one of them watching him at this very moment? He couldn't see any of them, so maybe they couldn't see him, either.

The Laird broke in on his thoughts. "I've sent south for more dragons. They're our one true advantage. If we can overpower the Buchanans from the air, they dinnae stand a chance."

Grant lowered the glass and eyed the old man. "That hasnae ever worked in the past. I dinnae like to stake our chances on it working now."

"It will work. We'll position our armies there and there." The Laird pointed along a promontory that divided the estuary from the open sea. The headland cut into the Boundless from the Buchanan side. "We'll flank them. We'll draw them down to battle on the beach, and when they come, we'll close them between the two flanks. Then, when we get them boxed in, we'll bring in our dragons."

Grant shook his head and turned his back on the Boundless. All this war talk made him sick to his stomach. "Dinnae ye think they'll anticipate that? They've fought us for generations. They'll expect us to take advantage of the promontory and the headland. They winnae let us trap them so easily. I'm surprised at ye, me Laird. The Buchanans arenae fools. Ye cannae plan a war assuming that they are."

The Laird only gave a slight smile and let his eyes drift half-shut. He didn't need a spyglass to see across the Boundless. He could see more with his eyes half-shut than Grant could see through a thousand spyglasses.

"They'll fall for it the same way they always do. They may not be fools, but they tend to lose their heads in battle. I've fought them countless times and it's always the same. Perhaps it has something to do with their cat nature. When they get into a fight and they shift, they go wild and they stop thinking the way men think. They always let themselves get boxed in. We've used that trick for decades and they always fall for it no matter how many times we use it."

Grant shook his head again, but he knew better than to argue. "Me Laird kens best."

Nothing pleased the Laird more than that. He smiled more than ever and drifted away downstairs. He left Grant and Lily alone on the ramparts.

Grant peered through his spyglass again. He gauged the Buchanans' territory with a clear head now that the Laird's presence no longer affected his judgment.

Lily came to his side and murmured in his ear. "He's really cracked his nut this time if he thinks that will work."

Grant indulged in a crooked grin behind his spyglass, but he didn't take it down. "One thing's certain. He's fought them more times than we have. He may be right about them losing their heads in battle. I've seen it before. The cats go all out. They get so passionate in a fight they'll likely fall for anything."

"I've seen them fight, too, and I disagree. They might be ferocious and passionate in battle, but clear-headed men will be making the decisions behind the lines. You can't bank on them making a blunder like that."

He lowered the glass and turned his grateful eyes on her. She eased his doubts. He could think as long as he had her at his side. He could face the coming war without getting mired in the Laird's schemes.

She didn't take her fierce eyes off the mountains. "I've been thinking. We still haven't gotten over there to find out what they know about Lady Rhona. Maybe the answers are over there instead of here."

"What are ye saying, lassie? Are ye saying ye want to break out of here and run over there at a time like this? I dinnae think that's wise."

"I didn't say that. I only said we don't know what's over there. We don't know what they know or if they might be involved in this. Neither of us think Lady Ilisa was Lady Rhona, but the Buchanans know something about Ilisa. They say she was married to their Clan Chief. They were willing to send people over here to fight and die to get her back. Maybe they're right about her. Either way, we'll never find out by staying here. I would give anything to talk to Neill Buchanan in person."

"That isnae likely to happen," he remarked. "Ye winnae likely even see him in person unless it comes to negotiating peace and that didnae happen the last time until after twenty years of war had passed."

She groaned and slapped her forehead. "God, don't even talk like that!"

"It's true, lass. Ye must face the fact. Most of these wars last a long time and cost countless lives before both sides have had enough to finally come to the table and talk. This one isnae likely to be much different."

"And we have to be in charge of that?" She snorted. "Great."

"Leastways, I have to be."

She slipped her arms around his waist. "Come on. Let's get out of here. Let's run for it right now. We don't have to do this. Let's ditch this popsicle stand."

He sniggered into her hair. He was starting to get used to her quirky sayings and colloquialisms. They always made him laugh even when he didn't understand what she was talking about. "I only wish we could, lass, but ye ken that isnae possible. He'd only find us and bring us back, and one of these times, he'd retaliate to make sure it didnae happen again. We're much better off staying put."

She leaned back and closed her eyes. "I know that. I only wish there was some way we could stop this. I don't want to get involved in another war. I sure as blazes don't want to get involved in planning one when I know it's been cooked up to punish the Buchanans for something they didn't do."

"I dinnae want that, either, lassie. Believe me. I hate the Laird and all his evil plans as much as ye, do but think on it for just a moment. Being here and in charge of the campaign puts us in a better position to do some good with it. We can check him if anyone can. We can use our positions to see the war doesnae get out of control. We can perhaps give the odd order here or there to change the course of a battle or perhaps throw the advantage to the Buchanans."

"Do you really think that's possible? I doubt it somehow."

He sighed and lowered his eyes. He couldn't lie to her or himself when she looked at him like that. "Perhaps no, but if ye think on it, ye'll realize we cannae do ought if we arenae here. If we're to do ought, we havenae any choice but to stay here."

"All right. I'll go along with it, but I won't let my guard down around the Laird."

"Neither of us will." He squeezed her shoulders again. "I'm glad I've got ye here to keep me sane, lass. I couldnae do this without ye."

She buried her face in his chest and gratitude flooded his heart. He couldn't do any of this without her. He couldn't face a future—any future—without her in it.

She had become his all, his everything. He didn't want anything but to be with her.

He couldn't confide in anybody else. They stood alone against the world, but on the battlements with her, even that seemed right.

He could face this devastating war. He might lose everything all over again, but he could face that as long as he faced it with her.

She took Elliot's place for him and Grant took the place of the friends and comrades she had lost. Grant and Lily became the center of each other's worlds and the place of each other's deepest trust and confidence.

Grant nodded toward the stairs. "Come downstairs, lass. The Laird wants me to join him to review the wizards and I need ye with me."

She followed him down into the castle. As long as he needed her, she would be there to support him until they found a way out of this together.

<u>End of Book 1.</u>

If you enjoyed this book, please consider leaving a review. You can also support me on Patreon at <u>www.patreon.com/InvisiblePublishing.</u>

Keep Reading

Highland Heroes Series: Book 2: Clan Chief

No one is tougher, more determined, and more committed to their code of service and self-sacrifice than the Last Division's commanding officer, Jaimee Abernathy. When their friend Lily is in danger on the other side of the time portal, Jaimee and Lily's brother Liam return to Scotland to rescue Lily, only for Jaimee to get caught in the middle of the deadly war between Clan Creighton and Clan Buchanan.

When the time portal device malfunctions and sends Liam and Jaimee into the heart of Clan Buchanan, Clan Chief Colton Buchanan and his brothers threaten to execute the intruders as spies.

Jaimee will have to use all her experience and training, not to mention her wits and tenacity, to convince Colton not just to keep her alive but to let her help him win the war against the evil Laird Balfour Creighton.

When sparks fly, Jaimee finds herself getting closer to Colton than she ever thought possible, but Colton has a secret that makes him deadlier than she realizes. Can two people from different worlds find a way to come together before disaster consumes them all?

You can find it at your favorite book retailer.

Sign Up Once--Get all Theo Mann's free books including brand new releases

S ign Up Once--Get all Theo Mann's free books including brand new releases

Ian Wallace is tall, muscular, magnetically handsome, heroic, and passionately in love with the lady of his dreams--Lady Ada Ross.

Too bad he's just a character in a romance novel......or is he?

When Dayna Roberts finds a mysterious letter tucked between the pages of her favorite book, she decides to write Ian back to warn him of his enemies sneaking up on him. Little did Dayna know that one act would sweep her into a world of the past--a world of danger, intrigue, and powerful forces she never imagined possible. Disaster strikes when Ian's archnemesis Gavin Macauley intercepts her letter and conquers Grimlock Castle with Dayna inside it--but how could he intercept the letter when she wrote it in the twenty-first century?

If Dayna refuses to marry Gavin in Ada's place, he'll take drastic measures that could leave this whole mysterious world in ruins. Forget about Dayna finding a way to get back to the modern world. She'll be lucky if she survives long enough to escape from the castle. Is there any way out--much less a way to get back to the family and the modern life she knows?

Sign up at www.theomann.com to read it for free

About Theo Mann

I write 70 books per year—and yes, before you ask, all these books are my original creative work. Nothing written under my name is AI-generated or ghostwritten because I write better than AI and any ghostwriter out there.

People don't read fiction for entertainment or to escape from reality. People read fiction to see their humanity reflected in another person's character and story.

This is my promise to you. When you read my books, you'll see your own humanity reflected in the characters and stories. I take this commitment to my readers very seriously. My books are an intimate form of communication between us. I would never disrespect my readers by turning that over to a machine or another writer. This is my bond between me and you as my reader.

I write 20,000 words per day as my daily work output. If anyone with a public platform would like to challenge me to prove this in a controlled environment, feel free to contact me on this website's contact page.

I worked as a professional ghostwriter for fifteen years. Now I'm on a mission to set a Guinness World Record by writing 700 books over the next ten years and 1400 books over the next twenty years, all originally written by me. See my website for the full book list.

I'm also the author of *Proof for the Existence of God* and the *Crimes Against Fiction* blog. You can find all my nonfiction work at www.crimes-against-fiction.com.

If you have a story idea, or if you would like me to explore a series in more depth, or if you'd like me to explore a character by writing a spinoff series about that character or world, leave me a message on my website's contact page. I answer all reader emails, so ask me anything, tell me what you liked and didn't like, and let me know where you'd like your favorite series to go. I would love to hear your ideas and find out what you'd like to read next.

Find out more at www.theomann.com.

Also by Theo Mann (so far)

<u>Standalone Novels</u>
Kingdom of Heaven
The Verge

<u>Series</u>
Onyx Series
Prideland Series (Books 1-5)
Ultra Meridian Series (Books 1-7)
Hellhounds Series (Books 1-7)
Battlefleet Series (Books 1-4)
Highland Heroes Series (Books 1-5)
Battalion 1 (Books 1-5)
Corrupted Coil (Books 1-6)
The Network (Books 1-6)

www.ingramcontent.com/pod-product-compliance
Lightning Source LLC
Chambersburg PA
CBHW071907220626
47052CB00002B/249